Dear Reader,

The Kowalskis are back! And so is Liz, who's tired of being far from her family while her cousins and brothers fell in love and started families. It might be awkward seeing the town's chief of police after they snuck away during her brother's wedding, but it's time for her to go home.

Take two people starting over in life, throw in family, s'mores, a classic Mustang and a little bit of doom, and it just might be the recipe for another Kowalski happily-ever-after.

Thank you to all of you who've enjoyed spending the time with the Kowalskis. If you're meeting them for the first time, I hope you like this rowdy bunch. It's been a pleasure sharing this family with you.

Happy reading!

Shannon

Also available from Shannon Stacey and Carina Press

The Kowalskis

Exclusively Yours
Undeniably Yours
Yours to Keep
All He Ever Needed
All He Ever Desired
All He Ever Dreamed

Holiday Sparks
Slow Summer Kisses
Mistletoe & Margaritas
Snowbound with the CEO

Harlequin HQN

Be Mine (anthology with Jennifer Crusie and Victoria Dahl)

Harlequin Anthologies

Snow Day (anthology with Jennifer Greene and Barbara Dunlop)

And Coming Soon from Shannon Stacey and Carina Press

Taken with You (The Kowalskis)
Falling for Max (The Kowalskis)
Her Holiday Man

shannon stacey

love a little *sideways*

ISBN-13: 978-0-373-00225-2

LOVE A LITTLE SIDEWAYS

This edition published by arrangement with Harlequin Books S.A.

www.CarinaPress.com

Printed in U.S.A.

Dedication

For Meesha. I've loved you since the day you were born and, even though as sisters growing up we couldn't have been more different, our friendship as adults means everything to me. Who else can you call, ranting and raving and venting, and then say "Thanks, gotta go," to but your sister? You're an amazing mother, sister and aunt, and I know Mark will agree you're a fabulous wife, too. As always, you are our sunshine.

Acknowledgments

Thank you to my editor, Angela James,
and my agent, Kimberly Whalen, for being wicked awesome.
And to the Carina Press team, whose hard work
and enthusiasm for the Kowalski series
means more than I can ever express.

And thank you to Vanessa, Judy and Sam,
winners of the Name That Kowalski Kid contest,
for naming Sean and Emma's baby boy!

SHANNON STACEY

New York Times and *USA TODAY* bestselling author Shannon Stacey lives with her husband and two sons in New England, where her two favorite activities are writing stories of happily-ever-after and riding her four-wheeler. From May to November, the Stacey family spends their weekends on their ATVs, making loads of muddy laundry to keep Shannon busy when she's not at her computer. She prefers writing to laundry, however, and considers herself lucky she got to be an author when she grew up.

You can contact Shannon through her website, shannonstacey.com, where she maintains an almost daily blog, or visit her on Twitter, @shannonstacey, her Facebook page, or email her at shannon@shannonstacey.com.

love a little *sideways*

ONE

LIZ KOWALSKI'S THIRTY-YEAR-OLD shitbox, loaded down with everything she owned, went by the Welcome To Whitford, Maine, sign trunk-first, bald tires hydroplaning as it headed for the ditch.

Knuckles white on the steering wheel, she swore as the ass end clipped a tree and the trunk popped open. Closing that sucker had been like shoving a twelve-inch Jack into a two-inch box and she could almost hear the sproing of her belongings popping out. *Welcome home,* she thought in the seconds before the Buick's nose smacked left-fender-first into the trunk of an old pine, stopping its slide with a bone-jarring jerk.

Well. That sucked.

Liz sat there for a minute, breathing hard and wondering how long it would be before she could pry her fingers off the steering wheel. Five minutes, maybe. Ten. She'd never been so scared in all her life.

The knock on her window almost made her

wet herself. An older man with a fisherman's hat perched on his head was peering in at her and she could see a woman—his wife, presumably—trying to see over his shoulder. Liz read the words *is she dead* on her lips.

Rolling down her window, Liz forced a reassuring smile. "I really appreciate you stopping, but I'm fine, thank you."

"You just sit tight," the man said. "My wife called 9-1-1 for you."

Oh, no. No no no. "You didn't have to do that. I'm okay. Really. Not even a scratch on me."

She wasn't entirely sure of that fact, but she didn't seem to hurt anywhere. Just a whole lot of muscles that had tensed up and were now relaxing. And maybe a little headache starting.

"It's no trouble at all, and we'll stay with you until the police arrive."

Maybe it wouldn't be Drew Miller. He was the chief of police in Whitford, after all, so maybe he didn't respond to minor traffic accidents. He probably sat at his desk and pushed papers while sending patrol officers to minor accident scenes. She hoped.

Liz pulled the handle to open the door, but Mister Good Samaritan pushed against it. "You shouldn't move around until the paramedics check you out."

"It's raining. You should get back in your car." So she could have relative privacy to scope out how many of her belongings were getting soaked. When the man shook his head, she bit down on a sigh of frustration. "I slid off the road and clipped a tree. It's not even a real accident."

"You could be in shock."

From sideswiping a tree? Not likely. But she couldn't be any more firm with her would-be rescuers without being rude. "I didn't even hit my head on the window."

"Better safe than sorry."

It was another five very awkward minutes before she heard the siren. Rather than being relieved rescue from her hovering Good Samaritans was imminent, Liz leaned her head back and closed her eyes. She didn't even bother hoping it wasn't the chief as the wailing grew closer. The way her luck was running, it would be Drew and everything was about to get a lot more awkward.

"Don't go to sleep, honey," Mrs. Good Samaritan yelled through the window. "You might have a head injury. Stay with us!"

She wasn't going anywhere, but she opened her eyes to make her rescuers feel better. And because she had her eyes wide open, she couldn't miss the Whitford Police Department cruiser that pulled up. It wasn't a sedan with the familiar striped scheme down the side. No, this one was a big, black, shiny, four-by-four SUV with a light bar across the roof and the town seal on the door. It was the kind of vehicle the top of the departmental food chain drove.

The door opened and the Whitford police chief stepped out. Drew Miller was tall and ruggedly built, which she found incredibly sexy because, at almost six feet herself, she didn't meet many men who could pull off the *me Tarzan* thing with her.

He wore the department's short-sleeved summer uniform, and a ball cap with WPD printed on it covered his dark hair. No rolling up onto the balls of his feet and hitching his gun belt for Drew. He commanded any room he was in whether he was armed or not.

He even commanded outdoor spaces, Liz realized as she watched him head toward her car with long, confident strides. He had sunglasses on, but she didn't need to see his eyes to know his focus was one hundred percent on her.

"Are you hurt?"

Liz wasn't sure if she heard him or was simply able to read his lips because she was staring at his mouth. He had an amazing mouth. It was the first thing she'd noticed the day of her brother's wedding reception.

"Liz, are you hurt?"

She shook her head in answer to his question.

"We didn't let her move," the husband and wife said at the same time.

"Thank you. It's always better to be safe than sorry and I can't tell you how much we appreciate citizens who go out of their way to help when they witness somebody in need."

While the couple talked over each other in a rush to tell Drew how she'd lost control of her car in the rain and parked it in the trees, Liz took advantage of their distraction to get out and survey the damage. There was a lot of crumpled sheet metal and the ground was littered with broken lens covers.

In a rare stroke of good luck, it didn't look like anything had flown out of the trunk. No underwear or toiletries or other personal belongings on display, though the top layer of bags and small boxes was going to take a while to dry.

"So she wasn't speeding, then?" she heard Drew ask, and she knew him well enough to hear the undertone of amusement in his voice. He said it loud enough for her benefit, too.

Liz waited, her cheeks hot with humiliation and maybe something else, while Drew called in a status update and gently but firmly sent her two Good Samaritans on their way. She called out a thank-you, managing a wave and a smile as they left.

"You're sure you're not hurt?" he asked her again once the official part of his duties were over.

"I'm sure." She couldn't think of anything to say after that, which annoyed her. She'd known Drew since she was a kid and, just because they'd had sex the one time, she was as awkward as a middle-school girl with a bad crush.

He moved closer, looking her up and down. She told herself it had to be a police thing—checking her for injuries—but his slow perusal didn't help cool her face any. Once he was satisfied with what he saw, presumably injury-wise, he took a slow walk around the car.

"Can't say what your total damage will be, but with the way that fender's crunched up against the tire, I know you can't drive it."

"Great." Hell of a way to kick off her brand-new life, she thought as he radioed in a request for a tow truck.

"Why does it look like you have everything you own in this car?" he asked when he was done.

"Because everything I own is in this car."

His face was so expressionless, she knew it had to be a deliberate effort on his part. Some kind of cop face, maybe. "Why?"

Liz found it hard to believe the chief of police in a town that loved gossip as much as Whitford hadn't heard. "I'm moving back for good."

"Oh." Seconds ticked by in awkward silence. "I didn't know that. Mitch has been traveling, but I was at the lodge weekend before last and nobody mentioned it."

Mitch, Liz's older brother, was Drew's best friend. And Drew's dad, Andy, was now shacking up at the Northern Star Lodge—the Kowalski family business—with Rosie, who was called the housekeeper, but had practically raised Liz and her four brothers. How Drew could be out of the family gossip loop was beyond her.

"I made the decision last weekend and it was pretty fast. As in, I got off the phone with Rosie and packed my car." She gave a rueful laugh and waved a hand at the car. "I probably should have taken the time to have the tires changed."

He didn't laugh. "What made you decide to come back?"

It was a reasonable question, since she'd lived most of her adult life in New Mexico, but she wasn't about to stand around in the rain and tell him how lonely and isolated from her family she'd felt. "Seemed like the thing to do. You don't have to stay, you know. I can wait for the tow truck."

"Actually I do have to stay. This is a bad spot

to be loading up a ramp truck, especially in this rain, so I'll need to do some traffic control."

Traffic was a bit of a stretch, but she had to admit he had a point. Because of the angle of her car, the nose of the tow truck would have to be in the road and that meant he had to stay and wait.

Standing in the rain, alone with Drew Miller. She'd come back to start her life over and, so far, it was off to one hell of a beginning.

DREW MILLER WANTED to get back in his cruiser, hit the lights and sirens, and drive as fast as he could to anywhere but here.

Liz Kowalski was back in Whitford. His best friend's little sister. The woman he'd enjoyed a rebound quickie with during said best friend's wedding reception with the unspoken understanding Liz would be returning to New Mexico. And, more importantly, she would be staying there.

Not forever, of course. But he'd thought enough time would pass before her next visit so he could look at her without instantly remembering the way she looked naked, with her hair tangled around his fingers and her hips arching up to meet his.

He wasn't sure how much time that would be, other than obviously more than the eight months or so that had passed since Mitch's wedding.

She was dressed for a road trip, in old jeans

that hugged her long legs and an even older T-shirt that was doing some body hugging of its own, thanks to the rain. Her thick, dark hair was pulled into a long ponytail and she sure as hell didn't need makeup to show off those brilliant blue eyes. With her strong, stubborn jaw and skin that was tanned by the New Mexico sun, Liz looked as delicious to him as she had the last time he'd seen her. And just look how that had turned out—he was keeping secrets from his best friend.

Standing with her on the side of the road in the light drizzle, all he could do was hope the tow truck driver made good time and to hell with speed limits. For now, more awkward conversation. "Are you moving into the lodge?"

It would make sense. Liz's family had owned the Northern Star Lodge for several generations, catering to hunters before turning their attention to snowmobilers and now adding the ATV crowd, as well. He knew Liz's childhood room was still pretty much hers, even though it was occasionally used by other family members, because he'd been in her room last October. It only made sense she'd save money by moving back into it.

That made things a little complicated for Drew, however. His dad had moved into the lodge and helped manage it after falling for the housekeeper. Since Andy was his dad and Rosie was like a mother to Liz, that was entirely too much togetherness for him.

"I'm trying to go forward, not backward," Liz said. "Ryan and Lauren put her house on the market now that she lives in Massachusetts with him, but they haven't had a decent offer so they agreed to rent it to me."

And since Ryan was her older brother, she was probably getting it for a good price. "And work?"

"I guess since Whitford got connected to the ATV trails, business has really picked up in town, so I'm going to help Paige out at the diner. Handy having a sister-in-law who owns the place."

"Good. That's…good." He lapsed into silence again but then, after watching her shift her weight from foot to foot while looking everywhere but at him, he laughed. "For God's sake, Liz, this is ridiculous."

A slow grin curved her mouth and he finally got a glimpse of the girl he'd known as a kid. "You're right. We're acting like idiots."

"So let's stop." Adult Liz was almost a stranger to him—except for the whole sex thing—but he'd grown up with the Kowalskis and he'd always liked Liz.

"We're adults," she said. "There was alcohol. We snuck off for a rebound quickie, which happens all the time at weddings. So what?"

So what? It was all he could do not to push her up against a tree and repeat the experience, that's what. Though, without the quickie part. He wanted to take his time. And, since he'd been playing designated taxi service that night, alcohol hadn't factored into his decision to whisper his bold invitation into her ear.

And, because he'd watched her the entire afternoon, he knew it hadn't really played into her decision to accept, either. She'd had a couple of drinks during Mitch and Paige's reception, but she'd been far from drunk.

But being chief had honed his acting skills and he was ready to put this eight-months-delayed morning-after awkwardness behind them. "Not a big deal. And now, I hate to be the bearer of bad news, but it doesn't look like you'll be driving this car anytime soon, so let's move your stuff into my SUV before the tow truck gets here."

He watched her chew at her bottom lip for a few seconds before she gave a resigned sigh. "I'll be lucky if Butch can get parts for it, never mind fix it in a hurry."

Butch Benoit ran the garage and gas part of the Whitford General Store & Service Station while his wife, Fran, ran the store part. He was an honest guy who didn't play games and very few residents made the drive into the city to save a few bucks on service. "I think he'll tell you to get whatever you can from the insurance company and use it as a down payment on something a little newer."

She swore under her breath, but leaned into the car to get her purse and assorted other belongings from the front seat. He pulled the SUV as close as he could and started transferring things from the truck. By the time Butch arrived with the ramp truck, her car was empty of everything except the trash a long road trip generated, and his SUV was loaded down with her damp boxes and bags.

Drew moved his vehicle to make way for the tow truck, their light bars flashing bright in the night, then watched while Butch ran the hydraulics and dragged Liz's car up the ramp.

"You sure know how to make an entrance, girl," Butch told Liz once the wreck was strapped down. "I'll look it over tomorrow, but even if you didn't muck up the frame, it ain't gonna be easy finding fenders for this one. Insured?"

"Yeah," Liz said.

She looked like somebody had kicked her dog, so Drew suspected she wasn't anticipating getting a lot from her insurance company. The car simply wasn't worth very much, even before she'd crumpled it up.

"You need a ride up to the lodge?" Butch asked.

Before Liz could answer, Drew stepped in. "She can ride with me. I've got all her stuff in my cruiser, anyway."

"Okay, then. Liz, you can stop by anytime and I'll give you an update. Make sure you call your insurance company tomorrow."

She nodded, and then Drew collected the orange safety triangles he'd set out before gesturing for her to get in. Trying to ignore how weird it felt to have Liz Kowalski riding shotgun with him, he put the SUV in gear and headed for town.

"Where are we going?" she asked when they'd hit Whitford and he turned away from her sister-in-law's house.

"Need to stop by my house first." Not that he'd be inviting her in, because that could be a recipe for disaster. And to make sure he didn't have a moment of weakness, he wasn't even going to unlock the front door.

It only took a few minutes to reach the small farmhouse-style home he'd had to buy half of from his ex-wife, and he was glad it was dark. Since Mallory had left, he was having a little trouble with her flower beds and all her hanging plants, so the property looked a little shabby around the edges.

She didn't say anything as he pulled up the

right side of his driveway and then reached up to hit the button to open the left-side door.

"Hold on a sec," he told her as the overhead door started to rise, and climbed out.

Once the door rattled open, he hit the light switch, illuminating his prized possession. It was a 1970 Mustang, the Boss 302, in brilliant orange with black racing stripes. He opened the door, slid into the leather seat and turned the key. It fired right up, the throaty engine purring like a kitten.

After letting it run a moment, he drove it out of the garage and parked it alongside the cruiser. After he got out, he closed the overhead door and gestured for Liz to join him.

"You can drive this until you figure out what's up with your car," he said, when she'd climbed out of the SUV and walked over to him.

Her eyes grew huge as she looked back and forth between him and the car, and then she shook her head. "I can't borrow your Mustang, Drew."

"Needs to be driven and I spend most of my time in the SUV, so you'd be doing me a favor. And it's insured."

"Nice try. Look, I appreciate the offer, but—"

"Did you know this car was the only one to beat Mitch's Camaro in the quarter-mile back in the day?"

She smiled, running her hand over the black-striped hood scoop in a way that made him think of sex. "He's always claimed he missed a shift."

"Maybe my car was better or maybe I was the better driver but, either way, seeing the car annoys him. You driving it would *really* annoy him and I like keeping Mitch on his toes."

Drew knew he was poking the sleeping bear, so to speak. The last thing he wanted was for Mitch to find out he'd slept with his sister. Parading Liz around in his Mustang probably wasn't a step in the right direction.

But she needed a car and he had a car. And if it gave him some kind of primal thrill seeing Liz behind the wheel of his pride and joy, nobody needed to know that.

ENVELOPED IN THE scent of old leather and Drew Miller, Liz followed the big SUV through Whitford. Her fingers slid easily into the grooves decades of the man driving the car had worn into the steering wheel and she tried not to dwell on how sexy everything about the car—the look, the sound, the smell—was as she focused on the road.

It was better to think about how bad it probably sucked on gas, although whether or not it was worse than her own car remained to be seen. And just how much it would suck if she put so much as a door ding in the thing.

She'd continued to argue with him for what had to be another half hour after he'd given her the lame spiel about him wanting her to drive it to annoy her brother. There weren't any car rental places within a reasonable distance of Whitford, but there had to be an extra vehicle kicking around the lodge she could borrow.

But he wouldn't take no for an answer and, eventually, she'd gotten tired of arguing with him. So now she was driving the car she'd drooled over from afar during high school, though she'd never wanted a tour of the backseat like most of the girls had. Not that it would have mattered. Even if she hadn't been nothing more than Mitch's little sister to him, Drew only had eyes for Mallory.

Unfortunately, when Drew's turn signal started blinking, Liz realized she hadn't been paying attention and they'd arrived at Lauren's small ranch-style house without her knowing quite how they got there. She'd jotted down the directions her brother Ryan had given her over the phone, but she suspected that scrap of paper was still in the console of her car, along with the fast food and gas receipts she'd accumulated along the road.

And Lauren didn't have a garage. Or rather, Liz didn't have a garage, and she could imagine Drew sitting in the SUV he'd just shut off, cringing at the thought of his baby being exposed to the elements.

He didn't say anything when they were both out of their vehicles, though. He just opened the back of the SUV and grabbed a box while Liz retrieved the key from where it had been taped under the mailbox for her. After unlocking the door, she opened it and felt along the wall for the light switch.

"It's very…empty," Drew said from over her shoulder, and she stepped aside so he could carry the box in.

Her new home was indeed very empty. There was a futon in the living room and, judging by the familiar quilt draped over the back, it was Rosie's doing. Next to it sat an upside-down milk crate with a pile of paperback books on top, probably to distract her from the lack of a television. She went into the kitchen and smiled at the smallest microwave she'd ever seen, so new it still had the stickers on it. It was the only thing in the kitchen besides the stove, the fridge and a basket covered by a towel and a note.

She peeked under the towel first. Banana bread and pumpkin muffins, freshly baked judging by the smell. Then she read the note, written in Rosie's familiar handwriting.

Welcome home! I know you said you didn't

need anything, but I brought in a few things so you could at least have a place to sit. Call me when you get in. Love, Rosie.

Home, she thought. Maybe all she had to sit on was a hand-me-down futon, but she was home.

The first bedroom she came to was empty, and the bathroom had the bare necessities. Liz smiled when she recognized the towels and hospitality toiletries used by the Northern Star. It cheered her up, knowing her family had ignored her when she said she'd be fine and didn't need anything.

The big bedroom almost made her cry. Somebody had been busy, basically disassembling her room at the lodge and moving it here. Her bed was made with her favorite quilt, and everything from her dresser to her ancient unicorn lamp had made the trip.

"Liz?"

She jumped, turning back to the hallway. She'd forgotten about Drew, who probably thought she'd abandoned him to carry everything in by himself.

"None of the boxes are marked, so I put them in the living room."

"Thanks. I'll help with the rest. I didn't mean to run off on you."

"It's done. You don't really own a lot, Liz."

"I'm starting over," she told him. "Sorry I'm not starting over in a place with a garage, though.

It's not too late to change your mind about the Mustang."

"It's a car. Won't kill her to sit outside for a few days." He shrugged. "I'm going to head out. If you stop by the station, we'll write you out a police report for the insurance company."

"Thanks for your help."

"All in a day's work, ma'am," he said, and she laughed.

Once he'd left and she was alone in the empty house, her amusement faded. She sat on the edge of the futon and rested her chin in her hands, staring at the pile of her belongings. What the hell had she done?

One minute she'd been on the phone with Rosie, listening to news about the family. And somewhere between hearing about her sister-in-law Emma's pregnancy and Rosie wondering whether Ryan and Lauren or Josh and Katie would make it to the altar first, the homesickness had hit Liz so hard she could barely breathe. Between her cousins and her brothers, the family was awash with love and marriage and babies. And since they'd all recommitted to helping Josh make the Northern Star Lodge a success, it seemed her brothers were closer than ever.

And there she was, all the way across the country with a dead-end relationship behind her and nothing but work ahead of her.

"I'm moving back to Whitford," she'd told Rosie before she could talk herself out of it.

The housekeeper had only been quiet a few seconds before she said, "Your room will be ready."

The idea of moving into the lodge didn't appeal to her, though, and her brother's fiancée having a house sitting empty had seemed like a sign she was doing the right thing.

She was still pretty sure she was doing the right thing, but it seemed a lot scarier now that she was sitting in a house so empty voices echoed. A house she was going to have to pay for all on her own. Hopefully the good citizens of Whitford were as generous with their tips as truck drivers could be.

With a sigh, Liz stood up. First, she was going to heat up some of that banana bread in the microwave because nothing improved a person's outlook on life faster than Rosie's baked goods. Then she'd start spreading her stuff out in the living room so it could all dry.

The glint of orange outside the living room window caught her eye as she walked to the pile of boxes. It had started raining hard again, but she forced herself not to cringe at the sight of the Mustang in the driveway.

And tried not to think about its owner.

TWO

A KNOCK ON his already open office door made Drew look up from a stack of a paperwork with relief. He hated paperwork and welcomed distractions, especially when the distraction was Mitch Kowalski.

"Hey." He gestured for his friend to come in and sit down. "I thought you were…somewhere. Working."

"I'm only home for a couple of days." Mitch sat in the visitor's chair and crossed his arms. "I need you to do something for me."

"Last time you said that, I had to repaint half my truck."

Mitch grinned. "I told you not to get caught."

Drew got his license before Mitch and the favor was to pick up Drew's girlfriend and deliver her to the pond where Mitch planned to take her for a ride in the canoe he'd "borrowed" from his old man. Sure, Mitch told him not to get caught. What he'd neglected to mention was that his girlfriend's dad was not only paranoid, but had impulse control issues and a shotgun loaded with bird shot. The girlfriend hadn't pulled off the sneaky part of sneaking out.

"That's just one of many times doing something for you has been a pain in the ass for me," Drew said.

"This time there are no women involved. Except my sister."

Drew concentrated on not looking like a guy who'd been caught with his hand in the wrong cookie jar. "What is it you want me to do for you?"

"I want you to tell me why there's a picture going around Facebook of your Mustang parked in Lauren's driveway with no lights on in the house and a time stamp of just after midnight."

"Since when are you on Facebook?"

"Paige is, since she has an account for the diner and helps with the lodge's."

"Was there also a picture of Liz's car on Butch's ramp truck with the fender caved in?"

Mitch leaned forward in the chair. "What happened? Is she okay? I got in late last night and I haven't talked to Rosie yet, but she would have called my cell if Liz was in an accident."

"She's fine and it wasn't much of an accident. I don't know if Liz has even told Rose yet. She hydroplaned and sideswiped a tree, so I lent her the Mustang until she can get the insurance stuff sorted out."

"You're letting Liz borrow your car? Why would you do that?"

"Because I'm a nice guy. It's just sitting in the garage and I'd rather it be out on the road where I can see it and remember the day I smoked that Camaro of yours."

"I missed a shift." Mitch relaxed in the chair again. "Since Paige knew Liz was supposed to arrive yesterday, she thought maybe you were there with her. Like spending the night. But I told her she was crazy."

There was nothing confrontational in the way he said it, but Drew saw the opportunity to come clean. More than an opportunity, it was the window for confession. If he didn't say anything now, it would be so much worse if Mitch ever found out.

They were all adults. He was almost certain Mitch would be reasonable if Drew and Liz wanted to be in a relationship, not that they were there yet, if ever. Their two interactions in the past year had been a forbidden quickie and his response to her accident. Whether he was attracted to her or not, that was hardly a relationship. But, hell, maybe Mitch would even be happy for them if they were.

But that little bit of doubt kept him from spilling his guts. He and Mitch had been friends a long time. Mitch had been his best man when he married Mallory and the shoulder he cried on the night she moved out.

If Mitch felt betrayed—if Drew saw that in his eyes—it would cut him to the bone.

"Crazy," he repeated to buy himself more time to think.

"I told Paige you'd never do that. You're my best friend and she's my little sister. I told her you'd cut your own balls off before you'd ever lay a hand on her."

So much for reasonable. If Mitch would rather Drew castrate himself than touch Liz, it was probably best he keep his mouth shut.

"I knew there was a good reason," Mitch continued. "Though I never thought you'd let anybody borrow that car."

"She needed one and I had one. Simple as that." More or less.

Mitch hit a button on his cell phone to check the time. "Gotta head to the diner. Paige isn't feeling so hot this morning, so I called in a takeout order."

"Feel free to take some of those tart things

over there." Drew pointed to the far corner of his desk, where a paper plate filled with some kind of baked thing with fruit in the middle and covered by plastic wrap sat untouched. Since his divorce, he'd noticed an upswing in the amount of baked goods brought to the fine men and women of the Whitford Police Department.

Mitch took a peek and then grimaced. "I'm all set, thanks."

Drew couldn't blame him. They'd both been spoiled by Rosie Davis. And, since Drew's dad had surprised them all by getting Rosie to fall in love with him and moving into the lodge, Drew got enough of the good stuff so he was reluctant to make do with not-quite-Rosie's baked goods.

Once Mitch left to pick up his wife's food, Drew looked down at the paperwork again, but the words on the papers didn't register in his head.

Maybe he should call Liz and give her a heads-up on the whole Facebook thing. Once the same people who wondered why his Mustang had been parked in the driveway of Lauren Carpenter's empty house realized Liz Kowalski had been in the house at the time, the needle on the gossip meter would redline.

Calling her would have been easier if he'd gotten her cell number, he realized. He could always take a ride over there and tell her in person. See how she was making out with the house. She might need to make a shopping trip for more stuff than would fit in the Mustang or something like that. He could check on her, at least.

I told her you'd cut your own balls off before you'd ever lay a hand on her.

Or he could do his paperwork and let Liz's family take care of her so he didn't get himself into any more trouble than he'd already swept under the rug.

LIZ STARED AT the unfamiliar ceiling, willing herself to get up and start the day. The only way it could be worse than yesterday was if she tripped and fell in front of a bus. Since Whitford didn't have any buses, except school buses and school had just let out for the summer, today was bound to be better.

After wallowing for another ten minutes without going back to sleep, she got out of bed and threw a mug of water into the microwave before hitting the bathroom. Then, with a grimace, she dumped one teaspoon of instant coffee and two of sugar into the mug. While she'd packed those into a small box of food in the trunk of her poor car, she didn't have any milk to add since she'd been too exhausted to run to the market. She hadn't thought instant coffee could be any worse, but it could. Without milk, it was very much worse.

After years of waiting tables in a truck stop and putting up with a boyfriend who did nothing but drain her of money and energy, her stomach and blood pressure had been a mess, and she'd been having trouble sleeping at night. Once she'd cut Darren and multiple pots of coffee every day out of her life, things had gotten much better. Now she had a one-cup-of-instant-coffee-in-the-morning-and-no-men rule and—other than a couple cups of high-test that left her jittery halfway through her drive east and that one incident with Drew—she hadn't broken it.

Time to make a list, she told herself when the meager amount of caffeine she allowed herself started kicking in. Calling the insurance company had to be a priority, as was checking in with Butch at the garage. The insurance company would probably want an official report so, as Drew had said, she'd have to stop by the police station. She desperately needed milk. Rosie would expect her to show up at the lodge for a real welcome-home hug before the day was over, and she should stop in at the diner and see Paige, who was not only her sister-in-law, but her new boss.

The Whitford Diner first, she decided. Eggs.

Bacon. Home fries. Raisin toast. It was enough to propel her into the shower and then out the door.

Where she lowered herself into the driver's seat of Drew's Mustang and stuck the key in the ignition. But she paused a moment before firing up the engine, looking through the windshield at the house she'd rented for who knew how long. It was small but tidy, with gray vinyl siding and white trim around the windows. There wasn't much for landscaping, but the lawn had been mowed recently and she wondered by whom. She hadn't explored the backyard yet, so she had no idea if there was a lawn mower lurking in a shed, if one of her brothers had done it, or if the real estate agent had arranged to have it done before Lauren took it off the market.

She'd felt pretty sorry for herself last night and before she rolled out of bed. She'd wrecked her car, her house echoed and she had to start a new job. But now she breathed in deeply through her nose and blew it out through her mouth.

She had a friend who cared enough to lend her his classic Mustang. She had a lovely house that wasn't filled with somebody else's stuff, but was waiting for her to find new treasures to fill it up. She had a family who loved her enough to make sure she had the bare necessities even though she'd told them she'd be okay. And, thanks to her sister-in-law, she had a job waiting for her.

For somebody making a fresh start, she had an awful lot going for her.

With a much better outlook on life, she backed the car out of the driveway and headed in the direction they'd come from the night before. She concentrated on shifting, making sure she didn't grind any gears while getting used to the clutch. It had been a while since she'd driven a standard. Since the town hadn't changed much, it didn't take her long to get her bearings and, before long, she was pulling into the parking lot of her sister-in-law's restaurant.

It wasn't busy, but Liz hoped to chat with Paige a bit, so she took a seat at the counter just as the swinging door to the kitchen opened. A young woman who wasn't Paige stepped out. She wore a Trailside Diner T-shirt with a little plaque that said Tori pinned to it. Tori's dark blond hair was pulled into a short ponytail, and her honey-brown eyes crinkled when she smiled in greeting. "You want coffee?"

What Liz wanted was to dump sugar and cream straight into the full, fresh pot and down the entire thing, but she shook her head. She'd had her cup of instant for the day. "A small OJ and a large ice water, please."

"So you must be Liz," Tori said when she returned with the drinks.

"What gave me away?"

"Tall, with dark hair and blue eyes like your brothers, and you're driving Chief Miller's Mustang." She laughed, pulling an order pad out of her apron pocket. "Plus, Paige told me you'd probably show up looking for breakfast."

"Rose left me some banana bread and pumpkin muffins, but I need bacon." She also ordered the eggs, toast and home fries to go with the bacon. "I take it Chief Miller doesn't let a lot of women drive his car?"

Oh, that was subtle. Liz wanted to kick herself, but sipped her water and forced herself to look only mildly interested instead.

"I've never seen anybody else drive it, but I figure for your family, he'd make an exception."

Right. Because Drew and her oldest brother were best friends. "A tree jumped out and crumpled my fender in the rainstorm last night."

Tori laughed. "Hate when they do that. I'd have wrecked my own car, though, if I'd known that beast was available as a loaner."

The cook yelled Tori's name and she left to deliver a tray of food to a table in the back. Liz sipped her water, trying to pretend it was coffee and failing miserably. She should have scrounged up enough change to get a newspaper from the rack out front or brought a book to distract her.

"Is Paige around?" she asked when Tori moved within earshot.

"She's off today. Mitch flew in last night to spend a couple of days, so she asked me to cover for her. Ava comes in for the afternoon shift, but you probably already know that. When are you starting?"

Liz wasn't sure, actually. "She told me to take a few days to settle in, so maybe next Monday or Tuesday. I'll have a few days to get my bearings before the weekend."

It occurred to Liz there was a possibility Tori wasn't her biggest fan and was hiding it well. If Paige had exaggerated how much business had picked up so she'd take the job, having Liz around might cut into Tori's tips.

"It'll be nice having you on board," the younger woman said, and she sounded sincere. "I'm supposed to be very part-time, just to get out of my apartment and meet people, but between the increased business and Paige cutting back to spend time with Mitch, I'm here a lot more than I intended to be."

The cook yelled Tori's name again and she walked away again before Liz could respond. She kept herself busy reorganizing the sugar packets in their container until Tori set her plate in front of her. The bacon went a long way in bolstering her new and improved positive attitude.

Once she was done, she left her money on the counter, took a menu from the stack by the register so she could familiarize herself with it, and walked out into the sunshine. It was getting hotter and the humidity didn't help. She'd forgotten how much more humid it was in New England, and she cursed herself for not putting her hair into a ponytail before leaving the house.

Since there was a good chance somebody was already telling Rosie that Liz had been spotted at the diner, she decided to make the Northern Star her next stop. She could visit for a while and still have time to do the rest of her errands in the afternoon.

Liz kept her foot light on the Mustang's accelerator through town, but once she was free of the downtown proper, she opened it up a little. The car was made to run, and, since it didn't have air-conditioning, she needed the extra air flow through the windows.

She was almost to the turnoff for the lodge and about to let up on the gas pedal when she heard the siren and glanced in the rearview mirror to see flashing blue lights.

LESS THAN TWENTY-FOUR hours, Drew thought as he watched Liz put on her blinker to pull over. Not even a full day and the woman was being a pain in the ass.

She hadn't even seen his SUV through the break in the trees where he was waiting to pull out after doing a wellness check down a long back road. He'd been in the process of looking both ways when the Mustang—*his* Mustang—had blown by him.

Cursing under his breath, Drew pulled in behind her on the shoulder and threw the SUV in Park. He got on the radio and told his dispatcher he was stepping out of his vehicle for a traffic stop, but then hesitated when she offered to run the plate. After assuring her it was a minor infraction and nobody would be getting a ticket, he got out and walked to the car.

He might want to handcuff her, pat her down and lock her in the truck with him for a while, but he wasn't going to give her a ticket. Not only had she suffered enough vehicular trouble lately, but he didn't want his tags on a violation tag.

Liz started to open the door, but he shoved it closed. "Stay in the vehicle. You know that."

He bent down to look in the window and got sucker punched by her smile. It was the Kowalski get-out-of-trouble smile and God knew he'd seen Mitch and his brothers use it on women so often he usually just rolled his eyes.

But with her head tilted a little sideways and her blue eyes crinkling, Liz's smile did something to his insides and he straightened again. Folding his arms over his chest as if they were armor, he glared down at her.

"I'm really sorry, Drew," she said in a soft voice.

"What is it with you Kowalskis? When I'm in uniform and you're in trouble, it's Chief Miller."

"Just how much trouble am I in?"

Not as much as he was, if she didn't stop looking at him like that. "You're speeding. In the police chief's car."

She held up her hand, holding her thumb and index finger a half inch apart. "Just a little."

"Isn't it bad enough there's a picture on Facebook of my car in your driveway at midnight? What's next? A picture of my car laying rubber down the main street?"

"I didn't lay rubber down…wait. What picture on Facebook?"

"You haven't talked to Mitch?"

That certainly wiped the charming smile off her face. "Not yet. Why is there a picture of my house on Facebook?"

"And my car. He stopped by my office this

morning. Wanted to know why my car was in your driveway at midnight with no lights on in the house."

"Oh. Well, at least there's an easy explanation for that, and not many people know I've moved in there. Yet."

He felt his jaw clench. "He says he won't be too fazed by gossip because he knows I'd cut off my own balls before I'd put a hand on you."

He watched her expression as the words sunk in, until she turned to stare out the windshield and drummed her fingers on the steering wheel. "Did he say that?"

"He did."

She took a deep breath and, since the angle he was looking down at her offered a window-framed view of her breasts, he forced himself to look at the trees over the top of the car. Having sexy thoughts about her while discussing Mitch's reaction to the idea of them having sex didn't sit well with him. Neither did lying to his best friend, even if only by omission, but there was no point in putting a strain on relationships for what had been nothing more than a quick rebound fling.

As happy as he was for Mitch and Paige, their wedding had been hard on him. Divorce sucked extra hard when you were celebrating a marriage, and he felt lonely and cold inside. Then he'd seen

Liz and turned hot in an instant. She was so vibrant and fun, dancing and laughing with her family but, behind the smile, he could see that she was lonely, too.

They'd circled around each other during the reception. Glances. Smiles. Touches. Then they'd run into each other in the house and found themselves alone. He still wasn't sure who moved first, but the kiss made him feel like that bird that rose out of the ashes and they went upstairs.

Liz was just as vibrant and fun in the bedroom, and Drew wouldn't want to ever confess how many times he'd thought about that day since. But he'd barely caught his breath before Liz heard her brother Ryan yelling her name and ran off like a teen who'd spotted her parents' headlights in a window. There had been cake cutting and more celebrating and then he'd been doing the designated-driver thing, so he hadn't gotten to see her again before she went back to New Mexico.

Maybe if she'd stayed, it would have amounted to something and they would have told Mitch they were a couple. Instead, the best sex of his life was an awkward secret.

"It's not a big deal," Liz said, and he wasn't sure if she meant the sex, the Facebook photo or Mitch's certainty his best friend wouldn't put the moves on his sister. "I'm not worrying about what people think. I'm starting a new life and I'm going to have fun and do what I want to do. If people want to plaster it on Facebook, more power to them."

"Do me a favor and don't do it at sixty miles per hour, okay?"

She smiled and looked up at him. "Does that mean you're letting me off with a warning, Chief Miller?"

He should give her a warning, all right. A warning not to look at him like that, with her pretty eyes and the smile that looked sweet, but held a hint of naughtiness. "Just this once."

After waiting to make sure she pulled the Mustang back onto the road and drove off at a legal speed, Drew did a U-turn and decided to head home for lunch. While most of the time being in the house alone depressed him, sometimes it was a crazy-people-free refuge and that's what he needed right now.

He made himself a turkey sandwich on wheat in deference to his uniform's belt, but then slathered on the mayo in deference to his mood.

Sitting on one of the two bar stools at his counter, since Mal had taken the dining room set, he ate his sandwich and tried to clear his head. He vaguely remembered, from some high school English class, a story about beautiful women who'd lure sailors in so they smashed their ships on the rocks. That's how he felt about Liz. Not that she was trying to lure him to his death, but he didn't seem to be able to resist thinking about her, even knowing it wouldn't end well.

Even without Mitch as a rock to crash up against, any relationship between Drew and Liz was a disaster waiting to happen. They were both starting over, but they were going in different directions. Liz wanted to have fun and figure out her new direction in life. Drew already knew what direction he was going in. He wanted children, so he was looking for a wife who wanted the same and he was tired of waiting.

He needed to stop thinking about Liz Kowalski every time he closed his eyes and start picturing the family he wanted to have. Maybe if he concentrated hard enough, he could imagine the sounds of young voices and the sight of bicycles left in the driveway. He'd wanted that for a long time, but had been married to the wrong woman. Now it was time to start making that dream come true, and being derailed by another wrong woman wasn't getting him any closer.

No matter how good she might make him feel, he had to remember Liz wasn't going to be the mother of his children.

THREE

LIZ PARKED IN front of the Northern Star Lodge and leaned against the car to look over her childhood home. Somehow it was still the same while not being the same at all. She knew her brothers had done a lot of major remodeling before the wedding eight months ago, but she could see they'd been making constant cosmetic improvements since.

The huge house gleamed white and the dark green shutters framing the new windows were in perfect condition. Traditional white rocking chairs were placed in conversational groupings along the deep farmer's porch, which was punctuated by hanging baskets overflowing with bright flowers. The landscaping was lush and inviting, and she could hardly believe this was the same lodge Mitch had sent her photos of back when it was in financial trouble and they'd had to make the decision to sell it or keep it. Even when she was a kid and her dad still ran the place, she didn't think it had looked this good.

The front door opened and her brother Josh stepped out into the shade of the porch. She ran up the steps and threw herself into his waiting embrace, so glad she'd decided to move home. Phone calls just weren't the same.

"Rosie's been waiting for you all morning," he told her. "And she gets up early."

"I needed bacon."

"Don't we all?" He held her out at arm's length. "You look great. A lot happier."

"So do you." The last time she'd seen Josh, he'd been sitting on her front step in New Mexico, sulking because he was trying to convince himself he'd done the right thing in leaving his best friend Katie behind to see the country, and failing. Luckily, he'd figured it all out and returned to the Northern Star Lodge and to Katie, who was Rose's daughter.

"Katie's at work," he said, looping an arm over her shoulder as they walked toward the front porch. "She was going to close the shop, but nobody was sure quite when you'd get here."

Katie Davis owned the only barbershop in Whitford, so it was probably a big deal when she closed it down for a day. "I understand. You two set a wedding date yet?"

"Not yet. We're trying to let Ryan and Lauren go first, but if they don't hurry up, we're going to stop being nice."

Liz laughed, then gave a squeal of delight when the screen door flew open and Rosie stepped out.

"My girl's finally home!" Rosie threw her arms around Liz, barely giving Josh time to get out of the way, and squeezed her hard.

Rose Davis had been the housekeeper at the Northern Star all of Liz's life and, since Sarah Kowalski died when Liz was seven, she'd been the mom of the house, too. She considered the Kowalski kids as much hers as she did her own daughter, Katie, who she'd practically raised at the lodge along with them. And while Katie had been a tomboy, running with Liz's brothers, Liz had spent her time with Rosie, helping her clean and bake and learning to knit. Now that she was home to stay, it was safe to admit to herself that she'd missed her horribly.

"When did you get in?" Rosie asked, practically pushing her through the house to the kitchen, where most of the visiting usually took place.

"Last night. I know I should have called then, but by the time I got settled, it was late enough so I thought you might be in bed already."

Rosie's eyes narrowed. "You stayed at Lauren's last night?"

Liz remembered the photo on Facebook. "Yes, but before you jump to any wrong conclusions, I had a small accident and—"

"An accident? What happened?"

"My car hydroplaned and sideswiped a tree. I'm fine." She put her hands up and made a slow circle so Rosie could see for herself. "Drew lent me his Mustang, which is why it was parked in the driveway at midnight."

Josh laughed, pulling a chair away from the table so he could turn it around and straddle it backward, ignoring Rosie's frown. "When people find out you were in the house when the picture was taken, they'll have something to chew on for a while."

Liz felt pinned down by Rosie's look. She knew Liz and Drew had history, however brief. They'd talked about it before Liz went back to New Mexico and they'd both agreed it was best Mitch not know about it. Liz could only hope Rose's opinion on that wouldn't change now that Liz had moved home.

"Of course not," Josh replied. "It's ridiculous. Drew's too good a friend to Mitch to try something with you."

It was ridiculous, all right, but not for the reason he thought. "How come nobody assumes I'd try something with him?"

"Girls having a crush on their older brother's best friend is typical. It's up to the best friend to keep his hands to himself."

"That's so insulting." When she saw Rose's mouth tighten, Liz realized she didn't really want to continue down this conversational path. "Not that it matters, but two adults worrying about what big brother will think is pretty juvenile."

She watched Rose put water on for tea and she thought about mentioning the caffeine thing, but then reconsidered. One cup of tea wouldn't hurt. Probably. Besides, she still had a lot on her to-do list and she could use the extra jolt.

"I'm glad we don't have to worry about that," Rose said, and it took Liz a second to realize she was still talking about the Mustang being in her driveway. "But speaking of Drew, I wonder where Andy got to."

"I saw him with the chain saw, so he probably went out to take care of that branch that came down on the edge of the tree line in that last storm. Shouldn't take him more than a few minutes."

Liz's gaze drifted to a counted cross-stitched sampler hanging on the wall that read Bless This Kitchen. According to Rosie, Liz's mom had stitched it when Sean was a baby, so it had been made before Liz or Josh were born, and it made her smile. This kitchen did feel blessed, and she was overcome again by the certainty she'd made the right decision in coming home.

"I know you didn't want us to fuss," Rosie was saying, "but we couldn't have you walking into an empty house with no place to sit or lay your head but on the floor."

"It's perfect. Especially my bedroom. As soon as I walked in the room, it felt like home, so thank you for ignoring me."

"Anytime." Rosie winked.

"So what's up with your car?" Josh asked. "You could have borrowed the plow truck. Nobody's using it right now, obviously."

"Let me see…old plow truck or a sweet little Mustang? Tough choice, Josh." She laughed. "Drew was pretty insistent, actually. He likes the idea of rubbing the car in Mitch's face."

"He's always said he missed a shift."

She rolled her eyes. "Men."

"Back to your car," Rosie said. "How bad is it?"

"Managed to whack both the front and rear fenders, and the back was bad enough so Drew said I couldn't drive it. He and Butch both implied I'd be better off replacing the entire car."

The back screen door opened and Andy Miller walked into the kitchen. He smiled when he saw her sitting at the table. "Hey, Liz. It's good to see you again."

"You, too." A little weird, since he wasn't allowed at the lodge for much of Liz's life, thanks to something he'd done decades before that pissed Rosie off. Now the housekeeper had not only forgiven him, but fallen in love with him and moved him into the lodge.

Definitely weird, she thought when he put his arm around Rosie's waist and kissed her cheek as the teakettle started whistling. When she swatted at his behind, Liz looked at Josh, who only shrugged.

"Liz was just telling us she went off the road last night and wiped out her fenders on a tree, which is why your son's Mustang was parked in her driveway."

That took the weird up yet another level, Liz thought, killing the wince before it could show on her face. Rosie and Drew's dad being a thing was just one more reason to forget she and Drew had ever had awesome sex that fell short of perfect only because they hadn't had hours more to spend together.

"Knew there was a good reason," Andy replied, stealing a cookie from the jar on the counter. "Can't remember the last time he let anybody drive that car of his, though. I don't recall Mallory even driving it."

Liz didn't want anybody spending too much time analyzing why Drew would let her drive it when his ex-wife didn't, beyond the superficial reason of annoying Mitch, so she steered the conversation away. "Butch thinks I should take whatever the insurance company will give me and run."

"One of the most honest guys I know," Andy said. "If he doesn't think it's worth hunting down fenders and repairing the vehicle, he's probably right."

Liz smiled her thanks when Rose set a mug of black tea in front of her, and half listened while Andy and Josh talked cars, insurance claims and junkyards. She wasn't holding out much hope of being able to find fenders in the right color for her car in a junkyard within driving distance, and she wouldn't be able to afford a new paint job, anyway. She should probably grab a newspaper at the market and see what vehicles were for sale in the area.

"Enough with cars," Rosie said, sitting down across the table from Liz. "How does it feel to be home?"

"It feels good," she said honestly. "I had breakfast at the diner this morning and met Tori. I think

I'll like working there, and Lauren's house is perfect. And I'm tired of sharing everybody's lives over the phone."

"I've already told Sean I expect him, Emma and the baby to come over from New Hampshire for Christmas this year. I know they celebrated with your aunt and uncle last year because Emma was pregnant, but this will be the first holiday with all of you home since I don't know when."

Liz could see the tears gathering in Rosie's eyes, so she tried for a conversational U-turn. Rose loved to manage things. "I guess since I'm staying, I need to see if I can get a 207 number for my cell. Should I bother getting a landline? And maybe I'll get cable. And a TV."

Rose grabbed a piece of paper and a pen while the men fled the room and got down to business. Liz drank her tea and let the woman do what she loved best.

"WAS THAT THE Kowalski girl I saw driving your Mustang?"

Drew looked up at Officer Bob Durgin, who had spoken from his open doorway without preamble. "I lent Liz my car, yes."

"Why would you do that?"

Drew arched an eyebrow, not caring for the guy's tone. Durgin had always had it in for the

Kowalski kids. Sometimes they deserved it, like the night a teenage Mitch leading him on a merry chase in his Camaro had led to Bob rolling the new cruiser. Drew was certain Bob still had no idea Drew was riding shotgun that night. And sometimes they didn't deserve it. They'd found out when Mitch first returned to Whitford to help turn the lodge around that Bob Durgin had been in love with Sarah and, apparently as part of never forgiving her for choosing Frank Kowalski, he held a grudge against her and Frank's kids.

"Since we're not exactly overrun by car rental agencies in Whitford, I lent a friend of mine a vehicle until hers is fixed," he said, careful not to let his annoyance show in his tone.

"You know how those kids are when they've got a fast car."

Yes, he did. Because he was usually in Mitch's passenger seat or running his Mustang up the road behind him. Except for that one time, of course, when he'd been in front. "Liz is a thirtysomething-year-old woman now, Bob. We've all grown into fairly law-abiding citizens."

It was probably best not to mention that he'd stopped Liz for speeding the day after he gave her the keys.

Bob made a disapproving sound and wandered

off toward the coffee machine. Drew watched him for a minute, then tried to return to his paperwork.

Despite his long-standing beef with the Kowalski kids, Bob Durgin was a good, steady cop. He'd be retiring in a few years, most likely, and when he did he'd have the distinction of having served his entire career, right from his first day as a rookie, with the Whitford Police Department. Even Drew had done several years in Portland before moving home again when a vacancy opened up at the same time his stepmother passed away from ovarian cancer.

Bob had been offered the chief's position, of course. It would have been rude not to offer it after all his years on the force, but the town had made the offer safe in the assumption he wouldn't take the job. The man had no patience for politics, haggling with the budget committee over new tires for the cruisers, or being polite to citizens when they were a pain in the ass.

Drew glanced up to check the time and, as if Bob Durgin had conjured her, Liz Kowalski appeared in his doorway. Her smile brightened his day considerably. "Hey, come on in."

"I think Durgin wants me in handcuffs." His reaction to the word *handcuffs* must have shown on his face, because she laughed. "I meant, as in under arrest. Don't even try to stick me with that visual."

"Nobody wants that. So, have a seat and tell me what's up."

She sat in the chair across the desk from him and sighed. "What's up is that Butch and the insurance company agree that it's time for my car to go to the great junkyard in the sky. Even if he could repair the front fender, he started calling junkyards to see about a rear fender and gave up when he got to New York area codes."

"Sorry to hear it. What's next?"

"I need a copy of the report, of course, to send to them. And then I wait for a check from them and start watching the classifieds."

Drew leaned back in his chair and tried to think of anybody he knew who was selling something decent for a reasonable price, but came up blank. "You can drive the Mustang as long as you need to, you know."

Pink tinted her cheeks and he knew she'd prefer not to have to rely on his help. "Josh said I could drive the lodge's pickup. The older one they plow with."

"The Mustang's a bit of a gas hog, but nowhere near as bad as that truck. You may as well have Paige write your paychecks out to the service station if you take him up on that offer."

"It shouldn't be long, if you're sure you don't mind."

He didn't. "I like seeing it go down the road. When I do get a chance to take it out, I'm inside, so I don't get to see how awesome it looks on the move."

"She does like to move."

He tried to give her a stern look, but it dissolved into a chuckle. "Officer Durgin has his eye on you, just so you know. He's pretty outraged I lent one of those Kowalski kids a fast car."

"Did you tell him—"

"No." He shook his head. "He doesn't need any more fuel in his fire when it comes to you guys."

"I wonder if my mom knew he had the hots for her? Rosie said they never dated as far as she knew, and she knows almost everything."

"I don't know. But I guess wanting a woman and not being able to have her sticks with a guy."

The second the words were out of his mouth, he wanted them back. Wanting Liz and not being able to have her was sticking with him, that was for sure. But she didn't seem to read anything into what he said.

The department's secretary stuck her head into his office. "Sorry to interrupt, Chief, but you have a meeting at the town hall in ten minutes."

"Thanks, Barbara. Hey, can you get a copy of

the police report I left on your desk this morning? Kowalski, Elizabeth S."

"That sounds very official," Liz said once Barbara returned to her desk. "It's still a little weird to me that you're not only a cop, but the chief of police."

"Sometimes it's still a little weird to me, too. I think Mitch and I were voted Most Likely To Be Felons back in high school."

Barbara came back and handed the paper to Liz. "I'm glad you didn't get hurt, honey."

"Thank you." She had very vague memories of Barbara as a child, but she couldn't quite place her.

"Elementary school secretary," Drew supplied helpfully once Barbara was gone again.

"That's right. I think I liked her." She gave the paper a quick scan and then stood. "I'll let you get to your meeting. Thanks again."

"It's my job."

She gave him a warm, genuine smile that made him feel like a mini marshmallow dropped into a mug of hot chocolate. "I think the car goes above and beyond."

"Not for you." The words hung between them, and he waved them off before she could question his meaning. He hoped. "You know, being Mitch's sister has to have some perks to make up for what a pain in the ass he is."

For a fleeting second, he thought she looked almost disappointed, but then she laughed. "As perks go, that car's pretty sweet."

After she was gone, he took a second to put his thoughts back in order. He had a meeting to go over a grant he was trying to get to buy the department an ATV so they could help, along with the ATV club's unofficial trail patrol, police the influx of riders they'd seen lately.

Instead, all he could think about was what a dumb thing he'd said. *Not for you.* It was pretty sappy, and he could only hope he'd covered it in time. Liz wasn't for him, and any kind of flirting or innuendo was strictly off-limits in the future.

"Chief." Barbara had her arms crossed, giving him the look that had almost made his first-grade self wet his pants. "Meeting."

"On my way."

It wasn't far to the town hall and the weather was nice, so Drew decided to walk. He'd still make it in time, as long as nobody tried to stop him on the sidewalk and bend his ear. Halfway there, he heard a familiar horn and turned to see his car coming up the street.

He watched as the Mustang rolled by, doing at least five miles per hour under the speed limit, and his body tightened when Liz gave him a saucy grin and waved.

He'd been right when he lent her the car. Seeing her drive it—seeing her fingers curled around the wheel so perfectly molded to his hand—triggered some deep, primal thrill inside of him. Maybe because, out of all of his belongings, the car was the most personal and seeing her in it meant something he didn't want to analyze too much. Or maybe it was just seeing a sexy woman in a sexy car. Either way, he liked it.

FOUR

NOBODY COULD PULL together an impromptu family dinner like Rosie. Liz was summoned to the lodge Friday night because Mitch was home, and Ryan and Lauren were driving up. They usually met Lauren's ex-husband halfway from their home in Brookline, Massachusetts, so her son Nick could visit his dad, but Ryan had cleared his afternoon to make the drive up for dinner.

His truck, with Kowalski Custom Builders painted on the side, was already there when she drove up the lane and she parked between it and Katie's ancient Jeep.

The aroma made her stomach growl the second she opened the front door, though she felt it rather than heard it due to the noise level. In honor of her return home, Rose had made a traditional New England boiled dinner and the blend of ham and cabbage and other goodies made Liz's mouth water.

When she stepped into the kitchen, the conversation and laughter stopped as everybody had to give her a hug and welcome her home. She went down the line, from Mitch and Paige to Ryan, Lauren and Nick, then to Katie, who squealed and threw her arms around her.

"Josh told me you seemed lonely when he visited you in New Mexico. I'm so glad you came home where you belong."

"Me, too." Though Katie had spent a lot more time outside than Liz growing up, they'd been the only girls against four boys, so they'd been thick as thieves.

Josh, the only sibling younger than she was, pulled her into a quick hug. "Sorry we're eating on the early side. We've got guests coming in tonight and the first ones will probably get here about six."

"I don't mind."

"You all go sit down," Rosie said, making a shooing motion with her towel. "It's almost ready and I can't move in this kitchen with you all underfoot."

Liz trailed the others into the big dining room, where Rose had already set out the good dishes. She cringed a little because the good dishes couldn't go in the new dishwasher Andy had installed for her and that was a lot of hand-washing.

There was a lot of shuffling before everybody

was seated where they wanted to be. Even though he was the youngest, as the one who'd stayed and run the lodge, Josh had sat at the head of the table since their dad passed away. Mitch sat at the foot and they all paired off around the table.

Somebody had counted wrong, Liz thought as she looked around the table. There were two seats across from her she guessed were for Rose and Andy, who would help her serve, and then there was a place set next to her with nobody in the chair.

Then Drew walked in and it made sense. And lucky her, she got to sit next to him since everybody else was paired off as couples.

Once everybody had hollered out a greeting to Drew and he'd popped into the kitchen to say hello before being shooed back out, he pulled out his chair and sat down. There wasn't a lot of space and Liz realized she'd probably spend the entire meal trying to avoid her leg brushing his.

They all cheered when Andy carried in the huge soup tureen filled with boiled goodness, and Rose followed with a basket of buttered bread slices from what Liz would bet were freshly baked loaves.

It wasn't the kind of dish that could be passed around the table, so they took turns standing and leaning in to ladle the ham and veggies into their bowls.

"It looks amazing," Liz said as she watched Mitch fill his bowl and then Paige's, before handing the ladle to Ryan who also filled Lauren's. "Smells good, too."

"I don't usually make it in the summer, but my girl's home, so her favorite dish it is."

"You're the best, Rose."

When the ladle came around the table, Drew stood and took it. He filled Liz's bowl first, and then his own, before passing it on.

"Thanks," she said, feeling oddly pleased he'd done the same for her that the other guys had done for their women. Not that she was Drew's woman, but it made her feel good to not be the only female who ladled her own soup.

Then she looked across the table and saw Rose watching her with what could only be described as rampant speculation. *Uh-oh.*

If Rose got it in her head Liz and Drew would make a good couple, especially considering she knew there was physical attraction between them, they were doomed. If not for the fact Liz'd watched her family mill around, deciding where to sit, she would wonder if being next to Drew was Rosie's doing.

"Did I tell you I Skyped with Emma yesterday?" Katie asked once everybody was served. "Johnny's getting so big."

"I need to go see them again soon," Rose said, and Liz was relieved to see her focus shift away. "My sweet grandbaby and he's hours away. And Nick's not only in Massachusetts, but teenage boys are fast on their feet when you're trying to smother them with kisses."

Even though she sounded mournful, Liz smiled. It didn't matter that there was no blood between Rose and the Kowalskis. She was Grammy Rose and Liz had no doubt Sean felt as strongly about that as Rosie did. They all would.

"I need some grandchildren here in Maine, too," she continued with a pointed look in Mitch and Paige's direction.

"Hey, we're working on it," Paige said. "Maybe Katie or Liz will beat me to it."

Liz swallowed a chunk of bread that went down hard, shaking her head. "Maybe you don't get how the whole making a baby thing works, Paige."

"Explains why she's not pregnant yet," Ryan said, and they all laughed.

But Paige was always the optimist. "Hey, you could fall in love tomorrow and start making babies."

Now Rose was giving her that look again, and

Liz fought the urge to squirm in her chair as the woman's gaze bounced between her and Drew. That so wasn't happening. "I really doubt I'll fall in love tomorrow but, even if I did, there won't be any babies. Not for a while. I'm doing other things right now."

"Like what?" Ryan asked.

"I don't know. I might go back to school or take some online classes or take up skydiving. Since I don't know yet, it would be pretty dumb to have a baby." She wanted out of this conversation. Badly. "I can picture a playpen in the corner of the barbershop, though."

Katie pointed her spoon at Liz. "Oh, no you don't. Josh and I aren't having a baby until after our honeymoon."

"Where are you going?" Liz asked.

"We don't know yet."

"When are you going?"

"After the wedding," Josh replied.

"Which there's no date for," Rose said. "I'm going to have to call Mary and arrange to go visit again so I can kiss my baby grandson."

And on that note, Liz decided it was time for a subject change. "Lauren, do you know who's been mowing the lawn? I didn't see a lawn mower anywhere and I wasn't sure if the real estate agent was having it done."

"The boy three houses down does it, actually," Lauren said. "He wanted to earn money mowing lawns but his mower didn't really work. When I moved I sold him mine in exchange for him working off the cost. I think you have two more mows and then you'll have to negotiate with him yourself or buy a mower."

"Good to know." She shifted in her chair, then shifted back when her knee brushed against Drew's. "I'll probably have him keep doing it."

"He's a really good kid."

They talked about the house a bit, while other conversations went on around them. She was aware of the rich timbre of Drew's voice as he talked to Josh about the ATV trails, which made it hard to concentrate on what Lauren was telling her about the heating system in her house. She'd probably have to ask her again when it was time to turn it on.

"It's a problem when my officers can't get to the folks doing something wrong," Drew was saying to Josh. "I'm trying to get a grant to buy the department a four-wheeler, but I think we're going to see more of a presence on the state level, too. We're drawing enough of a crowd to keep a game warden busy."

Liz leaned forward to take a couple more slices of bread out of the basket and, when she did, her entire leg brushed the length of Drew's. She was off balance, so she couldn't pull away, leaving her keenly aware of the contact.

Sitting back down, she slowly ate her bread, avoided making eye contact with Rose and tried not to touch Drew again.

IF LIZ'S LEG didn't stop touching his, Drew was afraid he'd jump out of his skin right there at the dinner table.

Even worse than the touching was her soft laughter. She was obviously enjoying being back with her family and, as she talked with each of them, she'd occasionally laugh and the sound seemed to vibrate through his entire body.

It was a reaction he had to completely hide, of course, since Mitch was sitting at the other end of the table. And he kept catching Ryan watching him, giving him a look that seemed to bore right through him and he wasn't sure why.

He made a mental note to have more police business scheduled at the same time as Kowalski family functions.

After wrapping up a conversation with Josh, who he worked closely with regarding the ATV trails they'd opened to give access to the town, he did his part helping to clear the table.

Mitch loaded up with an armful of cold beers

from the fridge and the men made a break for it as the women argued over who was doing the dishes. When they made it to the front porch without being called back, Mitch started handing out cans.

"None for me," Drew said. "I'm out of uniform but I'm covering a shift, so technically I'm still on duty."

"All work and no play, my friend."

"Are you calling me dull?"

"I think he was," Josh said.

"I get to carry a gun. That's not dull."

Mitch smirked and popped the tab on his beer. "I blow stuff up."

Drew wasn't alone in rolling his eyes. It was hard to win the whose-job-is-cooler contest when a guy owned a controlled demolition company. "Imploding's not as cool as exploding."

"Whatever you say. It all goes boom."

Drew relaxed into one of the rockers as the trash talk turned to sports, tuning them out a bit. The brothers could get rowdy when it came to second-guessing professional coaches and Drew didn't care enough to immerse himself in the debate. Especially sitting on the front porch on a beautiful summer afternoon.

He should put a porch on his house, he thought. It might not have the view the lodge had, but it wasn't a bad way to close out a day. It'd be nicer if he had somebody to sit out there with, but he hadn't put much effort in looking for that somebody.

Thinking of the way his body reacted when Liz's leg brushed against his, he shifted in the rocker. What he wanted was a woman who made him feel the way Liz made him feel, but who wasn't talking about going back to school or jumping out of airplanes before she'd even think about having children.

"Hey." Mitch kicked his ankle. "Where'd you go?"

"Oh, just thinking about work," he lied. "Paperwork and shit."

He hated lying to Mitch. There wasn't a single time in his entire life he could remember that he hadn't been totally honest with his friend, until he had a weak, stupid moment and slept with Liz.

The lying felt like crap, but all he could do was keep his relationship with Liz one hundred percent platonic in the future and focus on putting himself out there in the dating world a little more. Once his mind was on anybody but Liz, it would be a lot easier to face her brother.

They all shot the bull for a while, until Josh started checking his watch every few minutes and keeping an eye on the end of the driveway.

"We should get out of here," Mitch said, "before guests start arriving and Josh puts us to work."

"Yeah, we've got a long drive ahead of us," Ryan agreed.

"You're not staying here?" Drew knew the family rooms were still kept separate, so there was plenty of room.

"Not this time. We have a few things we wanted to get done around the house this weekend while Nick's with his dad."

The guys went into the kitchen, which was where most of the women were gathered. The dishes had been dried and put away, except for a plate on the counter covered in crumbs.

Katie smiled at them. "If you all hadn't run away so fast so you didn't have to help with the dishes, you would have known there were brownies. Now they're gone. Sorry."

"You don't look sorry." Josh slapped her on the ass.

Since it looked like the goodbyes were going to take a while, Drew took that opportunity to duck out of the kitchen for a bathroom break. He went through the living room, but as soon as he turned the corner to the hall, he almost ran smack into Liz.

He came to an abrupt halt, struck by how similar this moment was to the last time he and Liz had been in the lodge at the same time.

"Wow. Déjà vu, huh?" Liz said with a tight laugh, as though she'd been thinking the same thing.

"Yeah." The last thing he wanted was for the awkwardness to rear its head again. "Except this time the fact you ladies ate all the brownies will give me the willpower to keep on walking."

She narrowed her eyes and the corners of her mouth tilted up in a wicked little smile. "What if I tell you I didn't have a brownie?"

He should have run, he thought. Maybe not literally, but when he saw her, he should have stepped around her and kept on walking. He wasn't sure his willpower could withstand blatant flirtation from her, so he needed to nip it in the bud. "Not twenty minutes ago, I told your brother I was thinking about work when I was really thinking about you. Lying to him feels really shitty, so I don't want to add to the list of things I'm hiding."

"I was just playing, Drew." The tightness replacing the flirtation in the set of her mouth made him wonder if he wasn't the only one lying. "The last thing I want to do is cause any more trouble between you and Mitch."

She tried to brush by him, but he stopped her

by putting a hand on her arm. "You have no idea how much I wish things were different."

Her eyes met his for a few seconds and he thought he saw a shimmer of regret there, but then she shrugged. "It is what it is. I'm your best friend's sister and you're a guy who wants a lot more commitment than I have to offer. So we're going to be friends and stop beating ourselves up about something we can't go back in time and change."

She started walking again, but he said her name and she stopped. "Even if I could go back in time, I wouldn't change what happened between us."

"Yeah? Well, I not only had one brownie, but I had *three*." She gave him a saucy wink and went to say goodbye to her family.

LIZ WAS UP bright and early on her first day at her new job. Or maybe not bright, since the sun wasn't fully up yet, but definitely early. With her hair pulled up into a ponytail and her name badge pinned to one of the Trailside Diner T-shirts Paige had given her, she felt as ready as she'd ever be.

She wasn't too worried about waiting tables. It was all she'd ever done, and at some restaurants a lot busier and more fast-paced than Whitford could offer. She'd memorized the menu, and the boss was her sister-in-law. But a new job was still a new job, and low-level anxiety hummed through her.

An hour later, she'd shadowed Paige as she opened the diner for business and served the first wave of early birds. Carl, the first-shift cook, didn't say a lot, but Liz could see he put out an amazing-looking breakfast. And, since she wasn't much for cooking herself, she already knew they tasted as good as they looked.

Once the initial rush petered out, Paige started giving her a more in-depth tour. "I haven't decided if I want to invest in a computer system or not yet. Maybe next year. For now, it's old school. Write down the order, stick the sheet up in the pass-through window and then, when they're done eating, use the calculator to write down the total. Don't forget the tax."

Nothing she couldn't handle. A sheet of paper next to the register with a running tally of slash marks under the days of the week caught her attention. "What's that for?"

"Those are for Gavin's specials. He's saving up to move to the city and get into a culinary school. In the meantime, I let him try out new recipes on the good citizens of Whitford. Since we're not computerized yet, just put a hash mark down whenever somebody orders one of his specials.

I've thought about separating it out so non-residents, who seem to be a little more adventurous, are broken out, but this is enough to give us both a general idea of what works and what doesn't. He's had a few flops, but overall his recipes are well received."

"I'm still trying to wrap my head around the fact Mike Crenshaw's son is all grown up."

"And you know Tori is Jilly's niece, right? Her brother's daughter. She moved here last year from Portland because her parents' divorce was not amicable and she was tired of being stuck in the middle."

Liz didn't really know Jilly Burns Crenshaw. Mike met her while he was away at college and she couldn't remember when they'd moved back to Whitford. There was a lot of that throughout the morning. Faces she knew. Some that were vaguely familiar. Many she didn't know but who knew who she was.

Everybody, of course, had something to say about her driving Chief Miller's Mustang.

She was tempted to greet every customer with, "Yes, I'm Liz Kowalski and I've moved home from New Mexico because I missed my family and I'm driving Chief Miller's Mustang because I wrecked my car, but I'm okay, and he lent it to me because I'm his best friend's sister and no other reason."

But she didn't think that would go over well. Not with this crowd, anyway. They liked to ferret out information for themselves, with a whole heap of wild assumptions thrown in.

The chief himself showed up after the lunch rush was over, taking a seat at the counter. "Hey, Liz. How's it going?"

She hadn't seen him since he'd rejected her pretty overt attempt at flirting three days before, and she was worried things would be weird between them again. But he seemed normal enough, so she tried to relax. "I guess you'd have to ask Paige, but I think it's going good."

He ordered a salad topped with grilled chicken and a diet soda. "I went on a cheeseburger binge after my divorce, until I woke up one day and had to suck in my breath to button my uniform pants. Spent the better part of two weeks sitting at my desk because I could unbutton them and nobody was the wiser."

"I was sorry to hear you and Mallory split up." She had been, too. That was, of course, before she'd gotten him to herself for a few minutes.

He shrugged. "Wanted different things."

It was a lot worse than that, from what Rose had told her. Mallory kept putting off starting a family until Drew finally dug in his heels and told her he didn't want to wait anymore. She'd finally confessed she'd never planned to have kids and didn't tell him because she was afraid of losing him. He tried for a while after that, but besides the fact he still wanted kids, he couldn't get over the fact Mallory had started lying to him before they were even married and never stopped.

"Better cheeseburgers than alcohol," she told him, trying to lighten the mood again.

He chuckled. "Yeah, until you can't strap on your gun belt and live in fear of having to chase somebody down."

She handed his order slip to Gavin, who'd replaced Carl and was preparing for dinner. The special was a steamed haddock with a sauce in a language Liz didn't understand, so she suspected Ava wouldn't be putting many checkmarks on the specials sheet during the dinner hour.

Paige had disappeared into the office and they'd pretty much finished the prep work, so Liz poured herself an ice water and went back to talk to Drew. "So, based on customer comments today, we're quite the Facebook sensation."

"I swear there are people inventing reasons to talk to me just so they can ask about it."

"Does it bother you?"

He scoffed. "Of course not. This isn't the first

time the good folks of Whitford have speculated about my personal life."

"It's something I'll have to get used to again, I guess. I was a little more anonymous in New Mexico. In some ways it's freeing to live someplace where people haven't known you since you were born. But in other ways, it's lonely. It's nice having a shared history with people. Stories, you know?"

"Like the time I put the plastic wrap over the toilet bowl in the bathroom your brothers always used, but Rosie was cleaning the other one, so you used that one and peed all over yourself?"

She'd screamed so loud Rose had come running, with her father close on his heels. Drew had been sent home, which meant calling his father and asking him to pick him up out on the road, since Andy wasn't allowed on the Northern Star property. "I still haven't forgiven you for that. Someday there will be payback."

He grinned and butterflies started dancing around in the pit of her stomach. He'd always been handsome, but a little more serious than her brothers, so when he flashed that boyish grin, it really hit hard. "Your old man made me split a cord of hardwood for that. I paid my dues."

"Not to me."

Gavin called out her name, so she went to the

window and grabbed Drew's salad. He didn't want any dressing, which she thought was weird and said so.

"My dad doesn't like dressing, either. I'm not sure we ever had any in the house, so I'm used to it plain."

"Salads are made to be covered with cheese, bacon bits and ranch dressing."

He shook his head, sprinkling salt and pepper over the plate, which she thought was even more weird. "Pretty sure a cheeseburger would be better for you."

Paige emerged from the office, and Liz could tell by the rosy glow she'd been on the phone with Mitch. "Sorry to disappear, Liz. Everything going okay out here?"

"Except for the part where she harasses customers about their food choices," Drew said in a dry tone.

Paige's eyes got big for a few seconds before she relaxed with a shaky laugh. "It's funny, but because I only met you at our wedding and you just moved back, sometimes I forget everybody knows you. Here I am worried about how you're treating our police chief, when you guys already have this whole history together."

Drew choked and ended up downing half his

soda before he could talk again. “Sorry, went down the wrong pipe.”

Liz left Paige to fuss over him, but she gave him an eye roll behind her sister-in-law’s back. Hopefully Paige would never know just how much of a shared history they had.

FIVE

BUSINESS MEETINGS AT the Trailside Diner were the norm for Drew. At least a few times per month, somebody would suggest they talk over lunch to save time.

Today he was sharing a booth with Dave Camden, who served as the school resource officer, as well as the school principal. With another academic year behind them, Drew liked to look back at the department's relationship with the school to see what they'd done right and what they could do better in the fall. Since Dave was fairly young and it had been his first year as SRO, it was even more important than usual.

He managed to keep his mind on topic when the topic was school safety, but as the others digressed, so did his thoughts.

Liz had greeted them all warmly when they'd sat down, setting them up with menus and drinks, but he thought there had been a little extra warmth in the smile she gave him. Maybe it was wishful thinking, but he didn't think so.

She looked totally natural in the diner, he thought as he watched her work. It was only her third day, but she was obviously comfortable with the work and the customers. And she looked like she enjoyed it, too. With one ear on the conversation, in case it turned back to something important, he watched her clean up as most of the customers left and then turn to prep for dinner.

When his meeting finally broke up, he shook hands with the principal and told Dave he'd meet him back at the station in a while. Then he took what was left of his soda and moved to a seat at the counter. Liz was in the process of restocking the salt and pepper shakers and the sugar bowls, but she stopped when she got to him.

"I saw you walk in with that woman and thought maybe you were on a date," she said with a small smile that looked a little tight.

"I haven't dated anybody since my divorce. Except, you know. Not that that was a date, I guess." Rather than keep shoving his foot in his mouth, he shut up.

"Really? I'm surprised the single women in Whitford didn't jump all over you."

"We get a lot more baked goods dropped off at the station than we used to." Since she'd brought up dating, he figured it was a good time to ask the question he'd been wondering about. "So everybody in Whitford knows why Mallory and I split. What happened with you and…what was his name? Darren?"

She shrugged. "Nothing happened, which was a big part of the problem, I guess. I told him we were done and he said, 'Bummer.'"

"If that was his reaction to losing you, he didn't deserve you." It wasn't an empty platitude. He meant it and he hoped she could hear the sincerity in his voice.

"He was a good guy, really. We were friends, if nothing else, and he had a hard time taking care of himself. I believed in his art, so I did what I could to support him. He ended up with some minor success and I ended up…tired."

"What made you tell him it was over?"

She smiled, fiddling with a sugar packet. "I blame Sean and Mitch."

"I know Mitch never liked him, but I also know you spent fifteen years ignoring his opinion. What changed?"

"I talked to Rose on the phone a lot. We've always been close, even if I was too stubborn to give up on Darren and come home. She'd tell me stories about how Sean and Emma fell in love, with the whole fake fiancé thing, and then about

Mitch and Paige. I wanted that. I wanted to turn a guy inside out. I didn't know at the time I was going to come back to Maine, but I knew I wasn't settling for just friendship anymore."

He nudged her arm with his elbow. "For the record, I'm glad you came back to Maine."

"I am, too."

She was smiling when she said it, but he thought he saw some reservation on her face. "Are you, really?"

"I am."

"I guess it's not the kind of thing you want to talk about at work. Sorry about that."

She laughed. "It's fine. The place is about empty now, anyway. It's just that sometimes I feel a little…underachieving. I came out here to be with my family while they were getting married and having babies and running their businesses. But now I'm here not doing much while they're doing all that."

"What do you mean you're not doing much?" He shook his head. "You're setting up a new house and working a new job. Getting reacquainted with old friends and making new ones. I'd say you're doing just fine."

"I guess you're right." Her eyes softened, which did things to his insides. "I guess I just see everything they have and feel like I don't have enough."

"If you judge your life by what others have, you'll probably always feel that way. I feel that way, sometimes. It seems like everybody's got their shit together and here I am starting over, too. Like you."

"You're a smart guy, Chief Miller. Before you know it, some lucky lady will snap you up and you'll be putting that town seal on the door of a minivan."

He laughed at that visual. "I don't know about that. I'd never hear the end of it if I had to call Butch to tow me out of a snowbank so I could answer an emergency call."

His phone beeped, and he checked it to see a text reminder from Barbara. He was supposed to head out to Posthole Road and mediate a dog versus chickens situation and there was a brief window of time when both residents were home.

"No rest for the boys in blue?"

He smiled up at her and shook his head. "Got a dog chasing chickens and if we don't get it resolved, we're going to have to hire somebody just to field the complaints the owners are filing against each other."

"Sounds exciting."

He downed the last of his soda and stood. "It's not exactly LAPD exciting, but taking care of Whitford makes me happy. And that's the thing.

As long as you're happy, who cares what everybody else is doing?"

The warm smile told him she knew he was talking about her. "I'll try to remember that. Have fun with those chickens."

"See you next time."

He walked out in a good mood, because the next time wouldn't be too far away. As far as he was concerned, being able to see her just by stopping in to the diner was one of the best parts of her job.

AFTER WORK, LIZ dropped by the Northern Star to see Rose for a few minutes. She had a feeling it would become a regular thing, which was okay. They had a lot of face-to-face visit time to make up.

Rose had just finished dusting in the living room, and it amused Liz that, instead of just sitting on one of the sofas, they still went into the kitchen to visit. It was just how family visits were done at the Northern Star.

"How's work going?" Rose asked as Liz rummaged in the fridge for some water and an apple. She was hoping to fend off Rose breaking out the baked goods because she was going to need new pants if she didn't cut back.

"It's good. I haven't had any problems."

"I hear Drew's in there quite a bit."

Liz gave her an *are you kidding me* look. "This town is too much. I'm pretty sure Drew ate lunch there long before I moved home from New Mexico."

"Don't try to pull the wool over my eyes. I can see by the blush on your cheeks that there's still something going on with you two."

"There really isn't." And there couldn't be.

Rose pulled out a chair and sat across from her. "I think you should tell Mitch what happened."

"I don't necessarily disagree with you, but I'm leaving that up to Drew."

"That's not like you, to keep your mouth shut if you think something needs to be said."

Liz shrugged. "He has more at stake. I'm Mitch's sister. No matter how mad at me he gets, he can't push me out of his life. With Mitch and Drew, there's this whole stupid guy code thing and Drew *could* get pushed out. So I'm leaving it up to him."

"You two can't move forward until he knows," Rose said, giving her a pointed look.

"There's no moving forward, anyway. I'm not ready to start popping out babies and everybody knows that's what he wants."

"He doesn't necessarily want them *tomorrow.*

Mallory didn't want them at all. You want kids someday, don't you?"

"Probably." Liz shrugged, turning the uneaten apple over and over in her hands. "Not definitely, but probably. And not anytime soon."

"I bet he'd wait. You're worth it, honey."

"Don't you have anything else to talk about besides me and Drew?"

"No, not really."

Of course not. Rose couldn't be any more of a typical mother where Liz was concerned if she'd given birth to her herself. "Why don't you tell me about you and Andy."

The warm bliss that flooded Rosie's face made Liz both very happy for her and a little jealous, too. It was obvious the woman was very much in love.

"We're very happy," Rose said. "We love each other and, not only do I get to keep taking care of this house and you kids, but he really enjoys helping Josh with the lodge. It couldn't have worked out any more perfectly."

"Pretty strange considering how long you refused to let him on the property," Liz said. "Are you ever going to tell me what he did to make you hate him for decades?"

Rose tightened her mouth and shook her head. "That, young lady, is water under the bridge."

"Well, so is what happened between Drew and me. Just water under the bridge."

"I still think you should dive back in and see where the current takes you."

"Probably over a waterfall and onto the rocks," Liz said, and then she took a bite of the apple.

Rose shook her head. "You're just as stubborn as your brothers."

SIX

After a few days of popping into the diner for lunch, Drew realized he really liked Liz. Not just liked thinking about the amazing sex they'd had or her amazing smile or how great her ass looked in jeans. He liked her.

Because he liked to be in the office if Barbara wasn't going to be, he ate lunch later than the norm, and the diner was fairly quiet whenever he went in. He'd chat with Liz while she restored order after the lunch rush and got the place ready for Ava to come in and do the supper shift, and he'd discovered there was nothing Liz couldn't talk about.

Politics, books, movies, history. It didn't matter what random subject popped up, she'd talk about it. And if she didn't know a lot about it, she'd listen and ask questions.

The best part of his day was when Liz leaned her hip against the counter and talked to him.

He wanted to take her on a date. A real date,

with dinner somewhere other than the Trailside Diner. That would mean a long drive, but he wouldn't mind because he liked her company.

Part of him was starting to wonder how Mitch would take it. Maybe there was a way to beat around the bush and see how his friend would feel about Drew dating his sister without actually coming out and saying he was interested in her.

It had the potential for disaster, though. And some logical part of his brain really wanted to know if it was worth risking his relationship with Mitch when that same part knew that before Liz came back to town, Drew had promised himself he was going to stop feeling sorry for himself and go out and find the mother of his children. Liz had never said she didn't want kids, but that wasn't something that came up in casual conversation. But he did know, or at least strongly suspected, that it wasn't something she was thinking about now.

That meant there was a possibility Drew could invest himself in a relationship with her, at great risk to his friendship, only to have her realize down the road she had other things she'd rather do than be a mother.

It was a frustrating circle of what he wanted versus what he needed, and it was enough to keep his mouth shut.

"You're looking pretty serious today," Liz said, breaking into his thoughts as she set his bowl of chicken soup in front of him. Drew never missed Gavin's chicken soup days if he could help it. While it wasn't quite as good as Rose's, it ran a pretty damn close second and nothing beat a good bowl of chicken soup.

"Lot on my mind." Before she could open her mouth to push for more, he kept going. "You know, if you need to go into the city to stock up on more than what the Mustang can hold, just say the word. We can take the SUV. I just fill it on my personal card before I leave town and nobody complains."

It was almost a date. He wasn't a big fan of shopping, but at least he'd get to spend some time with her away from her family and the rest of the town.

"Thanks, but I stole Josh's truck and made a run the other day after work. There are enough vehicles there so he didn't miss it and, if he really needed a pickup, the gas mileage in the old plow truck doesn't hurt as badly if he was just running around town."

Deflated, he tried to shrug off the missed opportunity. "Settling in okay?"

"Yeah. I haven't done a lot of shopping for the house yet. Mostly I needed to stock up on staples and fill the fridge and pantry. As much as I love Fran, that kind of shopping gets expensive at the market and it's worth the trip to the city."

"I know you've got plenty of family, but you can still call me if you need anything."

She smiled, handing him a few extra packages of crackers for his soup. "Thanks. I appreciate it. Hey, did you see on the news they caught the guy that was breaking into the camps on the lake?"

They talked about the news while he ate his soup and he would have lingered, but dispatch called him out for a possible bear in a backyard report.

An hour later, he'd coaxed a massive black dog he hadn't seen around town into his SUV, and radioed ahead to Barbara to let her know he was bringing her another stray and to give her a description. She'd start reaching out to see if he'd been reported missing anywhere local, then take the poor guy home with her. They didn't have much in the way of animal control outside of the police department, and Barbara always fostered the rare displaced or lost pet. They almost always traced them back to a vacationing family.

Because nothing popped immediately and the dog had obviously been wandering a while, Barbara left early. She'd make the half-hour drive to the vet, then take him home and get him fed and bathed. That left Drew as police chief-slash-office staff.

As soon as he sat down at his desk, he remembered something he'd wanted to tell Liz. She'd probably left work and, after a little bit of hesitation, he decided to call her. He'd given her his cell number earlier in the week in case she needed anything, so it had been natural for her to give him hers at the same time.

She answered on the second ring. "Hello?"

"Hey, it's Drew. Are you busy?"

"Nope. I just left the diner. Still in the parking lot, actually. What's up?"

"I meant to tell you when I stopped in for lunch, but I forgot. There's an all-wheel-drive wagon for sale in the paper for short money."

"I saw that. I was thinking about calling them when I get home."

"Don't bother. The guy selling it picked it up dirt-cheap at auction because its previous owner accidentally put it in a pond where it sat for two days before he finally confessed it hadn't been stolen after all. I've had some issues with this guy selling questionable vehicles before and he might have managed to clean it up enough to sell it, but it's going to have problems."

"Wow. I should have known the description and the price didn't add up."

"Sorry to burst your bubble."

She laughed, the sound almost musical over the phone line. "I'd rather know now than after I gave him my money."

"If a deal doesn't feel right to you, make sure you call me. And my dad's got a knack for cars. You should take him with you if you go look at something. Not that you're not capable of a test drive, but a second opinion never hurts."

He knew he was talking just to keep her on the phone, but he couldn't help it. At the rate he was going, she was going to start thinking he was stalking her and wouldn't that be an awkward complaint for his department to field.

But then she mentioned she was on her way to see Rose and they talked about the lodge for a while, and then his dad and Rosie's relationship, which seemed to have come out of nowhere. Before he knew it, almost twenty minutes had passed.

"You're not still sitting in the parking lot, are you?" he asked when she finished telling him how she had a very hazy memory of being hidden at the end of the couch the day Rose told Frank Kowalski that if Andy Miller was allowed to visit the Northern Star, she'd quit. The fact they were thinking about eloping to Vegas still boggled their minds.

"Yeah, I am. I didn't want to start the car because your engine's a little loud, plus there's the whole talking on the phone while driving thing. I've heard the local police frown on that."

"They're real hard-asses," Drew agreed. "I'll let you go before Rose thinks you stood her up. I'll probably see you tomorrow for lunch."

"It's a date," she said nonchalantly, and hung up.

It was just an expression, he told himself. But he still got barely any work done that afternoon.

STILL IN HER Trailside Diner T-shirt, Liz drove up to the front of the lodge and killed the engine. She'd promised Rose she'd stop by after work and, after sitting in her car talking on the phone with Drew for far too long, she was running late enough so she didn't go home and change first.

Paige's car was in the driveway, too, which meant there would probably be tea and visiting before they got around to whatever it was Rose wanted a hand with, or to talk to her about or whatever.

Sure enough, the two women were sitting at the kitchen table when she went in, and there was a plate of fresh-baked brownies on the table.

"How was work, Liz?" Rose asked, going to the stove to pour her some tea.

"It was good. It's a different climate than the truck stop I worked at last and I really like it."

Paige drew her hand over her forehead in a gesture of exaggerated relief. "Thank goodness. I've gotten used to having a little more free time when Mitch is home."

They talked about the diner for a few minutes. Paige's schedule was going to be fairly fluid. She'd spend more time at the diner when Mitch was traveling or during times the ATV traffic would be heavy, but she'd be more hands-off when her husband was in town. That worked just fine for Liz.

"Speaking of schedules," Rose said, "I talked to Mary this morning and she had a wonderful idea."

Uh-oh. A wonderful idea cooked up by Rosie and Aunt Mary couldn't mean anything good for anybody named Kowalski. "Do I want to know?"

"Every year they go camping for two weeks. All of them—the kids, grandkids. It's become a family tradition, I guess."

Liz didn't hear anything but the words *camping* and *two weeks.* Her brain added the word *no.*

"That sounds fun," Paige said. "My mom had a boyfriend who liked to camp when I was a kid. We went a few times and I loved it, but then they broke up and we never went again. I should talk Mitch into camping."

Liz could see Paige playing right into whatever hand Rose was about to play, and she was tempted to kick her under the table.

"I'm glad you said that," Rose said, "because Mary and I want to make it a family reunion."

"I'll never get Mitch away from work for two weeks. And I know Ryan's busy."

"Everybody's busy," Liz echoed, trying to keep her expression regretful.

"With not a lot of notice and everybody's schedules, we know two weeks is out of the question, but we can all go over for a week."

"I bet Mitch can make that work if I push," Paige said. "And Ryan can delegate. What about the lodge? If Josh and Katie go, how can you and Andy go, too? You have to be there."

"If we go up on a Thursday and leave Wednesday, we'll only be away one weekend. There's a big ATV event in central New Hampshire the first weekend the family will be at the campground and everybody seems to be going there. That means we have no bookings to worry about and there's also plenty of room at the campground."

"This is going to be so fun," Paige said. "Doesn't it sound fun, Liz?"

Not really, but rather than come off as a wet

blanket, she tried going with the practicality first. "If the diner's so busy you were able to hire me to take up some slack, how can we both be gone for a week?"

"Ava and Tori will understand this is a big deal for the family, so they'll be willing to hold down the fort for a while. And, like Rosie said, most of the four-wheeling crowd will be at that other event anyway."

"I don't have any camping stuff."

Paige shrugged. "You could probably bunk down in somebody's RV. They all have couches."

Yeah, and they were mostly newlyweds, parents or—in the case of her uncle Leo—snored like the early rumbles of a major earthquake. But with Rose and Paige both looking at her so expectantly, practically vibrating in their eagerness to start planning this family adventure, she knew it was as good as done.

She tried to muster a smile to match theirs. "There will be s'mores, right?"

Within seconds, a notepad appeared on the table and the two women were talking over each other in a rush to make a list of everything they'd need. Liz sipped her decaf tea—which she liked a lot better than decaf instant coffee—and watched them work. Once they started coordinating with Aunt Mary, she knew this would be the best-planned camping trip in the history of the great outdoors. All she had to do was relax and enjoy the vacation.

"Somebody should tell Drew right away," Rose said, looking up from the list. "The department's small, so covering for him might be a problem."

Liz almost choked on her tea, but she thought she covered it well. Of course they were going to invite Drew. He was Andy's son. There was a good chance at some point in the future, he'd be Rosie's stepson.

But Drew was becoming a problem for Liz. She already knew they had great sexual chemistry, which was bad enough. Now she was slowly discovering they seemed to have great chemistry in general, and that was worse. If they lived anywhere but Whitford and he was anybody but her brother's best friend, they'd be spending a lot of time together. Maybe going out to dinner or to a movie. Sitting on her futon, talking about who knew what at the end of the day.

She knew they wanted different things right now. From what she'd heard, he was looking to be on the fast track to marriage and babies, and she was still hovering at the Start line, wondering if that was a path she was willing to take. But there was still something there, whether it made sense or not.

"It would be so much fun to have Drew along," Rose said in a totally innocent voice Liz knew was covering up a devious mind.

"I'll have Mitch talk to him today," Paige said, because there was no way Liz could ask Rose to rethink inviting Drew, of course. Not in front of her sister-in-law. "After I've broken the news to Mitch, of course, and knocked down all of his excuses."

"He went a few years ago, though only for a couple of days, and he had a good time."

"If I have to go, everybody has to go," Liz added.

A week in the woods with Drew. And Mitch. What could be more relaxing than that?

TODAY WAS ONE of those days when Drew wished time machines were real so he could go back and politely but firmly refuse the appointment as police chief. The budget was a constant wrestling match requiring mathematical gymnastics that made his head hurt. He'd fielded a complaint from a mother about the new part-time officer not understanding how things were done, such as looking the other way when her little darling tried to bribe an adult to buy her alcohol. Papers were multiplying in his inbox at an alarming rate and the number of emails to the department's address that had been flagged for his attention made him want to "accidentally" spill coffee on every keyboard in the station.

He never thought, back when he was a rookie, he'd ever long for the days of being out on patrol, listening to motorists spin creative tales to explain away their vehicular sins.

A cheeseburger would help, he thought. Especially if it had bacon on it. But the only place to get one, short of going home and grilling one for himself, was at the diner. Liz was working today and the more he saw of her, the more he wanted to see of her.

And not just see more of her, as in more of her skin. He wanted to spend time talking to her. Maybe take her to dinner in the city, or to a scary movie so he could play the big, brave cop and offer to check her dark home for boogeymen when he dropped her off. He wanted to read the newspaper with her, swapping sections as they finished, and then talk about what they read.

He wanted company. But with each passing day, it became less about just somebody to keep him company and more about Liz's company. Maybe she wasn't interested in the same future he was, but in the right here and now, she was in his thoughts whenever he wasn't concentrating on something else. He'd been working even more hours than usual lately.

After skimming through email to see if there was anything either urgent or something his standard copied-and-pasted response could deal with, he leaned back in his chair and put a hand to the back of his neck, rolling his head from side to side.

Mentally playing eenie-meenie-minie-mo with his to-do list while he stretched his muscles, Drew looked toward his office window in time to see Mitch walk into the station. He hated the way his normal happiness at seeing his best friend was now tainted by his guilt for thinking dirty thoughts about the man's sister.

But he smiled and waved him in when Mitch headed toward his office. Guilt or no, he was still enjoying seeing more of Mitch since he'd come home for a brief visit, only to fall for Paige and settle back in Whitford.

"I've come to make you an offer you can't refuse," Mitch said as he stepped into the room and nudged the door closed behind him with his foot.

"Does it involve a bacon cheeseburger?"

"No."

"Then it's an offer I can refuse."

"I guess it's not really an offer, anyway. Aunt

Mary decided to turn their annual camping trip into a family reunion and she got Rosie on board."

"In other words, you're going camping for two weeks." More importantly, Liz would be going camping for two weeks. Drew could use the break because pretending he was indifferent to her was exhausting.

"We can't get away that long, but we're going for a week. I want you to come, too."

Whoa. Drew shook his head. "Not happening."

"You used to be fun."

"Yeah, but I've never been crazy."

Mitch frowned. "My family's not that bad."

"I'm also not a part of it, so I don't really need to reunite with everybody," Drew pointed out.

"Since your old man has hooked up with Rosie, he's practically family and you're his son. You've also been my best friend for as long as I can remember. Why shouldn't you go?"

What was he was supposed to say? *Well, at your wedding, your sister and I snuck off for a quickie and now things are a little awkward between us.* And he wasn't sure he could keep his hands off of her, which would make things a whole lot worse than a little awkward.

"Look," Mitch said. "When's the last time you took a vacation?"

Drew rocked back in his chair and thought

about it. Taking the odd fishing or sledding weekend off the table, it would have been…huh. "I went down to Florida for Red Sox spring training."

"What year was that?"

"Ninety-four?"

Mitch leaned in for the kill. "Think about it, Drew. Mud. Wheelers. Meat cooked on sticks over an open fire."

"No cell phones."

"Crushing beer cans and tossing them over our shoulders."

"Like men do."

Mitch nodded. "We have to pick them up after, though, or the women will make us suffer."

Women. Kowalski women. Liz was a Kowalski woman. "I don't know, Mitch. I've got a lot going on."

"Everybody does. That's why it's a vacation. It's not a vacation if it's a break from doing nothing."

"I could use a break," he admitted, looking over the cluttered top of his desk. "But—"

"Before you start thinking up excuses, you should know Rosie has her heart set on you going."

"Shit." He may as well start preparing the station for his absence. "I think I have some camping stuff in the garage."

"Don't worry. My aunt Mary will probably write out a master packing list and make sure everybody gets a copy." Mitch stood. "I'll tell Rosie you're in. I'd stay longer, but I have to head to Portland tonight. Early flight in the morning so I can try to get ahead of schedule on some things before the trip."

Drew stood and shook his hand. "I'll tell you right now, if I get locked into this camping gig and you use work to back out, I'll shoot you. And I know how to get away with it."

"You're already locked in. Be on the lookout for a list from Aunt Mary. If nobody gives her your contact info, she'll just email it through the department's website."

Liz came by her stubbornness honestly, that was for sure. "Since I haven't been camping since before I was old enough to drink, I don't have a problem with lists."

"Dust off the fishing gear while you're digging around the garage." Mitch started walking toward the door, glancing at the clock on the wall as he went.

"Hey, Mitch," he called after him. "We don't really have to cook our meals on sticks, do we?"

Mitch shrugged. "Depends on how badly we

piss off the women. Word to the wise, behave yourself on burger night because it's a bitch to keep them on a stick."

Drew opened his mouth to tell Mitch to forget it—that he'd changed his mind—but the door shut and the moment was lost.

And part of him didn't want to back out. It had been a long time since he'd taken a vacation, and four-wheeling with the guys during the day and kicking back with a beer around the campfire at night sounded like a good time.

SEVEN

Liz looked down at the list her aunt had sent to everybody and then at the pile of stuff in her cart while mentally adding up the price tags. Then she put back the nice two-room tent that she could almost stand up in, and grabbed the small nylon tent with the red clearance sticker. It wasn't as though she'd be spending a lot of time in it, so all it had to do was keep her dry while she slept and save her from having to have any camping roomies.

Most of the stuff on Aunt Mary's list was probably basic stuff but, since Liz couldn't remember the last time she'd camped, she needed all of it. She doubled up on bottles of bug spray and splurged on a small battery-operated lantern, but went cheap on the sleeping bag. It probably wouldn't be thirty degrees below zero at night in July, even in northern New Hampshire.

Cringing as she paid for the items, she told herself it would be worth the cost. She'd moved home because she missed her family, after all.

What could be better than having her brothers and cousins all in one place?

Once she'd loaded her purchases into the Mustang, she assessed the rest of the list. Aunt Mary had included every imaginable item that could be classified as toiletries, most of which she already had. The food stuff she was going to wait and buy at the last minute. She was afraid it would go bad or she'd eat it all and have to buy the same stuff again.

She had also included a list of who was bringing which games, so they didn't end up with six Monopoly games and no cribbage boards. Liz didn't own anything but a deck of cards and they seemed to have those covered.

Books. That's what she needed. Rather than part with any more money, she decided to drive back to Whitford and get a library card.

She slowed down when she passed the town line. Bob Durgin had been out on patrol a lot lately and she knew there would be no sweet-talking her way out of a ticket from him. The last thing she wanted was to give him the satisfaction of busting her in his boss's car.

Judging by the parking lot, the library wasn't very busy, so hopefully it wouldn't take long. The one food item she'd bought was chocolate and, with no air-conditioning in the Mustang, she was beginning to fear for its survival. And she wanted to get the tags and stickers off everything she'd bought and repack it for her trip.

The librarian looked so happy to see her, Liz couldn't help but return her smile.

She and Hailey Genest hadn't been close friends growing up, but they'd known each other. And Hailey had been at Mitch and Paige's wedding, as well. From what Liz understood, she was very good friends with both Paige and Lauren.

"Liz! I heard you'd come back to town. I was going to let you settle in before I started hounding you to get a library card. The trustees love when I find new victims. Especially if you're in the habit of paying overdue fines."

Liz laughed. "Not too many, I hope. But I'm going camping and, from what I'm told, part of camping is sitting around reading."

"Camping? Ah, yes. I heard Rose and your aunt in New Hampshire decided to make your family reunion a trip into the woods."

"I've been promised s'mores."

Hailey gave her a thumbs-up. "I'm a big fan of s'mores. Especially without the marshmallow and graham crackers."

"I'll be bringing a private stash."

"Kind of a bummer to go on vacation and be related to every single guy there. Well, except

Drew, I guess. And his dad." Hailey paused in copying the info from Liz's freshly minted Maine driver's license onto a big yellow card to look up at her. "If there's only going to be one single guy available, Drew's not a bad one to have."

Liz wasn't sure what to say to that. "He's a great guy."

"He really is. I guess you're off-limits because of Mitch, which is sad. He's off-limits to me because I'm friends with his ex-wife. So much opportunity lost."

Liz wanted to ask why everybody seemed bound by rules left over from high school, but sometimes it was best to let sleeping dogs lie. "I don't think a family camping trip's the place for romance, anyway. I mean, Rose and Aunt Mary both told me if I had sex it would ruin my life forever. Granted, I was probably thirteen at the time, but that kind of conviction can stay with a girl."

Hailey's laugh echoed through the quiet library and got her shushed by a guy using one of the computers. "Oops. Embarrassing when the patrons have to tell me to be quiet. Okay, so tell me what you like to read so I can help you find some perfect camping books. Fun stuff, though. Books that go well with s'mores, like romance or horror."

"Both," Liz said, though she had no idea how either corresponded to s'mores.

"And you'll be there how long?"

"A week. I was thinking maybe four books, but I might start reading one before I even leave, so maybe five."

On a mission, Hailey perused the new release shelves, her head cocked sideways to read the spines. She must spend a fortune at the chiropractor if she did that every day, Liz thought.

Hailey would make a noise and pull out a book, handing it to Liz. She then looked at the cover and skimmed the blurb on the back before either handing it back or holding on to it. In no time at all, she had a half dozen books in her arms, ready to keep her company on vacation.

"Did Paige talk to you about movie night?" Hailey asked as they walked back to the checkout desk.

"Yes. I guess women are coming to my house to watch a movie?"

"Awesome. It's always fun to go to a new house."

Liz set the books down and slid them toward Hailey. "You guys know I don't have any furniture, right?"

"We'll have food and drinks. Who needs furniture?"

Liz shrugged, still not sure about this new turn in her social life. Fran had mentioned movie night when she was in the market the day before yesterday and Paige brought it up, but how it got to be Liz's party, she wasn't sure.

"That's a lot of books," Hailey said once she was done stamping the return dates for all of them. "You know, for only ten dollars you can have an official Whitford Public Library tote to carry them in. All the cool kids have one."

With her reading material tucked away in her new tote bag, Liz hurried back to the car. She wanted to get the chocolate bars into her fridge before they became chocolate blobs.

A car sitting in a parking lot across the way caught her eye and she smiled as she let the Mustang crawl out onto the main road. She stopped completely at the stop sign, counting all the way to five, and then gave Officer Durgin a friendly wave as she passed by.

"Maybe next time, Bob," she said to herself, and then hit the gas when she was safely out of his sight.

THE FOURTH OF July had been a lot more fun before Drew was personally responsible for the safety of Whitford's population, but it was still one of his favorite holidays. It was a day for barbecues and beer and lemonade and fireworks, and most of all for friends.

Though everybody was on duty that evening, it didn't really feel like work as Drew wandered on foot through the crowd gathered to watch the fireworks. Whitford put on a good show and he'd fought the budget committee to keep them from cutting the funds. The better the official town display, the fewer people who got hurt blasting them out of their own backyards.

There were various fundraisers going on, and Drew spread his money around the different bake sales and lemonade stands until he couldn't take any more sugar. Everybody said hello to him and he felt a sense of deep satisfaction. This community was almost like a family to him and he took pretty good care of them.

Excitement hummed through the crowd when the first test shot went up, but Drew estimated it would be another ten to fifteen minutes before it was dark enough for the real show to begin. Off in the distance, a baby cried and a dog barked, but overall the crowd was a happy one this year.

He spotted his dad waving to him and waved back, making his way toward him. The Kowalski crowd had carved out a space in the park's grass, marked with several old quilts. Besides his old man and Rose, Josh and Katie were there, along with Ryan and Lauren. Drew had already run into Lauren's teenage son, Nick, who was watching the fireworks with his dad, stepmom and little brother and sister. Mitch and Paige were on the far side of the quilts and, of course, next to Rose was Liz. Drew waved his hand in the general direction of all of them to say hello.

"Come to watch the show with us, son?"

He'd actually just been wandering aimlessly, but why not? "Crowd seems peaceful. No reason I can't hang around for a little while."

Rose opened the cooler sitting at the foot of her quilt and pulled out a bottle of water. He wasn't really thirsty, having had his fill of lemonade already, but he took it from her anyway. There was a lot of chatter around him, but he only half paid attention while keeping part of his focus on the crowd. Now that the test shot had been fired, the kids were starting to get antsy.

Finally, another round went up and Paige clapped her hands. "Everybody lay down! You should lay down to watch fireworks."

Paige hadn't had much in the way of family before marrying into the Kowalskis, and she seemed to take a lot of joy in things the rest of them took for granted, so everybody stretched out on the blankets.

Rose looked up at Drew and then pointed. "Hurry up, Drew. There's room there next to Liz."

There wasn't much he could do short of standing over them like an idiot or walking away, so he kicked off his shoes, set the bottle of water in the grass and stepped onto the quilt. There was some maneuvering to make room for him, but there still wasn't a lot of space between Liz and Josh. He scooted down into the opening and lay on his back, feeling as relaxed as a slab of concrete.

"Sorry about this," Drew said quietly, his head turned toward Liz. "It's a little tight."

"Trust me, she knew exactly what she was doing."

It took a few seconds for her words to sink in and, once they did, he had no idea what to say. It sounded like she was implying Rose had wedged him up against Liz deliberately, which didn't make a lot of sense, unless she'd picked up on some kind of vibe between them. Or she already knew.

Josh was talking to Katie and the others were all in their own conversations, so he felt safe talking in a low voice. "Did you tell her?"

"The morning after the wedding."

Rose had known the entire time. It was a tough thing to wrap his mind around, and he stared up at the sky. On the one hand, she hadn't told Mitch, which meant she must agree it was best he not know. But on the other, Liz had implied Rose put Drew next to her on purpose. If she was matchmaking, she must believe it would be okay when Mitch inevitably found out.

And if Rose knew, had she told his dad? They were a couple, so it was possible. But since Rose was like a second mother to Liz, maybe keeping her secret trumped telling the man she lived with. He was pretty sure his dad would have said something to him by now, so Rose was the only person who knew Drew and Liz had snuck away from the reception. It was interesting, but nothing he could talk to Liz about while lying on a quilt, surrounded by her family.

When the first big rounds exploded high overhead, ripples of ooh and ahh went through the crowd. There were some whistles and woo-hoos, while another baby joined the first in wailing and more dogs barked. He barely paid attention, focused instead on the proximity of Liz's body to his own.

By ten minutes in, everybody was starting to squirm. Rosie had nice thick quilts and the grass under them was lush, but the ground was still the ground and none of them were kids anymore. He shifted, trying to work the various attachments on his belt—especially the flashlight—out from under his body. His thigh pressed against Liz's, only for a moment, but he heard the quickening of her breath.

Being chief of police was more about politics and paperwork than great powers of deductive reasoning, but it didn't take a great detective to figure out she was just as aware of him as he was of her.

Color exploded in the sky, much to the crowd's delight. Around him, Drew was aware of the other couples on the quilts. Paige had her head rested in the cradle of her husband's arm, while Katie had her leg hooked over Josh's. Through his peripheral vision, Drew could see Ryan constantly turning his head to whisper things against Lauren's ear that made her blush. Even his dad and Rosie were holding hands.

He couldn't do that because the woman he wanted was off-limits to him, and that sucked.

Then her hand brushed his and, on the ground where their hands were hidden from everybody else by their bodies, he linked his fingers through hers. She was still for a few seconds, and he wondered if she'd pull away. But then her hand relaxed and she drew circles against his palm with the knuckle of her thumb.

Such a sweet, innocent thing, holding hands. But the secrecy of it—the feeling of doing something forbidden—made the small touch seem so much more erotic. The sizzle of chemistry was as strong as ever between them and he savored this little bit of her that he could get. Each stroke of her thumb pulled at something deep inside of him and he lost himself in the sensation as colors continued to fill the night sky.

Then the radio clipped to his shoulder squawked and everybody jumped. Liz jerked her hand away as her family and a good number of the people around them turned to look at him.

"Sorry, folks." As he pushed himself very awkwardly upright, hoping nobody would be looking below his belt, he radioed back to dispatch that he'd call in on his cell. In a town like Whitford, where everybody knew everybody else, he did his best to keep people's troubles from being broadcast.

"What's up?" he said into his phone when dispatch answered.

A big family barbecue had gone south and, fueled by significant amounts of alcohol, somebody had insulted somebody else's mother. Sides were taken, punches were thrown, and Officer Durgin felt like he might need some backup with muscle.

"Sorry, I have to run," he said to everybody. It wasn't easy, scooting backward off the quilt, and then he had to roll to his knees to stand up.

"Is everything okay?" Rose looked concerned. "Was there an accident?"

"Nope. Just booze making people stupid."

"Be careful," she said.

After making sure all of his accoutrements were still attached to his belt, he glanced at Liz. She was watching him, her head tilted back against the quilt so she was upside down to him. There was a hint of rosiness on her cheeks that intrigued him, but she just smiled.

"Bye, Drew."

There was a lot more he wanted to say to her. He wanted to ask her why they were pretending they didn't want each other. Was it only because of Mitch? Or maybe it was because, deep down, they weren't right for each other in the long run. There was no denying they wanted each other, though.

But it was neither the time nor the place, so he just smiled back. "See you later."

Then he walked off, picking his way through the crowd without stepping on anybody, and didn't look back.

LIZ WASN'T SURE who first brought up the idea of her hosting movie night. Apparently, the first Saturday of every month, some of the women met to watch a movie and socialize without men or kids around. Somebody else had suggested making it a movie night and housewarming party combo. She was a little fuzzy on who had said what and when.

She'd already bought a used TV/DVD combo unit from the thrift store, mostly because the thrift store was in Whitford and the nearest department store was an hour away, but that didn't mean her house was exactly ready for company. Paige had assured her attendance was always low in July, thanks to the holiday, and that they'd take care of everything.

Liz hadn't expected pool toys. Paige and Hailey arrived early to help her set up, bringing with them two folding card tables. Liz helped Paige set those up in the kitchen while Hailey carried in a blender, which she plugged in on the counter, and plastic cups with a little package of what looked like colorful umbrellas.

"There's a theme," Hailey said when she caught Liz looking at them.

Next came a tiny air compressor and the pool floats. Liz laughed when Paige blew up the first one. It was an inflatable recliner float to use in pools and, once it was fully inflated, she tossed it in front of the television and started on the next one. There were half a dozen of them by the time she was done, all of them a different bright color, and Liz's living room looked like drive-in night at the deep end of the pool.

"They have built-in cup holders," Paige said, pointing them out.

"For the umbrella drinks," Hailey added. "And to complete the beach theme—"

"No sand," Liz interrupted.

"Of course not. Paige said no. Anyway, to complete the beach theme, we're watching *How Stella Got Her Groove Back.*"

"Good choice." It had been years since Liz had seen it, but it definitely fit the beach theme.

"You need to get your groove back," Paige said, pointing at Liz. "How long has it been since you and that guy broke up?"

There was nothing wrong with Liz's groove. She and Drew had proven that at Mitch's wedding, not that she could say so. "The last thing I want in my life right now is another guy. I'm enjoying being single, thank you, even if it means being groove-less."

"I, on the other hand, am sick of being grooveless," Hailey said. "I'm going to have to move to the city and find my groove."

Paige snorted. "You always say that, but you're not going anywhere. You love your house and you really love your job."

"They're going to have to give me a raise just to cover the cost of batteries."

Liz was saved from having to respond to that by a knock on the door. She opened it to find Fran Benoit, wife of Butch and owner of the market, standing on the step with a dish in one hand and a small wooden bookcase in the other.

"Open the door. This is heavy."

Liz took the bookshelf, which was more awkward than heavy, and let Fran into the house. "Nobody told me movie night was bring your own bookcase."

"I hadn't told her yet," Paige said. "So we wanted this to be part housewarming party, so everybody is to bring one useful item from their own house they don't use anymore to give to you."

"That's the nicest thing I've ever heard." The sudden prick of tears in her eyes surprised Liz and she tried to blink them away.

She hadn't expected to be made so welcome into a group of friends so quickly. Sure, she knew them all, but most she hadn't seen in years. And Paige was her sister-in-law, but she'd only met her once. Since that had been the weekend Mitch and Paige got married, she hadn't had a lot of quality bonding time with the bride. The fact she and Hailey had set all of this up for her made her want to cry big, fat happy tears, but she sniffed them back.

Fran gave a big shrug, making her thick gray braid sway. "I also brought nachos."

Paige and Hailey went back out to Paige's car to carry in their contributions. Paige brought her a vacuum that was possibly older than her car, but she promised it worked, and Hailey contributed a toaster oven. Jilly brought her son's infamous Buffalo Chicken Dip, a bag of tortilla chips and an over-the-toilet bathroom organizer.

Tori brought a veggie tray and a small end table that was painted a glossy black, with neon flowers stenciled on it. "I'm a little weird. Sorry."

"I love it," Liz said, and she did. It was funky and, strangely enough, it matched her blow-up furniture perfectly.

Hailey made the drinks because Fran made them so strong they could only have one and, even then, driving could be an issue. Hailey made them more in the spirit of drinking, but light on the actual spirits. Then they popped the movie in.

Fran chose to sit on the futon, but Liz claimed one of the pool floats and set her drink in the cup holder. It wasn't the easiest thing to lower herself into while balancing a paper plate loaded with food, but it was fun and squeaked if she moved around.

"You ready for the big camping trip?" Paige asked as she performed the same balancing act.

"I think so." She hoped so, since they were leaving in a few days and she didn't want to spend any more of her meager savings on a vacation that didn't involve a real beach.

"I can't believe everybody can actually go. Even Drew managed to get the time off."

One of the reasons Liz had agreed to host movie night was to get her mind off Drew Miller for a few hours, but between talk of getting one's groove back and the camping trip, that wasn't really working out for her.

Luckily, Hailey finished making the last drink and hit Play on the movie before maneuvering into the lime-green float. At last, a distraction.

But nothing, it seemed, could stop her from thinking about the Fourth of July fireworks. Whatever had possessed them to hold hands, surrounded as they were by almost her entire family, she'd never know. But she'd liked it.

It was delicious, the way her hand felt in his. And when her thumb stroked a certain spot, his fingers would tighten around hers for a few seconds. She wanted to play with that spot some more. And she wanted to see what other spots on his body would get a reaction like that.

Since that night, she hadn't seen him at all. The Fourth being on a Thursday meant a long holiday weekend for most people, and long holiday weekends meant busy law enforcement. Or he was avoiding her, possibly scared off by learning Rose knew they'd been together. She wasn't sure which.

But she was about to have a week of being with

Drew twenty-four seven, and there would be no avoiding each other. And, once again, she'd be surrounded by her entire family. She wasn't sure her nerves could take it, but, like it or not, she was going to find out.

EIGHT

THE FIRST THING Liz saw when they pulled into the campground was the black SUV with the light bar on top, and she realized riding with Mitch and Paige had been a bad idea. She was essentially a hostage, with no way to escape if she felt the need.

But she hadn't felt right about taking Drew's Mustang on a road trip, and the thing got roughly the same gas mileage as a tank. Also, it wasn't really designed to be packed with camping gear. Not that she had a lot, but the Mustang was safely sheltered in Mitch's garage for the week and she was at the mercy of other drivers.

"Oh, that one's ours," Paige exclaimed, pointing to a very large RV with the name of a rental company emblazoned down the side.

Mitch, having substantially deeper pockets than Liz, had arranged for a rental company to deliver an RV to the campground and set it up. Liz would be setting up her clearance tent by herself.

After he parked in the shadow of the RV and

killed the engine, Liz waited for Paige to climb out of the truck and open the access door. When she finally climbed out, Liz's back and legs protested spending almost two hours in the small backseat of Mitch's truck and she stretched, twisting her body to work the kinks out.

She got to do that for about thirty seconds before the family descended on them. It had been less than a year since she'd seen them all at Mitch and Paige's wedding, but Aunt Mary cried a little, anyway. Uncle Leo hugged her so hard she could swear she heard cracking, and then she was passed through what amounted to a gauntlet. Her cousin Joe and his wife, Keri. Their daughter, Brianna, was almost two and played shy, turning her face away when Liz said hi to her. Her cousin Kevin's three-year-old daughter, Lily, was more friendly, though she stuck close to Kevin's wife, Beth. Joe's twin sister, Terry, her husband, Evan, and their fifteen-year-old daughter, Stephanie, were next. Liz wanted to kiss Paige for giving her the rundown on the drive over from Maine. She'd grown up with or near her brothers and cousins, but the kids were hard to keep track of.

Her cousin Mike and his wife, Lisa's, kids were the hardest. Four boys—Joey, Danny, Brian and Bobby—ranging in age from sixteen to nine.

"Where's Sean?" she asked when she didn't see her brother in the crowd.

"They're on their way down," Terry said. "They got the cabin up around the corner. Between the distance and the log walls, she's hoping Johnny won't keep everybody awake."

Johnny was the almost two-month-old nephew she hadn't met yet, and she could barely stop herself from grabbing him away from Emma when she and Sean finally brought him down. She barely took her eyes off his sweet, sleeping face while she hugged her brother and then her sister-in-law.

"He's so perfect," she breathed, wanting to touch his cheek but not daring to in case she woke him up. She didn't know a lot about babies, but she knew sleeping ones were a lot quieter than awake ones.

Because Mitch had just one more business call to make, they'd gotten a later start than he'd intended and they were the last to arrive, so it was quite a crowd to get through. But Bobby and Brian finally showed her where her site was. Thankfully, she noted, it was close to the bathhouse, which meant she wouldn't have to stumble around too far in the dark to go pee in the middle of the night.

Tent first, she decided. After lugging the bag

from the truck to her site, she unzipped it and pulled out her accommodations for the next week. Luckily it was designed for easy setup, with the thin, bowed poles already attached to the tent, so all she had to do was unfold it, square up the corners and pop it up. A few adjustments and ground pins later, and voilà. She had a tent.

With her hands on her hips, she tilted her head and pondered her accomplishment. It was a lot smaller than it had looked on the package. She and her one duffel bag would be very, very cozy, and anytime she was moving around in it, she'd have to be on her hands and knees.

She heard a chuckle off in the distance and looked over to see Drew, standing in front of his own tent, inflating an air mattress and watching her. His tent looked like something on the cover of a camping gear catalog. It was spacious and tall, made out of a rugged-looking canvas material. It had a fly over it, to protect from rain and sun while allowing ventilation. And it had a small screen house built out from the door.

Rolling her eyes, even though she wasn't sure if he could see it from that distance, she turned her back and made her way back to Mitch and Paige's site. From the humming sound, she knew they'd already fired up the air-conditioning in their RV and she mopped at her forehead before grabbing the duffel containing her clothes, toiletries and miscellaneous things from the back of his truck, along with the grocery bag that held some snacks and water to squirrel away in her tent.

"How much more is yours?"

Liz jumped when Drew spoke from just behind her. She hadn't realized he'd followed her. "The sleeping bag and ground mat, and then my pillow and a bag of books in the backseat of the truck."

He grabbed the items she pointed out and fell in beside her for the walk back. "I hope you measured this sleeping bag before you bought that tent."

"I did. It'll fit." Probably. It was going to be tight, though.

"I'm surprised you're not bunking down in one of the RVs. They've got plenty of room."

"That's not real camping," she said, because it was easier than explaining she didn't really want to be a third wheel to any of the other couples. "Those are like luxury hotels on wheels."

"Ah." He nudged her with his elbow. "So you're hard core."

"That's me. Hard-core camping."

They stopped in front of her tent and she set down her bags so she could unzip the door. He crouched to hand in her belongings once she was inside. "So hard core you don't need a cooler?"

"My family has, like, eight refrigerators. There's a limit on being primitive."

She watched him take a knife from his pocket to slice the plastic wrapping on the ground mat, relaxing a little. This wouldn't be so bad, she thought. Obviously she had the ability to hang out with Drew and chat like friends did. Friends who'd had sex and occasionally snuck little touches they didn't want her family to see, but friends.

Once he handed her the mat, she unrolled it onto the tent floor and then spread the sleeping bag on top. After she added her pillow and tucked her duffel, book and food bags along the side, she was done. Then she crawled back to the door.

"You anchored this well, right?" Without waiting for her to answer, he went around to each corner and checked the ground pins. "It looks like it'll blow away in a stiff wind."

"Surrounded by trees, so I won't go far."

He didn't laugh. Instead he kept scowling, looking around. "You're kind of close to the bathhouse."

"I see that as a plus."

"Yeah, except for the Dumpster next to the building. If bears come looking to rifle through the trash, they might smell the peanut butter you have in that flimsy little tent."

"I'll yell and you can come running with your gun," she teased.

"I'm not too far away, but yell loud." He turned to face her and she realized he was very serious, which made her laugh.

"What's so funny?" Andy asked, surprising them both.

"Drew's going to guard my peanut butter from the bears."

He slapped his son on the shoulder. "Good man."

"Where are you and Rose set up?" Drew asked him.

"I guess Mike and Lisa's RV is ours for the week. They usually put the two older boys in the pop-up, but Mike and Lisa are moving to the pop-up and putting the boys in a tent so we can be comfortable." Andy shrugged, looking a little embarrassed. "I wanted to argue, just to be polite, but if I sleep on the ground, it'll take a small crane to get me back on my feet again."

As Andy continued on to wherever he'd been going, Drew drifted away with him. But he turned back and smiled at Liz, giving her a wave.

Warmth curled through her as she waved back, but she did her best to ignore it. Friends. That's all they were.

Very deliberately, Liz turned back to her tent

so she wouldn't do something foolish, like stare at Drew's ass as he walked away, but then she realized she was out of things to do.

A mosquito landed on her arm and she slapped at it. Time to douse herself in bug spray and go join in the family festivities.

ON THE RARE occasion Drew was hanging out at a pool, he liked to do just that. Hang out. Sit on the edge and dangle his feet in the water with a cold beer in his hand.

But there was chaos around the edge of the pool, with kids everywhere and half the women sitting around the edges watching the little ones splash in the shallow end. And Liz was in the mix, looking hot and curvy in a one-piece bathing suit that made his mouth water. It had a tiny skirt that moved flirtatiously as she walked the length of the pool, emphasizing her long legs. And the top of it had that bunched-up look that kept drawing his eye to her cleavage no matter how hard he tried not to look.

He fumbled with the gate latch securing the fence around the pool which, of course, drew attention. Praying his swim trunks were baggy enough to hide his reaction to Liz in a bathing suit, he waved off their ridicule and made a running dive into the deep end.

The water felt arctic, shocking his overheated body as it closed over his head. After pushing off the bottom of the pool, he surfaced gasping. Better than a straight-up cold shower any day.

"Hey, you're blocking our water ball of doom game!" a young voice shouted.

An inflatable beach ball smacked him in the side of the head and, just like that, he was sucked into a cutthroat game that seemed to be a mash-up of water polo, soccer and volleyball. And, since they were limited to the deep end of the pool due to the little ones at the other end, it was one hell of a workout. After about fifteen minutes, he worked his way toward the edge and hooked his elbows up on the rim.

"You're weak, Miller," Josh taunted, right before one of Mike's sons climbed up Josh's back to smack at the ball and shoved him underwater.

It was a rough crowd. Drew watched for a few minutes, until he was breathing like a normal person again, and then dove back into the action. He wasn't sure how the game would end, since he had yet to figure out the actual rules, but he wasn't going to be the first guy out of the pool.

"Liz! Liz!" It was hard to miss Steph shouting right next to him, so he gave himself permission to look in the same direction the teenager was. "Come on! I'm the only girl."

For a few seconds Drew thought Liz was going to refuse and he was relieved. Water ball of doom, as the boys called it, was a very physical game and there was a lot of bumping and grabbing.

Then she grinned and threw herself into the deep end with a splash. There didn't seem to be any time-outs in water ball of doom, so she surfaced in the middle of a melee. Just when Drew was going to yell at her to be careful, she dove under again and he lost track of her.

He felt her before he saw her—the glide of her naked leg across his thigh—and then her head broke through the water near his shoulder. She slicked her hair back and laughed. "Are there rules to this game?"

"Don't drown. Other than that, I think it's just an excuse to spike the beach ball in each other's faces and water wrestle."

"Are there points?"

The ball was heading toward them and Drew slapped it hard, bouncing it off the back of Sean's head. "The score, last I heard it yelled out, was two hundred thirty to two hundred nineteen, but I'm not sure how you score. It's a very complicated system that's pretty fluid, from what I've gathered."

"In other words, Mike and Lisa's kids invented this game."

"I've only been here less than a day and I've already figured out if the word doom is involved, so are Joey, Danny, Brian and Bobby. And Steph, too, though she tries to pretend she's an innocent bystander."

"Ooh!" She was watching the ball come toward them in a high arc. "Throw me!"

He clasped his fingers together and, before he could think about whether or not it was a good idea, she had her foot in the cradle of his hands and he tossed her high into the air. She slammed the ball back toward the buoy line marking the deep end and Ryan missed the return by a fraction of an inch.

"Point!" Brian yelled, and Liz gave a triumphant yell when she surfaced.

"Dude, she's not on our team," Ryan yelled at Drew.

"There are teams?" Drew threw his arms up in the air. "How can you tell?"

"You're not very good at water ball of doom," Bobby said in a very serious voice.

The penalty for helping the other team score appeared to be drowning since, after that incident, Drew spent more time under the water shoving people off him than he did treading water. His muscles were burning but he knew the Kowalski family well enough to know if he crawled out of the pool in defeat, he'd never live it down.

It was a relief when Mary whistled and called everybody out of the pool. His muscles were getting shaky and it was only the trash talking from Mitch and the other guys that had kept him in so long. He swam to the opposite side of the pool from Liz, just so he wouldn't be tempted to watch for her swimsuit's skirt riding up while she climbed the ladder.

Brian scampered up in front of him, then ran down the side of the pool with his fists in the air. "S'mores time!"

Wishing he had a quarter of the kid's energy, Drew hauled himself up the ladder and winced at the soreness already setting into his leg muscles. He couldn't remember the last time he'd been swimming, but it was obviously too long ago.

"Rematch tomorrow," Mitch said, slapping Drew's shoulder so hard he almost fell back into the water.

"Can't wait." He'd come up with a good excuse before then. Maybe run himself over with a four-wheeler somehow.

Leo, who'd been smart enough to claim a chair on the sidelines, tossed towels at them. "You think that was bad, you just wait. After everybody's changed, it's time for s'mores."

Drew Miller was no fool. Not being a fan of the overly sweet traditional camping dessert, he took his sweet time showering, shaving and throwing on a pair of flannel sleep pants and T-shirt. Then he threw on a lightweight zip hoodie because, not only did it get a little chilly at night, but the mosquitoes started getting aggressive as the sun dropped.

He didn't take long enough, though, and when the crowd around the group campfire spotted him, they didn't accept him waving off their invitation. After stowing his toiletries back in his tent and draping his swim trunks and towel over one of his tent's ropes, he grabbed a bottle of water from his cooler and went to join the insanity.

"Want a s'more?" Bobby asked him, swinging an almost-liquid marshmallow on a stick in his direction.

Drew flinched away. "No, thanks. You should get that onto a cracker before—"

The melted marshmallow slid off the stick and hit the ground in a white, sticky lump Drew knew would end up on the bottom of somebody's shoe before the night was over.

"Oops." Brian wandered away. "Mom, I need another marshmallow."

From his vantage point just outside the perimeter of the circle of camp chairs, it looked to Drew as if there were at least a half dozen marshmallows being waved over the fire, so he stayed where he was. Liz was sitting across the fire from him, laughing with her aunt and Rose, and he watched her for a while.

She looked relaxed. Happy. Drew enjoyed seeing her surrounded by her family, and the bond she'd managed to keep with them despite being all the way across the country for so many years impressed him. Family was obviously important to her.

"You know they'll keep offering you s'mores until you eat one," Mitch said, stepping up beside him. "The sooner you give in, the sooner they stop waving flaming marshmallows at you."

As if she'd heard him, Steph moved toward them, holding a s'more in her hand. "Drew, do you want a s'more?"

This one was premade, not offered up in the form of molten marshmallow dangling from a stick, so he figured Mitch was right. It was probably easier to give in. "Thanks."

He had a mouthful of very sticky sweetness when Brian looked over and saw him. "Hey! How come you didn't want my s'more?"

He shrugged, unable to talk even if he'd wanted to, and Mitch came to his rescue. "Because Steph had put it together already. You know, I don't think Ryan's had a s'more yet. He loves s'mores."

Since Ryan was over near Liz, they'd have a few minutes of peace. "Brilliant move."

"Being with these kids makes me wonder how Rose kept her sanity. I think we were almost as bad."

"There were some moments for sure." He saw Ryan trying to get marshmallow out of his hair, glaring in their direction over the top of Bobby's head, and nudged Mitch. "There's going to be payback."

"Remind me not to ride behind him."

Drew laughed, and his gaze shifted from Ryan to Liz. She was watching him and, when his eyes met hers, she gave him a warm smile. She had a smudge of chocolate at the corner of her mouth and he wanted to cross the distance between them and wipe it away.

Maybe it showed, because her cheeks got a little pink and her gaze flicked to Mitch before she turned back to Mary and Rose.

"We're going to get sucked into going on a big group ride tomorrow," Mitch was saying, "but once they're all in the pool or hiding in the air-conditioning, we'll head back out on the trails and blow off some steam."

Sounded like a good plan to Drew. He definitely had some steam to blow off, though he wasn't sure if one tank of gas in the ATV would be enough. He might have to do laps around the trail system before he found any relief.

IT TOOK ABOUT two minutes for Liz to come to the realization she was maybe a little too old to sleep on the ground in a cheap, nylon tent.

Privacy had been first on her priority list and, since both cabins were rented and she couldn't afford an RV, her own tent had seemed like a brilliant idea. Now she realized comfort should have ranked up there, too. And judging by the damp chill setting in, she should have sprung for the nicer tent.

When her hip started throbbing because the foam pad under her sleeping bag offered a lot less protection from the ground than the label had advertised, she rolled onto her back. Maybe she should take a walk to the bathhouse and then accidentally wander into one of the RVs, with their lovely pullout couches. She could claim she was sleepwalking.

Unfortunately, running through the options of alternate accommodations to sneak into made her think of Drew and his big tent. Or, to be more precise, the very comfortable-looking, very large air mattress she'd seen him inflating earlier. It would easily fit two, especially if there was cuddling.

Liz groaned and threw her arm over her eyes as if she could block out the images that popped into her head. Thinking about Drew and cuddling wasn't going to help her sleep. All that would lead to was tossing and turning and, with the crappy mat under her, she'd probably be black and blue by morning.

She'd tried her best to ignore him at the campfire, but he'd been in her line of sight. And once he'd relaxed and started talking to the other guys and laughing, she'd barely been able to keep her eyes off of him. He fit in with her family so nicely, probably because he'd always been around them, and she was tempted to leave her chair and join in the conversation. But her aunt had been determined to make up for all the years Liz had been away by talking to her all night. Which was fine. She'd missed Aunt Mary, who'd done her best to co-mother them along with Rosie after their mother died.

But with everybody else being part of a couple, it was hard not to imagine sitting next to Drew around the fire, holding hands like some of the others.

When she opened her eyes to find the sun beating down through her cheap tent, Liz was surprised to realize she'd not only fallen asleep, but slept through the night. Then she rolled onto her side and groaned.

The water ball of doom game had to be responsible for the heavy sleep, just as it was for the muscles screaming in protest. The hard ground had just been the icing on the cake.

After a few minutes, she managed to get turned around to face the door, snagging her bathroom bag along the way. After working the zipper up, she crawled out of the tent into the already humid morning.

"Do you need help?"

Liz tilted her head back to look up at Katie. "I haven't actually tried to stand up yet, so I'm not sure."

"I'll wait." Katie, who was staying in the small cabin with Josh, had her shower bag with her and her hair was wet. None of the cabins had bathrooms, so she had to walk back and forth. "There's a set of bunk beds in our cabin, you know. You could sleep in there."

Sure, because nothing spiced up a vacation for a new couple like the guy's older sister sleeping in the same room. "I'm okay, really. I like camping. I just need to never, ever play water ball of doom again."

"There's a reason it took so many women to watch the little ones in the shallow end."

"Lesson learned." Liz finally pushed herself to her feet, grimacing as her muscles stretched.

"You'll be happy to know breakfast is almost ready. Probably less happy to know they're already dragging out the riding gear."

Liz actually groaned aloud. "There aren't enough ATVs for everybody. I'll be noble and volunteer to stay behind."

"Um, they're getting around that by making it a couples ride. That way there's two to a machine."

"Nothing makes a single girl feel more included than tacking the word *couple* before an event."

"Mom said you can just ride double with Drew, since you're both single."

Since Katie's mom happened to be Rose, Liz bit her tongue. Hard. She hated matchmaking, especially when it wasn't subtle and they were trying to hide the fact they'd already made that match once. And having her legs wrapped around Drew for half the day? They were trying to kill her, obviously, and the water ball hadn't done the trick so they'd upped their game.

"Hey, you're both single," Katie said in a voice that dripped with suggestion. But then she laughed. "I guess not. He's Mitch's best friend, so that's out."

"Ten minutes," they heard Lisa yell from her site, which doubled as breakfast central.

"Crap. I need to hurry or I'll be licking the crumbs off everybody's plate."

Liz was ready in fifteen minutes, so she managed to snag some scrambled eggs and a couple slices of bacon before the horde went back for seconds. She even treated herself to a mug of real coffee instead of making a cup of the instant she'd stashed with Mitch and Paige. After sleeping on the ground, she deserved it and, as long as she only had one, it wouldn't bother her too much.

Much too soon, the breakfast debris had been cleaned up and it was time to hit the trails. It was tempting to come up with an excuse not to go, but the only thing they'd accept would be not feeling well and she had no doubt either Rose or her aunt would give up their riding to stay with her. She sucked it up and took the helmet Paige handed her.

"What are you going to wear?"

Her sister-in-law shook her head. "I'm not riding."

"That's not fair. If I have to go, so do you."

"If anybody but Rose or Aunt Mary asks, I just don't feel like it, but—"

"Oh my God." Paige was pregnant.

"Shh!"

"Sorry. Do you know for sure? At dinner, you didn't say anything."

"I was starting to be hopeful by then but I didn't want to jinx anything. Now I'm sure, but I'm not very far along at all, so we don't want everybody to know."

"I want to hug you and jump up and down and cry."

Paige smiled. "That'll look odd since you can't tell anybody why."

Another baby. This was why Liz had come home, so she could be a part of these family moments, and it took all of her willpower not to tear up. While jumping up and down. "I'm so happy for you."

Everybody was waiting, so Liz put the helmet on and buckled the chin strap, then took the goggles Paige offered. When she turned toward the machines, she realized she didn't have to spend half the day with her legs wrapped around Drew after all.

"I'll ride with you," she said to Mitch.

He gave her an *oh, hell no* look. "Why?"

"Because your machine is bigger than Drew's." It was a sound excuse.

"His has a passenger seat on it."

Damn. "I can sit behind you."

"Until you fall off the back."

She crossed her arms over her chest and glared at him, hoping he got the full effect through the goggles. "I'm not going to fall off."

"You will when I wheelie and dump you off because you're uncomfortable on the rack and won't sit still."

"Fine." She walked to the machine Drew was already sitting on and climbed into the passenger seat. Luckily there were handholds, so she was spared having to wrap her arms around his waist, but there was nothing to be done about the fact he was sitting between her legs.

"Chicken," he said in a low voice, so only she could hear him.

"Just trying to save us both some awkwardness."

He shifted on the seat, pushing back a little against her. "I don't find it awkward at all."

Because they were surrounded by her family and slapping him upside the helmet might draw attention, she reached down and pinched his ass hard. "Behave."

"It was Rose who suggested you ride with me."

"That's what Katie said." She regretted now telling him Rose might have maneuvered him next to Liz deliberately on the Fourth. It could be a little weird for him.

"Do you think she told my dad?"

So he wasn't really thinking about the matchmaking. He was worried Andy might say something to Mitch, even an accidental slip, because the more people who knew a secret, the less likely it was to be kept. "I'm pretty positive she didn't. And we know she didn't tell Fran, since the entire town doesn't know."

He laughed and hit the throttle, falling behind the line of four-wheelers heading out of the campground to the trails. When he hit the first bump, Liz realized she was going to spend every single mile bracing herself to keep a little distance between her body and his. With her muscles already beat to crap by the water ball game, she anticipated a very long, cozy ride.

NINE

DREW HAD TO admit the view from the picnic area they'd ridden to was worth the mile after mile of being painfully aware of Liz's body pressed up against his. He could see for miles, the horizon line made jagged by northern New Hampshire and Vermont's mountainous terrain and the hills littered with splotchy shadows made by puffy white clouds.

With his stomach full from hot dogs on the hibachi they'd strapped to the grill of Leo and Mary's machine, Rose's macaroni salad and Mary's brownies, he found a mostly flat-topped boulder he could sit on fairly comfortably and watch the others.

It wasn't long before Liz's laughter caught his attention and his gaze moved to her as if she was somehow magnetized. She was standing with Mitch, Sean and Josh, and her brothers were obviously regaling her with one hell of a story, based on the expressions and exaggerated hand gestures.

It would be criminal to do anything that might come between Liz and Mitch, he told himself. Even if Mitch could eventually come to terms with the fact his best friend and little sister had some kind of thing going on, it would cause friction and she didn't need that so soon after coming home. She was still rebuilding the family bonds after years of a long-distance relationship with them and, no matter how much he might want to, Drew couldn't throw himself in the middle of that.

In his peripheral vision he saw Ryan approaching and tore his attention away from Liz and her other brothers. "Did you have one of those brownies?"

"I had three of those brownies and I'm sure I'll be sorry later." Ryan loomed over him. "Sitting over here feeling guilty?"

Drew glanced up at him, then looked around nonchalantly, as if he wasn't trying to make sure nobody else was within earshot. "About what?"

"The fact you never told Mitch you slept with our sister?"

He didn't want to lie to Ryan and deny it, but he didn't want to offer up a confirmation, either, in case the guy was just fishing. So he said nothing.

Ryan snorted and shook his head. "Doesn't take a genius, you know. You and Liz both left the reception and when she came downstairs for the cake cutting, it was pretty obvious what she'd been doing. And who she'd been doing it with. I guess I was the only one paying attention."

"It's not that big a deal. We're not teenagers."

"If it's not a big deal, why didn't you tell him?"

Drew would have walked away, but there really wasn't anywhere to go and he didn't want Ryan's family thinking they were arguing. "Why didn't you tell him?"

"My brother, his best friend and my sister? You couldn't pay me to jump into that drama, thanks."

"But you're in it now."

Ryan turned and leaned against a tree, so his back was to his family. "Because you're not doing as good a job as you think of hiding how you feel about her. And if things blow up in your face, it's going to make Rosie and Aunt Mary unhappy. Nobody wants that, especially this week."

Since Drew wasn't really sure how he felt about Liz, he didn't know what it was he wasn't hiding. "Liz and I are friends. There was a thing. It was short and it's over and it hasn't happened again."

"But you want it to."

What he really wanted was to throw Ryan over the side of the hill, but he shoved his hands in his pockets and smiled at Lauren, who was watching them from across the clearing and probably wondering what Ryan was talking about so intently. "Who wouldn't want to? She's hot as hell, you know."

"Shit. No, I don't know. Don't want to."

"Hey, you brought it up." Drew chuckled when Ryan gave him a sour look. "But I'm looking to get married and start a family. That's no secret. Your sister's enjoying her life as it is right now and has no interest in a relationship. So, like I said, we're friends."

Ryan stood up straight, shaking his head. "But seeing Mitch and Liz together is making you feel guilty and I'm telling you that you need to bury it. Bury it deep and then bury the shovel, or it's going to be an ugly mess."

"Trust me, if I could bury the guilt deep enough, I would. It feels shitty. But it's not a one-time thing I can shove under the bed. Every time I see her, I want to see her more, which makes my guilt as far as Mitch is concerned ongoing."

"If you think you and Liz might go somewhere, which I have to admit is a little weird, it's on you to pull him aside and talk to him. Don't blind-side him."

Drew would have said more, like maybe reminding him that Mitch's feelings were pretty damn important to him, too, but Kevin and Beth were gravitating toward them now and this wasn't a conversation he cared to have overheard.

"Having a good time?" Drew asked them when they got close enough.

Kevin nodded, even though his face scrunched up a little. "Pace is a little slow, but it's still better than working."

Kevin owned a sports bar in the city as well as being a partner in a restaurant in snowmobile country, so work wasn't too much of a hardship for him. "How about you, Beth?"

"Still not sure I'm a fan of four-wheeling, but I'm a fan of getting a break from Lily." She sighed. "I should feel bad about leaving her. She's a handful."

"Emma and Paige can handle Lily, Brianna and Johnny." Kevin looped his arm around his wife's shoulders. "Even if they just throw them all in Liz's tent and zip it up."

They all laughed, but still didn't miss Leo yelling, "Let's pack it up!"

Drew shoved himself off his rock and made himself useful helping pack up the debris of their picnic before reuniting with Liz at the machine they were riding.

She grabbed her helmet from where she'd tossed it on the rack, but paused before putting it on. "You and Ryan looked pretty serious for a few minutes. Everything okay?"

He ignored the fact she'd been watching him

and focused on the conversation he'd had with her brother. There was no reason to make things any more awkward. "Just business stuff, I guess. The ATV trails back home and stuff."

Fortunately, she seemed to believe him. "Time to ride them now, not talk about them."

"You want to drive for a while?"

She laughed, then shook her head. "I'm a bit rusty, so I probably shouldn't have a passenger."

He was relieved. Not only because he preferred to have control of the machine himself, but because her sitting between his legs seemed even more intimate than him being between hers.

Once she was settled behind him, he fired the engine and waited for the others to pull out. After a couple of miles, he felt her relax against him. Her hands rested at his hips and he found himself seeking out the smoother paths on the trail, avoiding rocks and ruts, so she wouldn't pull herself back from him again.

Ryan's advice about the shovel ran through his head, but it was hard advice to take when Liz's body was draped against his. The aches and pains of water ball and tent sleeping were forgotten and he could have ridden all day.

LIZ WASN'T SURE what was up with Drew, but he'd definitely been giving off a weird vibe since they got back from the ride. He'd been so relaxed while they were riding, even resting his left hand on her knee for a while during a smooth section of trail, but as soon as they got back to the campground, he practically ran away from her. She'd barely seen him other than when they'd all eaten supper together.

He either wanted her and he was going to have to man up and face her brother, or he didn't and he needed to stop touching her. In the meantime, she and Katie were going to sneak into the pool while the kids were trying to kill each other with tetherball.

She felt ridiculous sneaking around the far side of the campground after she'd changed into her suit, but if the kids found out there was an adult in the pool, they'd be cannonballing in from all sides before she even had her feet wet.

Katie was waiting at the gate and Liz chuckled when she did the latch as quietly as possible. Then they tossed their towels on the ground so they wouldn't advertise their presence hanging on the fence.

"I'm almost afraid to talk," Katie whispered. "I'm convinced they have some kind of super-hearing radar system."

"I know what you mean." Liz sat on the edge

and dangled her feet in the pool, sucking in a breath at how cold the water was.

"I mean, they're great kids. And fun. But sometimes they can be a bit much."

Eventually both women worked their way into the pool, until they were floating on the surface, staring up at the sky. Liz couldn't remember the last time she'd been so relaxed, and she found herself smiling at a small cloud that looked vaguely like a rabbit.

"Josh and I have been talking about kids a lot," Katie said after a few minutes. "He said Andy's getting older and he needs sons to chop wood and mow the lawn so they don't have to do it anymore."

Liz laughed, but then remembered they were in stealth mode and slapped her hand over her mouth. "That sounds like my brother."

"He's kidding, of course. I mean, they'll have to do that, but that's not why he wants to have kids."

Treading water, Liz pushed her hair back out of her face. "What about the barbershop?"

Katie sighed. "I'd keep it open until I was very pregnant, then maybe do a couple of hours a day. Then everybody would have to survive five or six weeks without a haircut. Josh and Rose are convinced that together they can take care of a baby, especially if I cut back the shop's hours a little."

"I have no doubt Josh and Rose can take care of a baby, but it sounds like a lot on you."

"I think, with four of us at the lodge, we can make it work."

Liz tried to imagine having a baby come into her life and couldn't. She felt so unsettled and, while she couldn't imagine a better support system than her family and Rose, she wasn't prepared for that kind of commitment. But the idea of Josh and Katie raising the next generation of Kowalskis at the Northern Star with Rosie's help made her throat tighten a little. At least she wouldn't miss it.

"Hey," a male voice said from outside the fence and Liz sighed as they both turned to see Sean leaning on it. They'd been found. "Just wanted to give you a heads-up that some of us guys are heading out for a ride, but the kids have talked the other adults into bringing them to the pool for a swim before they start getting ready for bed. They'll be here any minute."

"It was fun while it lasted," Katie said mournfully.

They wrapped up in their towels and left the pool area in the knick of time. The kids whooped and hollered as they ran by, which always made

Liz laugh. The running did them no good since they couldn't go in before the adults got there and they were taking their time.

Liz and Katie parted ways, since the cabin and her tent were in opposite directions, and Liz took a shortcut around the bathhouse. She was rounding the corner, paying attention to her wet sandals slipping in the fallen pine needles, when she ran into a very solid chest.

She almost lost her footing but Drew grabbed her by the elbows and steadied her. "You okay?"

"Yeah. I wasn't looking where I was going. Sorry." She sounded breathless to her own ear and felt ridiculous.

"Have I told you how much I like that swimsuit?"

She realized her towel had slipped and was in a terry puddle at her feet. "I don't think you have."

"I like it a lot."

They couldn't be seen from either the pool area or from where the guys were getting the ATVs ready to go out, and she realized this was as alone as they'd been since they got there. "I heard you guys are going out for a ride."

"Yeah. We're all going to pretend we're teenagers again without getting ourselves killed."

His grin made her want to melt up against his

body, which wasn't too far away since he was still holding her arms. "Don't get *too* stupid."

"I'm trying not to do anything stupid."

He was staring at her mouth and, with a shiver, Liz realized he wasn't talking about four-wheeling anymore. As much as she'd resolved earlier he needed to be all in or stop touching her, she couldn't bring herself to step back. Instead, she inched closer.

"What are you doing, Liz?" he asked in a low, husky voice.

"I'm trying not to do anything stupid."

His hand moved from her elbow to her hip and he tugged a little, pulling her up against him. When he brushed his cheek over hers, his breath hot against her skin, she shivered.

"I shouldn't kiss you," he whispered.

"I shouldn't let you." She tucked her arms under his so she could run her hands up his back. Even through his T-shirt, she felt his muscles quiver at her touch.

"Why can't I stop thinking about you? Why do I *have* to touch you?"

She could hear the battle he was waging with himself in his voice. He obviously felt like he was doing something wrong, but didn't have the strength to stop doing it. Maybe it was up to her.

If she shut him down, that would save them both some angst and drama.

But she thought about him, too. She wanted him to touch her. Before either of them could do what may or may not be the right thing and back off, she turned her face and pressed her lips to his.

"Where the hell is Miller?" Mitch yelled, and Drew physically flinched.

"I have to go."

She pointed at his shirt. "Your shirt's a little damp. From my bathing suit, I guess."

"I'm putting a sweatshirt on before we go out, anyway." He took a couple of steps, then paused and looked back, as if he was going to say something else.

"They're waiting." She didn't want to hear whatever it was. An apology. A reminder nobody could know Drew had been kissing Mitch's little sister at the bathhouse.

She wondered if that's how he thought of her in his head while he was beating himself up. *Mitch's little sister.* Screw that. She had her own identity, thank you very much.

Without saying another word, she ducked into the closest bathroom and bolted the door. After a few minutes, she heard the gravel crunch as he walked away. She stayed where she was until she heard the roar of the four-wheelers driving away.

POUNDING THROUGH THE woods, Drew had no room in his head for woman or best friend issues. His concentration was focused on the trail—every rock, bump, rut and corner rushing at him—and it felt damn good.

He leaned through a tight corner and then came to a rise in the trail. Goosing the throttle, he enjoyed the brief sensation of all four wheels leaving the ground. Then his headlights were cutting through the trees as he leaned into a hard left turn.

When Evan's taillights dropped in front of him, Drew slowed down for the waterbar, and then they were running hard again. They'd been out two hours and they'd already done more than twice the miles they'd done as a group earlier in the day.

By the time they slowed for the last bit of trail into the campground, Drew was tension-free and ready for a shower and a beer. Then he was going to sleep like a baby.

After pulling the ATV into the overflow site they were using for parking, Drew took a back path to his tent to gather his things. Luckily most of the other guys who'd been out had RVs with private showers, so it wasn't a race.

Outside his tent, he pulled off his boots and sweatshirt. He debated on dropping his pants, too, since it was fairly dark, but the presence of a teen girl somewhere in the campground sent him inside. Trying to keep his filthy pants from brushing against anything, he gathered what he needed and shoved his feet into sandals for the walk.

Drew grimaced when he saw the light shining out from under every door along the front of the bathhouse. Between sweating and the dust on the trails, he felt as if dirt had been ground into every nook, cranny and pore of his body, and he was desperate for a shower.

Before he got there, though, a door opened and Sean—who'd been riding at the front so had beat him back to the campground—walked out, framed by a billow of steam. The guy's skin was practically pink from the heat and scrubbing, and Drew silently vowed to kick his ass if he'd used all the hot water.

Sean waved to his wife, who was talking to a couple of the other women over by the clothesline they'd strung to cope with endless wet towels and then walked off toward his camper. Drew ducked into the steamy bathroom before anybody could beat him to it and bolted the door.

He'd stripped down and was about to turn on the shower when he saw the sticky note stuck to the frame of the still-foggy mirror.

After the baby goes to sleep, I'm going to...

Drew slapped his hands over his eyes like a kid who'd seen his parents kissing. Obviously Sean had left that note for Emma, who he'd thought would be following after him. But she'd gotten sucked into a conversation and Drew was the recipient of the square yellow sexual promise instead.

Lucky him. Nothing like a written reminder he *wasn't* having sex with anybody.

He turned the shower on lukewarm and spent a few minutes rinsing the surface grime off. Then he lathered his hair and scrubbed the hell out of his scalp to get rid of the sweat and grit his helmet seemed to grind in.

When it came to soaping his body, it was tempting to linger below the waist. Maybe just take the edge off his sexual frustration a bit. But it was weird, since there was a sex note from Sean to Emma a few feet away and, since he'd read it, it felt weird to now take matters into his own hand, so to speak.

Instead he cranked the knob over to cold and almost yelped when the water turned icy. He finished rinsing off and then leaned his head against the shower wall, letting the cold seep into his body.

Kissing Liz has been a stupid thing to do. He'd known it. She'd known it. But his wanting her was like a runaway train and, even though he knew the whole thing would derail on them, he was helpless to stop it. No matter how often he tried to apply the brakes, even if only mentally, they didn't stick.

Once he'd dried off and dressed, he braced himself for a visit to the campfire. It would be burning low, with the kids either in bed or allowed some quiet electronics time, and the adults would be sitting around talking.

He took the sticky note with him when he left the bathroom. The Kowalskis didn't really need that kind of reputation if one of the few campers not with them wandered in.

After dumping his stuff in his tent, he grabbed a beer and wandered down to the campfire. As he got near, he started scoping out which empty chair was best to sit in, and then he saw Liz. She was holding Johnny and the sight made him stop in his tracks.

An electrified cattle prod couldn't have moved Drew from that spot. She cradled Sean and Emma's son against her chest, singing to him in a soft voice. There wasn't a Kowalski born who could carry a tune as a rule, but there was something about her singing to a sleepy baby that made it a beautiful sound.

It made his chest ache, the way Liz looked down at Johnny. He'd been waiting to be a dad his entire adult life and seeing the woman he was in some crazy, undefined not-quite-a-relationship with holding the infant made him feel as though his world was shifting. He wanted that—the visual in front of him—and he had to remind himself that not only was that not his baby, but Liz wasn't even really his woman.

"Hey, Drew." Sean was leaning back in a chair, waving him over.

Drew shook off the emotions threatening to show all over his face and walked over to take the empty chair to the left of Sean. Emma was on the other side.

Sean leaned close so he could whisper, "So, uh, you went in the bathroom after me?"

Drew chuckled and slipped him the sticky note, which he'd folded into quarters. "Thanks for the offer, but you're not my type. I also don't have that body part."

"I didn't even see you. Emma was waiting to go in after me because she didn't want both of us away from the baby at the same time, but she started talking."

Drew laughed, then turned toward the conversation about tractors Leo and his dad were having because they were in the opposite direction of Liz and the baby and he wouldn't be able to see them.

He saw them when it was time for bed, though, and he was stretched out on the air mattress with his eyes closed. He tried not to, but nothing else on the planet mattered enough to replace that image in his mind.

That's what he wanted. Not some faceless woman whose most important trait was wanting to be the mother of his children. He wanted Liz. He could picture those kids now, with her blue eyes and their dark hair, running wild with their cousins playing games that involved no rules but always doom.

But even if he manned the hell up, looked Mitch in the eye and told him he was falling for his sister, his gut told him Liz wasn't lying in her tent, imagining what their children would look like. She had bigger things in mind for her life, apparently.

And he knew what he wanted well enough to know a relationship with a woman who didn't want kids would be, as the Kowalski kids would call it, a romance of doom.

TEN

A COUPLE OF days passed in an easy rhythm of laughter, riding, swimming and dodging projectile marshmallows, and Liz was glad she'd let Rose and Paige talk her into coming. Maybe Drew was being a pain in the ass, with his running hot and cold, but the total-immersion method of re-bonding with her family was a huge success.

Today it was quiet. Joe, Keri, Kevin and Beth had taken all of the kids out for pizza, which meant Mike and Lisa had disappeared someplace private. Uncle Leo, Aunt Mary, Rose and Andy were playing cards inside. A bunch of them, including Drew, had taken advantage of having no kids or older folks to go for a ride.

Liz had opted out. She hadn't been sleeping well, thanks to Drew and her less-than-high-quality camping gear, and she just wanted to kick things down into a lower gear and relax. She read for a while, slowly working her way through the pile of books Hailey had chosen for her, but eventually she went looking for company.

After grabbing a water from the cooler, she joined Paige and Emma in the screen house on Mike and Lisa's site. A shady, bug-free zone and the company of her sister-in-law and her cousin's wife were just what she was in the mood for.

"I'm surprised you didn't go riding," Paige said when she'd zipped herself in with them.

"Just wasn't in the mood." While everybody else seemed impervious to it, the tension between her and Drew was as taut as an overstretched rubber band and she was enjoying the absence of it. "I'm sorry you can't ride, though. Bad timing on the baby's—"

She covered her mouth, a few seconds too late, but Paige just smiled. "Emma knows."

"Oh, good. Maybe in the future, you shouldn't tell me any secrets." She watched Emma's foot, gently rocking the baby carrier at her foot where Johnny was sleeping. "Were you drunk when you agreed to come camping with an infant, or are you just flat-out crazy?"

Emma laughed. "If we hadn't taken over almost the whole campground, I'd be worried about him bothering other people. But I have most of the comforts of home and no shortage of people willing to help me take care of him."

"I noticed playing pass the baby is a favorite family game. Although it's a blessing they don't call it pass the baby of doom."

"I do have to be pretty firm if it gets out of hand. It makes him fussy and, oh good lord, the germs." She smiled at her son through the netting. "But I'm going back to work soon and, even though Sean and I are coordinating our schedules so one of us is always with him, it's nice to have this last bit of quiet family time. Or quiet-ish, anyway."

Liz leaned forward to peek at Johnny. "I've noticed the kiddo can sleep through anything."

"Self-preservation. If loud kids woke him up, he would have been a hot, twitchy mess by the time he was two weeks old." She smiled down at her son. "And he may as well get used to the crazy now. Lily and Brianna will be a bit older, but he and Paige's baby will be close in age. Kevin and Beth are trying for another. And Katie's working her way around to being a mom soon, from what I've heard."

That ticking biological clock Liz never paid a lot of attention to came to sudden, clanging life and she sat back in her chair. Maybe there'd been *too* much immersion-method bonding. Just because they were all having babies didn't mean she had to.

Sure, she wanted kids someday. She had time. But having kids that would grow up as bonded and close as her siblings, cousins and Katie had would be fun. If only she was in a place in her life where having kids was really an option.

"So, Liz," Paige said after they'd all watched Johnny sleep for a few minutes. "How do you like working at the diner? Be honest."

"You're my boss *and* married to my brother. But, luckily, I can honestly say I like it. Great staff, great food, busy enough without being crazy."

"It's probably not the highest-paying job you've ever had."

"It's not, but it doesn't need to be. Lauren's only charging me enough rent to cover her costs on the house and it's not like I have a fancy car payment." They laughed, but then Liz got serious again. "And I *like* working there. I don't wake up dreading the day and then spend the hours after my shift dreading the fact I have to get up and do it again the next day. Trust me, that matters."

"It does," Emma agreed. "I think we've all been there at some point."

"Yeah, well, try being the underachiever of the family. Everybody owns their own damn businesses, except me. I wait tables."

Paige held up a finger. "But you do it exceptionally well."

"And it makes you happy," Emma added.

All true, but she still felt as if she should want more. She wasn't sure where the feeling came from. Maybe because she'd spent her adult life to date working to support a guy whose desire to be an artist came from an unwillingness to have an actual job rather than artistic drive. But now that she only had to want things for herself, she felt some pressure to want something. She just didn't know what yet.

"Hey, did anybody tell you tonight's dirty Scrabble night?" Emma asked.

"I'm almost afraid to ask what that means. Dirty, depending on the context, may or may not be more enjoyable than doom."

"No doom. And only the grown-up women can play. And there's alcohol. It's basically a girls' night out without going anywhere. Or so I'm told. Paige and I haven't played it yet, either. They only play during their camping trips, I guess."

"Do we lock the men in the bathhouse?"

Emma laughed. "No. I guess they have a men-only campfire far enough away so it's like a guys' night out. Only here."

"What makes it dirty?"

"I guess it's regular Scrabble, but you get a

double word score if you wouldn't say the word in front of the kids. And if it's a word you wouldn't say out loud, it's a triple word score."

"So the alcohol might make a difference," Paige said.

"And whether or not Aunt Mary or Rosie play, too," Liz added.

Emma nodded. "Anyway, start thinking up naughty sex words, ladies."

Liz snorted. "I have three sex words. Not. Getting. Any."

"You need to start dating," Paige said. "Who do I know who's single in Whitford? Oh, there's Max Crawford. He's a little odd and works out of his basement. It has its own security system and nobody knows what he does, so the popular theory is that he's a serial killer."

"Great. Give him my number." Liz rolled her eyes.

"But he's *smoking* hot."

"But wait," Emma said. "How would being a serial killer make him money?"

"Don't poke logic holes in our gossip."

"I don't want to date Max Crawford the alleged serial killer," Liz said.

"I mentioned the smoking-hot part, right? Just sex. You don't have to go in the basement." Both

Liz and Emma gave her a raised eyebrow. "Okay, fine. Who else do I know…"

"I don't really want to date anybody."

"But you said yourself your only sex words are *not, getting* and *any.* Why don't you want to start dating?"

Because I only want to date your husband-slash-my brother's best friend and he seems to have a split personality when it comes to reciprocating that feeling. "I just moved back. Let me get settled in before you start pimping me out to odd guys with locked basements."

"He likes sports," Paige added.

"Not going to happen."

"Fine. There aren't that many single men in Whitford, though, so if you see one you like, act fast."

Oh, she'd seen one she liked, all right. And they'd both acted fast. Now, though, they seemed to be spinning their wheels, rocking back and forth but remaining stuck in the same rut.

The worst part was not being able to pour out her troubles and get advice. Certainly not from Mitch's wife. And secret keeping wasn't exactly a dominant Kowalski trait. So she kept her mouth shut and let the subject veer off in a different direction.

Inevitably, with a new mom and a soon-to-be

mom, the conversation turned to baby stuff and Liz rested her head back against the chair and half listened. The others would be back anytime, so she was determined to enjoy the peace and quiet while she had it.

And, as with any game, she played to win, so she started building up a collection of naughty words in her head. She might not be having any sex, but that didn't diminish her vocabulary in any way.

"There aren't any hyphens in Scrabble, are there?" she asked, breaking into a debate on cloth versus disposable diapers.

Convenience versus bleach buckets were forgotten as they got down to the serious business of dirty Scrabble strategy.

THIS WAS WHAT Drew had signed up for. A roaring campfire, a comfortable chair and a cold six-pack. The kids were in bed and the women were almost out of earshot, playing Scrabble. And it was one hell of a game, judging by the laughter echoing through the trees.

"I don't remember Scrabble being that funny," Drew said, popping the tab on beer number one.

"They're making sex words," Mike said. "They get extra points or whatever if nobody will say them out loud. But I don't think we're supposed to know that's what they're doing."

Drew couldn't help glancing over, wondering what sex words Liz might be spelling. She was as cutthroat as the rest of her family when it came to competition so, judging by the furrow between her eyebrows, she wasn't coming up with anything too raunchy. If she was winning, her face would show it.

He'd be happy to educate her on all manner of things people didn't say aloud outside of the bedroom.

"Speaking of sex, Drew," Mitch began, and Drew's entire body tensed. "When are you going to jump back into the dating pool?"

He forced himself to relax into his chair, taking a long swig of his beer. "The divorce has only been final six months, Kowalski. There's no rush."

"Six months is a long time to go without dirty Scrabble fodder, if you know what I mean. Hell, almost a year actually, since you split last August."

There were two ways this conversation was going to go. One, he'd nod and have to take a bunch of crap about his drought. Or, two, he'd confess there hadn't been an eleven-month drought and subject himself to a lot of questions about who in Whitford's very small dating pool he'd been swimming with. Questions he couldn't—or wouldn't, rather—answer.

He could practically feel Ryan's stare boring a hole through him, as if the guy was trying to psychically remind him of their conversation at the picnic area. "Job keeps me busy."

Mitch laughed. "You're the chief of police in a town with crime statistics that don't even make a slice of pie, never mind a whole pie chart. I should sign you up for one of those online dating services."

"If you do that, I'll arrest you for impersonating a police officer."

Joe looked up from the cooler, where he was fishing through the beer cans to find a soda. "Is it technically impersonating a police officer if he's pretending to be you personally rather than professionally?"

Drew held out his hands so Joe could toss him another beer while he was in the cooler, then he set it next to him. He'd probably need it soon. "Semantics are for juries. They can figure that out after he's been cuffed, fingerprinted and had his name in the paper."

A burst of squeals and shocked exclamations from the women drew their attention, and then they heard Rosie's voice above the others. "Elizabeth Sarah Kowalski!"

"Whoa," Evan said in a low voice. "How bad does a word have to be to get you middle-named during dirty Scrabble?"

Drew's brain scrambled as guesses started running through his mind. Then he had to shift in his chair because he still had on his jeans instead of his baggy sleep pants and things were getting uncomfortable below the waist.

"Leave it to Liz," Mitch said, shaking his head.

"Usually Aunt Mary stays in her camper while they play," Kevin said. "Rose must have talked her into playing. Or being a spectator, at least."

"Makes for a lot more words they won't say out loud," Evan said. "More points."

Josh chuckled. "I've heard your wife's good at dirty Scrabble."

"Hey." Joe shook his head. "His wife is our sister, so we don't want to hear how many dirty words she knows."

"Sisters and sex is off-limits," Mitch agreed. "Nobody wants that."

Sure Ryan would be staring at him again, Drew stared down at his beer and prayed for a subject change. Sports. Weather. Best bathroom cleaner for hard water stains. Literally anything else.

"Did you see what Mike did out on the trail

today?" Ryan asked, and Drew let out a slow, relieved breath. "Out by the moose pond?"

"That wasn't my fault," Mike said.

"I saw him in my mirror for a second," Josh said. "He looked sideways, but by the time I was going to stop and go back, he was behind me again."

"I hit a rut the wrong way and it threw me. That's all."

"Took a detour through the woods," Ryan added. "It was probably funnier if you heard him screaming the whole way."

The chagrin on Mike's face made them all laugh, and Drew relaxed as that story segued into another and then another after that. He even told one himself, about the ATV rider he'd busted for riding into Whitford in his underwear. The guy had gotten muddy and, rather than make a mess in the diner, he'd stripped down to his boxers and used a bungee cord to strap the ball of dirty clothes to his rack. Since he was drunk as well as almost naked, it had made perfect sense to him at the time. Less so when he'd sobered up and had to call his wife.

It was several hours before they let the fire burn down and called it a night. Drew tossed his empties into the bag with the others, then looked around to make sure there were no others. "Since

I have to go by it anyway, I'll dump these in the recycling barrel."

"Hey." Mitch draped his arm over Drew's shoulders. "I'm glad you came. We don't get to spend enough time together."

"I'm having a good time." Mostly. But he'd enjoyed tonight. It had been too long since he and Mitch had just kicked back and talked, other than the night Mallory had left and Drew went looking for a shoulder.

"You and I should go on a fishing trip soon. Tents, beer and fishing poles. Nothing else."

"Since neither of us can fish worth a damn, maybe a package of hot dogs, too."

Mitch laughed and slapped him on the back. "That's a plan."

It was a plan that would probably sound less appealing with fewer beers in them, but Drew agreed and started the long walk back to his tent. The campground was dark and quiet, since they'd outlasted the women, so he did his best to be quiet. Rather than dump the cans into the barrel, he set the bag next to it to add tomorrow, then walked around the bathhouse to take a leak, doing his best to stay in grass and avoid the gravel.

LIZ SHOULDN'T HAVE had that second rum and Coke. Actually, she shouldn't have had *any* of the rum and Coke. Terry had started handing out the drinks and it dawned on Liz way too late that the rum wasn't the problem. Coke not only had sugar, but it had lots of caffeine.

Now she was wide awake, damn near twitching, and she had to pee. Again.

It took her a couple of minutes to get out of her sleeping bag and crawl out of her tent, and the zipper sounded incredibly loud in the still night. Not that it would matter to the rest of them, since they had the white noise of all those lovely rooftop air-conditioning units.

She was getting ready to push open the door when she heard a rustling next to her and froze. Bear? Maybe it was just a raccoon.

Slowly turning toward the sound, she bit down on a yelp as a dark shape—too tall to be a raccoon and too skinny to be a bear—came toward her. "Drew."

He jumped and she heard him suck in a breath. "Liz. You scared the hell out of me. What are you doing out here?"

"Probably the same thing you're doing."

"I was leaving the beer cans next to the recycling barrel."

"Okay, then maybe not. I have to pee."

"Oh. Okay." He didn't keep walking, though,

which would have been the polite thing to do. "Want me to stand guard?"

"I'm good, thanks." She went into the bathroom without giving him the chance to say anything else.

When she came back out, she saw him sitting on a rock waiting for her in the spill of light from the bathroom before she flipped the switch. He was persistent when he wasn't running in the other direction, she'd give him that.

After a lot of blinking, her eyes adjusted to the darkness again and she made her way toward him. "What are you doing?"

"I wanted to make sure you got back to your tent okay." He shrugged, then she saw the white of his teeth when he grinned. "And ask what word got you middle-named by Rose during your dirty Scrabble game."

"Ah, the truth comes out. Too bad. We don't spell naughty words and tell."

"You look pretty tonight."

"Since it's too dark to really see me well, let me describe to you the raggedy T-shirt and sloppy braid for sleeping."

He got off the rock and moved closer to her. "Since you always look pretty to me, it was a safe bet."

"How much have you had to drink?"

"I had a few beers. How about you?"

"I had a couple of rum and Cokes which I'm regretting now. I don't really do caffeine anymore, so the caffeine and sugar combination is why I'm roaming around wide awake."

"Want to go for a walk?"

As appealing as that sounded, she needed to zip herself back up in that little tent before she did something a lot more stupid than kissing him. "That's probably not a good idea."

At least where they were, it was only a semblance of privacy. If they went for a walk and ended up someplace where they were *really* alone, she might forget she was irritated with him.

"I guess you're right." He shoved his hands in his pockets. "Look where drinking got us last time."

She started to walk away, but turned back. "Drinking didn't get us in a bad place, Drew. I liked that place. It's where we are now that kind of sucks."

"I know. I'll go home if you think that'll make it easier."

She didn't want that. As much as his presence tied her up in knots, she'd miss him if he left. "I don't want you to do that. Maybe I should just tell him."

"No. If he finds out, it has to come from me."

"That's stupid. He's my brother. We're adults."

"It's a guy thing, Liz. A code."

She snorted, then waited for him to continue. To say he'd talk to Mitch tomorrow or when they got back to Maine. Anything to signal he wanted her enough to risk pissing off her brother, but he was quiet.

"Let's go sit on the swings for a while and talk," he finally said, which wasn't what she'd been hoping to hear.

"I don't know. It's probably not any better an idea than going for a walk."

"We'll be in full view of anybody who cares to look, so I'll have to keep my hands to myself."

She arched her eyebrow. "So, to recap, we'll be in full view of anybody who cares to look."

"We've known each other forever, Liz. We're allowed to talk."

He was right, and she felt silly about her paranoia. "I'm not going to sleep anytime soon, anyway."

They kept a respectable distance between them as they walked down to the playground, sticking to the grass as much as possible. She could hear the hum of the air conditioners running all through the campground and knew that, as hard as the family played, everybody was probably sound asleep already.

She sat on one of the swings, smiling as he took the one next to her. "I haven't been on a swing since I was a kid."

"Me either, but it beats trying to sneak chairs out of the campsites."

Looking up, she gazed at the star-speckled sky and sighed. "You're like a yo-yo, you know. You flirt and then you run away. You kiss me and then you run away. I'm starting to not like it."

"I know." His swing was swaying back and forth, his toe dragging in the dirt. "I'm not trying to play games with you. But there's Mitch to consider, and being here with him has reinforced how much his friendship means to me."

Rose had warned her there would be no going forward with Drew until one of them had told Mitch, but at the time she'd still been able to convince herself they weren't really going forward, anyway. But now she knew whatever was between them might be stronger than she'd thought.

But, as she'd told him, she wanted to turn a man inside out. She wanted a man who'd walk through fire for her, and Drew wouldn't stand up to her brother. "I don't want to come between you and Mitch. You've been friends for as long as I can remember."

"You know I want you."

The quiet words tugged at her heart, but she

kept her gaze on the dark shadow of the tree line. "It's too messy."

He was quiet for a few minutes, the only sound the slight creak of the swing chains. Then she heard him inhale deeply and blow out a slow breath. "Your family's really great. I've enjoyed them. Even the kids. Maybe especially the kids. They're tough to keep up with, but I like them a lot."

"I know you and Mallory split up because she didn't want children, so it must be a little hard to be around them if you want kids that badly."

"It was the lying about wanting kids someday that ended the marriage. Sure, I want them, but who knows how things would have turned out if she'd told me up front how she felt."

"But you've always wanted to be a dad?"

"Yeah." His swing stilled as he stared out at some point in the darkness. "I'm an only child. My parents were pretty quiet people and, after my mom left, it was even quieter. My stepmother was a good woman, but I felt a lot like a third wheel. Then it was Mallory and I. So quiet and neat and orderly."

"Some people like that."

"I want loud and messy and crazy. I want crayons on the wall and bicycles in the driveway and playing ball in the backyard. I want to teach my kids to read and climb trees and drive a standard. I want noise and laughter and yelling and the kind of love that can't ever be broken."

Her heart ached for him, even though it was a strong reminder that Mitch wasn't the only thing between them. "You're still young, Drew. You'll find the right woman and, before you know it, you'll be scrubbing your walls and listening to the gears in that Mustang grind."

"I'll find the right woman, huh?" He looked at her then, his gaze holding hers in the darkness.

"She's out there." The idea of him finding that woman made her stomach hurt, but Drew already knew Liz wasn't on the fast track to babies, baseballs and bicycles.

"It's hard to find her when all I can think about is how much I want you."

But not enough to risk his friendship with Mitch. Rather than continuing down what was turning out to be a depressing conversational path, she forced a humorless chuckle. "Pretty sure a baby would be a hard secret to keep from my brother."

"Yeah."

He didn't seem inclined to say anything else, so Liz let the silence envelop them again. But sitting on the swing, wishing there weren't so many stumbling blocks in the way of the chemistry neither of them could deny, just made her feel cold and she couldn't stop the shiver.

"You want my sweatshirt?"

"No, I'm good. I think if I go crawl into my sleeping bag and get warm now, I might actually be able to sleep."

"It's probably pretty late, so I'll turn in, too." He stood at the same time she did, but didn't move closer to her. Whether it was because he was afraid somebody was watching or because of her telling him the right woman was out there somewhere, he'd pulled back again. It was for the best.

"Good night, Drew." She walked back to her tent without looking back and zipped herself in.

Once cocooned in nylon again, she heard his slow walk back to his tent and screwed her eyes shut. It didn't help. The look in his eyes when he talked about finding the right woman still haunted her, the tears of frustration still leaked out, and sleep still didn't come.

ELEVEN

GETTING OUT OF bed the next morning was a little rough, so after dragging herself out into the sunshine and into the shower, Liz was good and made one cup of instant coffee. No more soda for her, rum or no rum.

Everybody else was running a little slow, too, so at least she didn't miss breakfast. She helped the others get it ready, buttering pancakes as Terry took them off the griddle and passing them off to Keri and Lisa, who were adding sausage links to the plates and handing them out. Finally, Rose and Aunt Mary stopped making more batter and she got a chance to have a couple herself.

Feeling a little restored, she helped clean up and then flopped onto one of the chairs. "Today is going to be a lazy day."

There were a lot of murmured agreements, but they were quickly drowned out by the kids listing off all the things they wanted to do that day. Everything from riding their ATVs all the way into town for lunch to a croquet tournament to more water ball of doom.

"Love these kids, but right now I'm so glad they're not mine," Liz said, tipping her head back against the chair. "Because I might not move until it's time to go to bed."

"Me, either."

She realized Drew was sitting next to her and rolled her head sideways to look at him without picking it up. "I shouldn't have had a second pancake."

"I won't tell you how many I had."

She pushed herself upright in the chair again, mostly so she wouldn't nod off. Everybody seemed to be scattering in a dozen different directions, probably getting ready for whatever activities they were going to do. It made her even more tired just watching them.

"Hey, Liz." Drew's voice was very low, which put her on guard as she turned back to him. He was about to say something he didn't want anybody else to hear and, honestly, she wasn't sure she wanted to hear it. Her heart still felt a little bruised from last night. "I'm going to talk to him."

For a few seconds, she wasn't sure she'd heard him right, but the intensity in his gaze held hers and she realized he was serious. "Why?"

"Why? Why do you think?"

"Are you going to talk to him so you don't feel guilty anymore about what happened at his wedding or…why?"

"I'm going to talk to him because I want to take you out. I want to take you out to dinner or a movie. I want to walk down the street holding your hand, not just settle for little touches when we think nobody's looking."

Her heart tumbled hard and, when he smiled at her, she knew her return smile was a little shaky. "Really?"

"Really. But I don't want to do it here, with your entire family around. And if it gets ugly, it'll ruin everybody's vacation. When we get back to Whitford, I'll have him stop by my place and we'll talk."

"I think that's a good idea." She didn't want to wait, but she knew he was right. And what mattered was the fact his desire to take her out was stronger than his desire to hide his transgression from her brother.

"In the meantime," he said, "I'm going to do my best to behave, but it won't be easy."

"Anticipation makes it all the sweeter."

He laughed. "If I anticipate any more than I have been, I won't be able to walk."

She didn't get to respond to that because his

laughter had drawn attention and there were two boys bearing down on them.

"Drew, Uncle Joe wants to know if you're riding today," Brian said.

"I don't know. I'm pretty beat."

"Uncle Kevin said if you said no," Bobby said, "to ask you if you lost your ba…uh, testicles in a tragic accident overnight."

"Oh, really?" Both boys shrugged. "I might do a few miles."

"Sucker," Liz said when the boys ran off to report to their uncles.

"If I don't go do something, I'll just fall asleep sitting in this chair and then I won't be able to sleep tonight. Again. How about you? You going to ride?"

"I'm out of jeans. I have to stay here and do some laundry because I was lazy yesterday."

Drew stood and she let herself watch him stretch because she didn't think anybody was paying attention and because she wasn't going to have to deprive herself of touching him very much longer. Just a few more days and then he could stop beating himself up every time he looked at her a little too long.

He looked down and what she was thinking must have shown on her face because his smile turned decidedly naughty. "Soon."

She would have watched him walk away, but female voices were closing in so she stood and started putting the chair away. They liked to have their morning coffees and breakfast in the early sunshine, but then the chairs went under the huge tarp. If it rained, they'd stay dry and sometimes people used the tarp for shade if they didn't feel like wrestling with the screen house zipper.

Three hours later, she'd at least started her load of laundry. She'd also read for a while and taken a nap. Then she'd remembered her clothes were sitting in the washing machine and forced herself to get up, only to realize she was out of quarters.

Strongly suspecting she wasn't the only one napping, Liz decided to walk down to the campground store for quarters instead of going from camper to camper scrounging for some. It was hot and humid once she left the trees that shaded her site, and she didn't like the clouds that were rolling in. The riders in the family must not have, either, because she could hear them approaching in the distance and they were going a little faster than usual. The first machines were pulling into the overflow site when she reached the store.

She traded a ten-dollar bill for a roll of quarters, then gave four of the coins back to buy a fudge pop. Standing inside, she soaked up some air-conditioning and took her time eating her ice cream while reading the day's newspaper.

Halfway back, the rain started. And it wasn't a drizzle. The sky opened up and the rain fell in what could only be described as a deluge. She broke into a jog as it soaked through her T-shirt and shorts and headed for the bathhouse. There was a small overhang over the bathroom doors where she could hang out for a few minutes and wait for the worst to pass. These kind of humidity-busting storms were fierce, but didn't last long.

She didn't see anybody as she ran, so she assumed they were all smart enough to take shelter. By the time she reached the bathhouse, the deluge had eased up, but the rain was still coming down pretty steadily.

When she reached the overhang, she stopped, panting a little. Her work kept her on her feet all day, but she wasn't much for running. As she squeezed water out of her hair, the bathroom door she was standing in front of opened and Drew stepped out. He was fresh out of the shower and he stopped short when he saw her.

His gaze skimmed down her body and when it returned to her face his eyes were hot. "You have about five seconds to change your shirt before I push you up against that tree behind you and give the chipmunks a show they won't ever forget."

Liz looked down at her chest, displayed quite well by the soaking-wet light pink T-shirt. "I got caught in the rain, obviously. And if you want to give the chipmunks a show, that's between you and your right hand."

He set his shower bag down and took a few steps toward her, his gaze focused on her so intensely she felt like she was under a spotlight. "Is that right?"

"I have four brothers. I can hold my own, so you don't want to mess with me."

"I have police training."

"Are you abusing your power, Officer Miller?"

Drew moved fast, but she was ready and at the last second, she turned. Taking him by the shoulders, she gave him a shove and he fell back against the tree. Ignoring the rain, she planted a foot on either side of his leg, pinning it between her knees. "Oh, I don't think so."

She realized her mistake a second too late. He hooked his foot behind hers and they went to the ground, his arm under her head to protect it from impact. His body pinned hers and there wasn't a damn thing she could do about it.

"It's *Chief* Miller."

"Does that mean I'm in trouble?"

"I don't know about *in* trouble, but I know you *are* trouble." He was staring at her mouth and she shivered. “Now that I have you in custody, got anything you need to confess?”

She hadn’t robbed any banks lately, and he didn’t need to know she was still having a little trouble adjusting to the lower speed limits in Whitford. What else about her didn’t he know? “I wasn’t drunk at Mitch’s wedding.”

His gaze shifted from her mouth to her eyes, and she tried to ignore the weight of his body on hers. “I don’t believe I’ve ever heard anybody confess to not being drunk before.”

“I mean, I wasn’t sober. But I wasn’t drunk.” She wasn’t sure why she was telling him this. Maybe he had some kind of police officer superpower when it came to confessions. “I know, the day I wrecked my car, I tried to laugh it off as too much alcohol, but that’s not why I went upstairs with you.”

“And I was a designated driver so I obviously didn’t drink, but if letting you blame booze got us over that whole awkward thing we had going on, I decided to let it slide.”

“It wasn’t booze.”

“Why are you telling me this now?”

Because his body was hot and hard and she wanted him again. “I plead the Fifth.”

“I’m a police officer, not a judge.”

"Fine, then I'm using my right to remain silent."

He slid his hand down her side until his fingertips found the gap between her T-shirt and her shorts. Stroking that tender strip of skin, he lowered his face almost close enough to kiss her. "If you're going to be uncooperative, I'll have to frisk you."

"Do you guys learn cheesy, clichéd cop pickup lines at the police academy or do they come to you later?"

"Okay, that was lame. I'll give you that. And we're getting rained on."

"We're also outside. In full view." Not to be a mood killer, but he had made it clear he didn't want to ruin anybody's vacation with family drama.

"Everybody's inside, except us, because it's raining. Or they're under the tarp, which is halfway across the campground." He pushed himself up and then took her hand to haul her to her feet.

She expected him to pick up his stuff and head back to his tent. Maybe give her a quick kiss first. Instead he kept her hand and pulled her into the bathroom he'd just vacated.

The room was warm and humid from his shower, and she shook her head. "The bathroom?"

"It's here. It's private." He spun her to face him,

backing her against the wall and kissing her so hard it took her breath away.

She yanked his T-shirt up and he broke off the kiss only long enough for her to haul it over his head. Then his mouth was back on hers, hard and demanding. She moaned as his hands slid under her shirt, his skin hot and a little rough against hers.

As his tongue danced over hers, he shoved her shirt higher so his hands could cup her breasts. His thumb stroked her nipples through the damp fabric of her bra, and she grasped the loose waist-band of his flannel pants, yanking them down. He kicked them off, along with the sandals he wore to the shower, and pressed his body—now bare except for navy boxer briefs—against hers. Trapped between him and the wall, she buried her hands in his hair.

"Someday we're going to take our time doing this," he murmured against her mouth.

"Next time," she gasped. She was through with waiting.

He slid his knee between hers and nudged her foot, opening her legs as he started kissing his way down her neck. Groaning, she reached be-tween them to undo the button on her shorts.

"What the hell?"

Oh, no. Drew jerked away from Liz so fast she

almost fell over and she saw Mitch staring at them from the open doorway.

"What the hell is going on?"

"Mitch," Liz started, taking a step toward him, but Drew put his arm out, keeping her behind him.

"Get your hand off her," Mitch said in a low voice. He was moving toward Drew, who pushed Liz back toward the sink and started circling around.

"Calm down and let me talk," Drew said.

"Calm down? Really? When I find you in here pawing my sister?"

"Liz and I—"

She gasped when Mitch swung, even though Drew easily dodged it. He'd circled his way around so he was at the door and he was backing toward it.

"There's no Liz and you. You're my friend. She's my sister."

"And she's an adult."

Liz saw Mitch's muscles bunch and knew he was about to throw himself at Drew. But Drew must have seen it coming, too, because he cleared the door and took off. Her brother took off after him and Liz ran to the door.

"Mitch, don't." They were moving fast and already rounding the corner as she struggled to pull her wet T-shirt down. "Mitchell Kowalski!"

He didn't even slow down. Cursing men in general—and Drew and Mitch specifically—under her breath, she took a minute to make sure she was decent and then took off after them.

When she turned the corner, she was surprised to see the other women sitting in their camp chairs along the side of the road. They were sharing big umbrellas instead of sitting under the tarp that wasn't ten feet back from the road.

"Did you guys see which way Drew and Mitch went?" They all pointed toward the bend in the road that led up a hill. "Thanks. What are you guys doing, anyway?"

"Honey, Drew Miller just ran by here in his boxer briefs," Keri said.

Emma nodded. "And since he's the only hot guy here not related to or married to one of us and that road doesn't loop all the way around, we're going to sit right here and hope he runs by again."

Unbelievable. Her brother was going to kill his best friend with his bare hands and they were lined up to catch a second glimpse of Drew in his underwear. Not that she blamed them, of course, but there was a time and a place and this was neither.

"This is the best damn family camping trip ever," Terry said.

And they wondered why she'd lived in New Mexico for so long? Her family was insane.

She only had to detour about twenty feet off the road to knock on the door of Aunt Mary's camper. When she heard a welcome called out, she wiped her feet on the mat and went inside. Not surprisingly, Mary was in the RV's kitchen.

"You look flushed, honey. And you're soaked."

"I need to borrow a wooden spoon." There were several right there in the dish drainer, so she plucked one out.

"Since I highly doubt you're baking anything, can I assume you're having man troubles?"

That was an understatement. "I need to knock some sense into my brother."

"Which brother?"

"Mitch."

Mary opened a drawer and pulled out the wooden spoon. The big one, worn from decades of use and known to strike fear in the hearts of young Kowalskis. And not so young ones. "You're going to need the big spoon. And good luck."

DREW HEARD MITCH lagging behind him and started slowing his pace. Even with anger fueling him, his friend wasn't much of a runner and he was breathing hard. It was why Drew had chosen the hill he had. The more he could physically exhaust Mitch, the better.

When he reached the clearing at the top of the hill, hopefully far enough away from everybody else to be out of earshot, he stopped and turned to face the music. Mitch stopped, too, glaring at him while he bent over to rest his hands on his knees and catch his breath.

Drew figured it was best to just get it out. "Liz and I were together once before. When she came home for your wedding."

"Bullshit. She never left the lodge the whole time she was…" He stood up straight, disbelief clouding his expression. "Nobody could find her when it was time to cut the cake. You slept with my sister at my *wedding?*"

"It was a rebound thing. We were both feeling lonely and a little down and…I guess we cheered each other up temporarily."

"That was then. What's your lame-ass excuse for this time?"

Hell if he knew. No matter what his brain said, Drew's body couldn't seem to shake off its need for Liz. "I was going to talk to you when we got back to Whitford. I wanted to sit down and tell you."

Mitch shook his head, shoving at his hair with

one hand. "We laughed about it. When that picture of your car in her driveway was on Facebook. You said you'd cut off your own balls before you'd touch my sister."

"No. *You* said that, not me. And I should have told you then, but I thought it was just a onetime thing and didn't want to lose our friendship over it."

"Friendship? You're a lying sack of shit."

Drew felt a flare of temper, but he squashed it. It was a skill he'd learned on the job, and he did his best to stay calm and use an even voice. "By omission, maybe. But it doesn't change the fact that we're both adults and when we get home, I'm going to take her out."

"Like hell you are."

Drew saw Liz coming up behind Mitch. She was winded and had what looked like a wooden spoon in her hand. He shook his head, trying to signal to her to leave them alone, but she was on a mission.

"Leave him alone, Mitch."

Her brother turned, pointing down the hill. "You go back with the others."

"Excuse me? You kiss my ass. How's that?"

"This is between me and Drew."

She folded her arms across her chest, tapping the wooden spoon against her upper arm. "No, what there is right now is something between *me* and Drew. I'm sorry you found out this way, but it's my life."

"You don't understand," Mitch began.

"If you tell me there's a damn *code* or any bull like that, I'm going to smack you so hard with this spoon when you wake up your clothes will be out of style."

"Liz." Drew took a step forward, wanting to defuse the situation. Liz's temper was as bad as her brothers' and it wasn't going to help. "You should go back and let us talk."

Mitch whirled back to him. "Don't tell her what to do."

"It's the same thing you just told her to do."

"She's my sister!"

"And her sex life is none of your business!"

It was a critical error, just when he thought he'd been doing so well keeping his emotions in check. While they were talking, he and Mitch had gotten closer than he'd realized and he didn't have time to dodge his friend's fist. He managed to evade the full impact, but he took a glancing blow to the jaw that hurt like hell.

He didn't hit back. He wouldn't, even though they'd scrapped a few times when they were kids. Maybe it was partly guilt and on some level he felt he deserved to get his ass kicked. But Mitch was also Liz's brother and if Drew forced a situation where she might have to take sides, Drew would lose.

"Ow!" Mitch spun, rubbing the back of his head, and Drew realized she'd hit him with the spoon.

"If you hit him again, I won't forgive you for it. I know you're my brother and I love you, but you're being a bullheaded idiot right now."

"I don't want to hear about your sex life. And my best friend."

She held up her hands. "Swell! Then don't. Go make s'mores or take a dip in the pool."

Drew wanted to beat his head against the nearest tree. Mitch and Liz could bicker a long time once they got started. And he was cold, wet, half-naked and his jaw was throbbing. At least it had stopped raining at some point.

"Liz, I know he's your brother, but you need to let us talk this out." She actually rolled her eyes at him. "Please."

She pointed the spoon at Mitch. "Promise me you won't hit him again."

Drew knew his friend well enough to see some of the initial anger-fueled fight was going out of him. That was good in a way, because he didn't really want to get hit again, but in another way

Drew was sorry to see it. Anger was a lot easier to deal with than hurt and betrayal.

"I'm not going to hit him again."

She gave them both a hard look, then turned and walked back the way she'd come. Both men watched her leave until they were sure she wasn't coming back.

"I'm sorry," Drew said quietly. "Not in a million years would I have guessed that your sister and I would…end up where we are."

"Where is that exactly? Besides making out in a bathroom, of course."

He blew out a breath and rubbed the back of his neck. "I don't know, to be honest. We're attracted to each other. We enjoy each other's company. But it hasn't been an actual relationship because of you."

"Don't blame me when you didn't even have the respect to let me figure out how I'd feel about it. Instead you let me walk in on…I'm not the bad guy here."

"You're right. It wasn't because of you. We were afraid, or mostly I was, that you'd react badly. As long as you didn't know about it, I didn't have to choose between you and her."

"Which would you choose?"

Drew hadn't expected that and it threw him. He hesitated, trying to wrap his mind around a choice he'd avoided making at all costs. "You. We've been friends our whole lives."

Mitch pointed at him. "Then you don't deserve her."

Ryan stepped out of the trees, catching them both off guard. The path was a shortcut to the clearing and neither had heard him coming. "Everything okay?"

"Yeah." Mitch gave Drew a look that was full of anger and hurt and questions, and then turned away. "I'm done here."

Ryan followed Mitch down the hill, leaving Drew alone. He sat on a boulder, which wasn't especially comfortable considering his lack of clothing, and gingerly touched his jaw. It wasn't broken and, other than some bruising and throbbing, wasn't a big deal.

His life, on the other hand? That had gone to hell in a hurry.

TWELVE

LIZ WENT BACK to the bathhouse, where she gathered up Drew's clothes, and then walked to the big drink cooler they kept at Mike and Lisa's site. She scooped some ice into a towel and almost bumped into Rose when she turned.

"What's going on?" Rosie asked, her eyes scanning Liz's face like an interrogator's spotlight.

"Nothing."

"Nothing? The others thought, when they ran by, that they were horsing around, but Ryan went to see what was going on and he said punches were thrown. And you're holding Drew's clothes. Mitch found out, didn't he?"

"Only one punch was thrown. And it's nobody's business."

"If anybody was ever my business, it's you kids. I told you before that you should tell him."

She hadn't thought that would be enough to put Rose off, but Liz really didn't want to talk about it right now. "Mitch should learn to knock."

She knew Rosie had more to say—probably a lot more—but Liz stepped around her and kept walking. Mitch and Ryan passed her on the way, but they didn't say anything to her. That was fine. She had nothing to say to them, either.

Drew was sitting on a rock, holding his jaw. His eyes tracked her approach, but his expression was as hard as the boulder under his butt.

"I brought you some ice." She held it out to him and, after a few seconds during which his pride and his pain were probably having an epic battle, he took it and held it to his jaw. "I'm sorry, Drew. I thought you locked the door."

"I didn't want to slow down that long," he mumbled.

Flattering, but a serious error in judgment. "Thank you for not hitting him back."

Even if he did feel like he deserved that punch on some level, she could see it really pricked at his pride to take it. It said a lot about his feelings for Mitch, and maybe for her, that he hadn't even raised a hand in retaliation.

"He'll get over it," Drew said, and she wasn't sure if he was talking to her or to himself. "A lot of the anger is shock. That was the absolute worst way to find out."

"Actually, in another ninety seconds or so, it

would have been way worse." Her lame attempt at humor didn't make him smile.

They heard the low rumble of an ATV slowly climbing the hill, so Drew stood and grabbed the clothes she'd brought him. He started with the pants, then pulled the T-shirt over his head.

Liz saw him wince when he shoved his feet in his sandals. There was a lot of gravel between the bathhouse and the top of the hill.

Their visitor turned out to be Andy and, thankfully, he was alone. "I'm too old to walk all over this campground."

"Hey, Dad."

"I heard there's a problem."

Liz watched Andy climb off the four-wheeler so he could check out his son's jaw and, when she heard their voices in very low conversation, she figured it was her cue to leave. "I'm going to go, uh...finish my laundry."

She took the path Ryan had used, which would save her from making what would feel like a walk of shame through the campground. It dumped her out of the woods slightly above her aunt and uncle's camper and she could see Aunt Mary and Rose standing in front of it, having what looked like a serious conversation. No doubt about her and Drew and Mitch.

Rather than veer off and hide in her tent, she

walked down to the camper. Maybe she'd score a sympathy cookie, at least.

Since the rain had stopped and the kids were running around, the two women bustled her into the camper, where the air-conditioning chilled the surface of her skin.

"I'm still pretty damp," Liz said when Aunt Mary sat on the couch and patted the seat next to her.

"It'll dry. Sit."

Liz figured a lecture was coming and she debated whether or not a cookie was worth it. Two cookies, maybe. Or a brownie. "Did you make any blond brownies?"

"Talk first. You save the goodies for after the tears."

"I'm not going to cry." She almost never cried. It was probably a holdover from growing up with four merciless brothers.

Then Rose sat in the swivel recliner and reached across the space to touch Liz's knee. Before long, Liz found herself curled up on the couch with her head in her aunt's lap. Aunt Mary stroked her back and Rose held her hand while she spilled out the entire story for her aunt's benefit. With tears.

"You can't stay up here forever."

Drew knew his dad was right, but it was pretty

peaceful at the top of the hill now that Mitch and Liz were somewhere down at the bottom of it. “It takes about a half hour for the worst of Mitch’s temper to burn itself out. Not everything will be all better, but I don’t want to have a scene in front of the kids.”

“Says the guy who just ran through the campground in his underwear.”

Drew chuckled, but that hurt his jaw so he stopped. “I wasn’t sure how bad things would get and if Mitch and I really went at it, I didn’t want it to be in that tiny bathroom where Liz could get hurt. And once I moved, I figured I should wear him out a little before giving him the chance to swing. I was always the stronger runner.”

“So, this thing with Liz…did it just happen or is it serious? What’s going on?”

Drew told the entire story to his dad, who winced when he got to the part about sneaking away from Mitch’s reception and then again when he talked about Mitch coming to his office and laughing off the idea Drew would touch Liz while Drew kept silent.

“Ouch.” Andy shook his head. “That’s going to be a sticking point there. That’s as close to an outright lie as you can come without opening your mouth.”

"I know. And I don't know how to make it better."

"A lot's going to depend on what you do next. And then the rest is just time." Andy sighed. "I think you've got to give him enough space to wrap his head around it, but not enough space so it's easier to shove you away and be done with you."

Drew sat sideways on the seat of the ATV, wanting to get off his feet. Now that the adrenaline was waning, they were really starting to hurt. His face didn't feel much better. He wanted, more than anything, to go check on Liz, but he wasn't sure what the current climate was in the family circle and he didn't think Mitch had had enough time to cool off yet.

A couple minutes later, Ryan returned, this time walking up the road. He had a couple of water bottles and he handed one to each of them. "Lauren said you need to hydrate, so here. Hydrate."

He cracked open the top and downed half the bottle in one shot. "Tell her I said thanks. So, what's going on down there? Where's Liz?"

"Paige took Mitch into their camper where, hopefully, she's listening to him rant himself out and calming him down. And Rosie and Aunt Mary have Liz. Probably stuffing her full of cookies. The others are kind of giving the kids the bum's rush toward the pool, not that they're complaining."

"So the coast is clear to grab my stuff and get the hell out of here, then."

Ryan tilted his head, giving him a scowl. "I don't think that's how to handle this."

"If I leave now, you can all salvage what's left of your vacation."

"If you leave now, you and Mitch are estranged. Probably forever. You'll be working, he'll go back to traveling. You won't call him and he won't call you and time will pass until it's too awkward to even say hello to each other if you pass on the street."

"I have to agree with that, son," his dad said.

They were right and he knew it. And he didn't want that. "But me being here will make things harder for Liz."

Ryan chuckled. "Don't worry about Liz. As long as neither of you push her into a corner and try to make her choose one of you over the other, she'll be fine. She's a pretty tough cookie."

Drew knew he wouldn't do that to her, but he wasn't sure about Mitch. "Maybe I should go talk to him."

"Let Liz get to him first," Ryan suggested. "He needs to be reminded our little sister is a grown woman who's free to have sex with whoever she wants and that argument coming from you will probably get you punched in the face again. She'll push back at him but it'll be okay because they're blood. You don't have that unbreakable bond."

"I'm not going to hide in my tent while she cleans up the mess I made."

"Look," Ryan said, annoyance obvious in his clipped tone. "This is why you don't mess around with your best friend's sister. Now you've got this messy triangle thing where Mitch and Liz's relationship is not your problem and your relationship with Mitch is not Liz's problem and Liz's relationship with you is not Mitch's problem, but really it's just one huge goddamned problem because you're all bound together."

"If Mitch knows he and Liz are okay," Andy added, "he's more likely to listen and try to be okay with you."

"So what am I supposed to do in the meantime? Sit on this rock?"

"I'd recommend running to Rosie," Ryan said. When they both scoffed at him, he held up his hands. "What? I'm serious. Let her fuss over your face and your feet and feed you cookies. Don't forget, she loves Mitch and Liz like her own, but you're Andy's son. She loves Andy. They live together so you're like her almost stepson."

"That's a good plan, Drew. Ryan's right."

"I have a teenage almost stepson. Trust me, it's like a crash course in navigating awkward family politics."

Drew downed the rest of his water and screwed the cap back on the bottle. "I guess you're right."

As much as part of him wanted to go to Mitch and push him for the opportunity to explain and make things right, he knew the other men were right. And if ever he'd needed some fussing over from Rose, it was now. She'd known their secret all along and had still tried to throw them together, which meant she must be on his side.

He just hoped Liz didn't eat all the treats first.

LIZ SIGHED AND shoved the last bite of her third blond brownie in her mouth. She was in dry clothes, thanks to Rose making a trip to her tent, but she still felt like a wet washcloth that had been wrung out hard.

After getting through the entire tale of woe, both women had tried to talk through it with her. Their joint advice was, of course, best summed up as Mitch would get over it and if she and Drew were meant to be, it would all work out.

Meant to be *what,* was the question.

If they were meant to be having some fun sex with no complications, that wasn't working out too well for them. If they were meant to be more than that, well, she wasn't sure that's what either of them were looking for.

Rose, who'd been in and out, probably taking everybody's emotional temperatures, entered the camper and smiled. "Most of the family has evacuated to the pool. And Paige thinks Mitch has calmed down enough to have a conversation now."

"Good." Liz chugged down the milk remaining in the glass Aunt Mary had poured for her and slid out of the dinette. "I'm going to go converse with him right now. Is he in his camper?"

"Yes," Rose said. "But you need to keep that temper of yours in check or you'll set him off again."

"I'll be good."

Because most of them were down at the pool, she didn't feel like a sideshow attraction as she made the walk to Mitch and Paige's RV. That would no doubt come later when the family game of telephone had had time to complete the circuit.

When she tapped on the door, Paige stepped out. She was wearing a swimsuit and had a towel draped around her neck. "I'm going to join the others. Mitch is inside."

"How is he?" Even though she was mad at him, she was trying to empathize with how it would feel for your best friend and sister to sneak around keeping secrets.

"He's hurt. Angry. A little embarrassed by his temper. Confused, I guess."

Liz drew in a deep breath and let it out slowly. "I guess I'll go in."

Her oldest brother was sitting in the corner of the RV's couch, leaning against the back of the dinette's bench. She could have sat in the small swivel rocker, but she chose to sit on the other end of the couch. It wasn't very long, so she had to nudge his legs a little to make room. She wanted the physical proximity, even if they were a mile apart emotionally at the moment.

"Drew told me yesterday after breakfast he was going to talk to you when we got back to Maine."

"He should have told me immediately."

Liz shook her head. "At your wedding? What, shake your hand and say, 'Congratulations and, oh by the way, I banged your sister while they were bringing out the cake'?"

Red tinted his neck and face. "Don't talk like that, Liz."

"Okay. Here's the thing. He didn't want to lose your friendship over a nothing fling. And when I came home and that chemistry was still there, it was kind of too late for him to tell you, so he's been trying to keep his distance from me. With varying degrees of success, of course, but some of that's on me. And this happy family camping trip didn't help. But he did try to walk away from me."

"It's weird."

It was a funny word to use, but at least they were working their way down from bluster to real feelings. "Why?"

His scowl grew more intense with each passing second, until he shrugged. "I can't explain it. It's just weird."

"If we were still teenagers and all of a sudden you had to be the third wheel to the two of us, I can see why it would be weird. But we're not. You're married and you own a business that keeps you busy and you're going to be a dad. You guys aren't running buddies anymore."

"There's still a code."

She wanted to shake him until his teeth rattled. "Fine. There's some stupid code left over from high school I'm sick of hearing about. And, yes, he broke it."

"He disrespected you."

"Oh, hell no. He didn't disrespect me. He disrespected *you* and he owns that, Mitch. He knows it and, whether you believe it or not, he's suffered for it."

Mitch propped his elbow on the back of the dinette bench and rested his head against his hand.

"You guys never messed around when we were kids?"

"No. I don't think we even noticed each other that way. But at your wedding, at that point in our lives, it was just…it happened."

"And what's happening now? You guys weren't keeping your distance from each other in the bathhouse."

"That was the buildup of weeks of trying to keep a distance neither of us really wanted. *That* I'm sorry for. Not being with him, but that you had to find out that way."

"Do you love him?"

Whoa. "That's a little premature, I think. I mean, I like him. I like being with him. But it's hard to see what's going on in a relationship when you're spending the entire time trying *not* to have one."

He was quiet for a few minutes, staring off into space. She let him have the time to think rather than poking at him some more. At least the anger vibe had stopped emanating from him in waves.

"You should know," he said quietly, "that when he was talking about not wanting to choose between us and I asked him which of us he'd choose, he said me."

That hurt. Probably more than Mitch intended it to. Rather than let him see it, she swallowed hard and thought about what she wanted to say. "He's your best friend, Mitch. If he chose you, he could avoid me and eventually you guys would be okay again. If he chose me, you guys wouldn't be friends anymore and that would put a strain on my relationship with him *and* with you. It would come between you and me. The whole thing would be doomed anyway, but a lot more painful in the end."

"Is it, I don't know...casual? Is it serious? You know he wants to get married and have kids, right? Like, yesterday."

"I know that." She just wasn't sure how she felt about it yet. "Our relationships with you have been in the middle of anything we might have since the beginning. We need the time and space to see if we have something real or if we're just burning off residual chemistry."

He shifted his leg so it pressed against hers. She leaned her head against the back of the couch and smiled at him. "Just try to be okay with us dating. Please?"

"I've never been able to refuse you, imp."

"You refused to let me drive your Camaro."

"And now you're stuck driving a second-rate Mustang."

She laughed and slapped his knee. "It beat you in the—"

"Don't." His smile was reluctant, but he couldn't hold it back. "He's letting you drive that car just to piss me off. You know that, right?"

"Why do you think I agreed to borrow it?"

His chuckle was like a healing balm to her shredded nerves. "I love you, Liz. I promise I'll *try* to be okay."

And that was enough. "Aunt Mary made blond brownies."

"Those will help." He looked at her and narrowed his eyes. "Or did you eat them all?"

"I only had three."

"Speaking of baked goods, that freakin' wooden spoon hurts." He rubbed the spot on the back of his head where she'd whacked him.

"I know." She gave him a sweet smile. "I'm going to buy one of my own as soon as we get home."

THIRTEEN

IT WAS ALMOST two more hours before Drew got to see Liz again. And, unbelievably, he got to see her alone. Or as alone as they could be in a campground surrounded by her entire extended family.

Rose and Mary had finally gotten tired of fussing over him and stuffing him full of brownies, so he was on his way back to his tent. He wasn't sure what to do with himself or where he was welcome, so his intent was to go stretch out in his tent, close his eyes and relax.

Liz was carrying her laundry bag from the bathhouse to her tent and he changed course to intercept her. She smiled when she saw him and, though she looked as beat as he felt, it was warm and genuine.

"You doing okay?" he asked, taking the bag from her.

"Yeah. Mitch and I are okay, so…yeah. How about you?"

"I wasn't tarred, feathered and ridden out of

town on a rail, so I'll count it as a win." He set the bag down at his feet. "I could use a hug, though."

She didn't hesitate before stepping into his embrace. He wrapped his arms around her and rested the unbruised side of his face against her hair, breathing in the scent of her shampoo. Her arms looped around his waist, so her hands were pressed against his back.

"I'm sorry this blew up," he said. "The last thing I want to do is cause friction between you and your family."

"Me and my family will be fine. We always are." She squeezed him. "And, even though it wasn't the best way, I'm kind of glad it's out there now."

He guessed he was, too. It would have been better to sit down with Mitch and yell it out in the privacy of his home, but at least now he could look his friend in the eye again without feeling like an ulcer was eating him from the inside out. And he could hold Liz in his arms without looking over his shoulder like he was committing some kind of crime.

"I promised Joey I'd go for a walk with him," she said, backing out of his arms. "He's looking at colleges and he wants to ask me about the west coast. I can't tell him much about colleges, but he has a lot of questions about the climate and the whole art thing."

"He wants to be a writer, like Joe, right?"

She laughed. "I guess he's more of a literary book club kind of writer, though he's admitted making millions of dollars writing horror novels like his uncle isn't a bad plan B."

"I was going to go lay down for a little bit. Decompress and get my head on straight."

She kissed him quick on the mouth, then picked up her laundry bag. "I'll see you later, then."

Drew's step was a little lighter as he continued the rest of the way to his tent. Despite the drama of the day, it was nice not feeling as if his feelings for Liz were some dirty, shameful secret.

After straightening up around the tent for a while, he flopped down on the air mattress and closed his eyes. He was still too wound up to actually nap, but he tried to let the tension flow out of his body.

"How the hell do you knock on a tent door?"

It was Mitch's voice, which kicked up the tension again. He got up and undid the zipper, intending to step outside.

Mitch took the flap and blocked his exit. "I'll come in."

Drew sat carefully on the plastic bin he'd packed his clothes in and gestured for Mitch to sit on the cooler. Mitch opened it first, pulling out two cans of beer. After tossing one to Drew, he popped his open and had a seat.

"Everybody's unanimous in wanting you to stay the rest of the week," he said after taking a drink. "Let me rephrase that. Everybody *else* is unanimous."

"If you want me to leave, I'm gone. But that won't be the end of it. I'll call you when you get home and I'll keep calling you until you talk to me because I'm not sweeping almost forty years of friendship under the rug."

"You'll leave if I tell you to? Sure. Run away and leave Liz to take all the crap and teasing the family's going to dish out."

Drew held up his hands, careful not to spill his beer. "You want me gone, but you're giving me shit about going?"

"Because I don't want to see your face right now, but running out on Liz is a dick move," Mitch growled, yanking off his hat so he could push back his hair. "See? This is why you're not supposed to sleep with my sister. It puts me in the middle."

"Bullshit. This isn't about you, and you put yourself in the middle." Drew felt his temper rising and it was mirrored on Mitch's face, so he took a deep breath and tried to dial it down a notch. "I'm sorry I'm falling for your sister. It would be better if she was anybody else, but if she was anybody else, she probably wouldn't make me feel the way she does."

"So you *are* falling for her?"

"I think so. I don't know how she feels. I know she feels like she's still looking for what she wants out of life, but I can't walk away from her if there's a chance it's me."

"I can't control what's between you two. But between you and me? You lied to me." Mitch shook his head, staring down at the can in his hand. "I always trusted you to have my back."

"And I still have your back. You can call me every name but nice and throw me out of here, but if you call me next week and have a problem, I'll still be there. Always. I did you wrong, but for just one second try to put yourself in my shoes. I don't remember a time we weren't friends and that matters to me. But on the other hand there's this amazing, vibrant, sexy-as-hell woman I can't stop thinking about. And she's your sister. If you think this has been easy for me or just some stupid lark, you are dead wrong."

Mitch stared into his eyes for a long time, looking for who knew what, and then he nodded. "I promised my sister I'd try to be okay with you guys…dating or whatever."

When he stood and set his can down on the cooler, Drew stood, too. The conversation felt unfinished and he didn't want Mitch to walk out without feeling as if they'd resolved anything. He wanted to work toward them being okay.

Then Mitch put out his hand. Drew recognized the gesture for the huge step it was in the right direction and clasped hands with his friend.

Mitch squeezed, looking Drew dead in the eye. "I don't care how long we've been friends. If you break my sister's heart, they'll never find your body."

"If that happens, and I pray it doesn't, act fast or you'll have to wait your turn in line. Probably behind Mary and that damn spoon."

Mitch actually barked out a laugh as he released Drew's hand. "Liz said she's buying her own as soon as she gets home. Good luck with that."

After Mitch left the tent, Drew inhaled the first easy breath he'd had since the bathhouse incident. Everything might be okay, after all.

"SHE LOOKS CUTE. Like a little blue-eyed hedgehog in a pink sundress."

Keri looked up from her daughter to glare at Liz. "Yes. So cute."

The toddler had inhaled her pancakes, managing to smear maple syrup all over her face, hair and arms while she ate. Then, in the process of going to throw her plate away, she'd tripped over her uncle Mike's foot and went sliding through the fallen pine needles like a runner stealing third base. She came up screeching and looking like a porcupine, though Liz said hedgehog because it sounded nicer.

Of course, in her full-blown state of drama, the sticky hedgehog wrapped herself around her mother. Then Liz tried to help and now all three of them were sticky.

"Joe, come help me with Brianna," Keri called to her husband, who was deep in conversation with Joey.

"Hold on. Joey's helping me with a plot problem."

"If you don't come get your daughter, you won't have to plot your next horror novel because it will be your autobiography."

"We need hot water," Liz said when Joe had taken one of Brianna's hands to detach her from Keri.

"We'll go to the bathhouse. Less fabric and more easily washable surfaces than the camper."

Since Joe had Brianna's hand, Keri and Liz followed along behind on the trek to the hot water.

Liz didn't have a lot on her, but when it came to maple syrup and pine needles, it didn't take a lot.

"So," Keri said when they'd left the breakfast circle. "You and Drew are a thing, huh? I can't believe I didn't see it. That *nobody* did."

"We were trying not to be a thing."

"It's a little weird," Joe said over his shoulder. "He's been a friend of the family for, like, ever."

"Oh please." *Weird* seemed to be the word of the week. "Nobody has a problem with Josh and Katie being together and she's Rose's daughter. She practically grew up in our house with us."

"That's different. Katie always loved Josh and everybody knew he'd catch up eventually."

"I think it's great," Keri said. "I like Drew and he fits right in with the family."

"Because he's practically one of us," Joe muttered.

"Heard that." Liz rolled her eyes at Keri. "Somehow I suspect the divide on the me and Drew issue will run pretty evenly down gender lines."

She wasn't far off. As the day went on, it was obvious that the men who were willing to pick a side were siding with Mitch—cautiously accepting—while the women were probably planning her bridal shower already.

Leo decided they all needed another family

ride after lunch, and this time Liz didn't feel awkward about riding double with Drew. She climbed behind him and let her legs surround him without worrying about bracing herself. He rubbed her knee, then pulled into line with the others.

Talking wasn't easy with the helmets and engine noise, but at least there was a little privacy. "How's today going?"

He shrugged. "A little awkward and I'm getting a lot of the side-eye from your brothers, but better than I thought it would be."

She rubbed her hands over his shoulders before grabbing for the handholds so he didn't buck her off on a waterbar. "Well, the women are all rooting for you, if that helps."

"I guess. It's a little uncomfortable being the center of attention, though."

"I know what you mean." And she did, which was why there had been small touches, like a hug or holding hands or a quick kiss good-night, but that was it.

Her brother was trying his best to accept this change in the natural order of his life, so Liz was trying not to make it any more traumatic than necessary. She had really, really wanted to crawl into Drew's tent last night, but she figured Mitch had been traumatized enough by her sex life.

The irony, of course, was that now that she was

free to openly be with Drew, they still weren't having sex. But she could wait. They'd go home soon and then they could maybe have a normal relationship.

At about the halfway point of the loop they were riding, they pulled into what passed for a rest area on the ATV trails. A swampy pond to look at, one ancient picnic table to sit on and lots of trees to pee on.

Within seconds, there was riding gear littering the entire area, which seemed overrun with kids. Liz set her helmet on the back of the machine next to Drew's, and then slipped her hand into his. His fingers locked with hers and he gave her a little squeeze.

"So much dust today," Beth said to her husband, slapping her clothes so big puffs of dust drifted into the breeze. "I'm glad we left Lily with your parents."

Liz pulled Drew back as the boys ran between them and her cousin, with Steph in hot pursuit, screaming about giving back her hair elastic.

Kevin looked at Drew and shook his head. "I know what you must be thinking. Camping with this crew is a great advertisement for birth control."

Drew's gaze swept over the horde of shouting, laughing kids and he shook his head. "I was thinking that you're all really lucky guys."

Liz felt a pang deep inside. He probably wasn't aware of how much longing he let slip into his voice and his expression. And it was a poignant reminder that, even though they'd somewhat managed to clear the hurdle of Mitch, he'd never been the only stumbling block in their path.

"Yeah, we are pretty lucky," Kevin agreed. "Now that my business partner and his wife have the new pub running smoothly and Jasper's Bar & Grille is as strong as ever, Beth and I are thinking about adding another to the horde."

"Boy or girl, I hope the addition's got a strong constitution," Drew said. "Lily's one fierce little girl."

"Yeah." Kevin's dimples popped into view when he thought about his daughter. "Maybe a little less time in a sports bar for that one. She likes to sneak out of the office and *help* Paulie sometimes and she fits right in. But hanging out with the whole family, what with Emma having a new baby and Paige being pregnant—um, you guys knew that, right?—and Katie thinking about it has Beth determined to get pregnant now, too."

Liz was keenly aware Drew had let go of her hand and shoved his hands in his pockets while Kevin was talking. Maybe it was a coincidence, or maybe there was a reason he'd pulled away from her while there was talk of having babies.

"It'll be quite the pack of kids if Rose and Mary decide to make this family reunion thing an annual tradition," Drew said. "Assuming the couple that owns the campground don't run away in the middle of the night."

Kevin laughed. "They're good people. They're getting up there in years, though, so we're worried they might sell the place to somebody with less tolerance for juvenile exuberance."

"Of doom," Liz muttered.

"Let's go!" Leo yelled over the noise.

"That was fast," Liz said.

"We don't have much in the way of snacks with us, other than granola bars, so it's best to keep the kids moving," Beth explained. "And we might be trying to wear them out so they're not hiding in the woods, trying to dodge bedtime tonight."

"Parenthood is fun," Kevin told Drew. "Really. You should have five or six of the little buggers."

Drew laughed. "I was thinking two or three, but why not field a hockey starting line, right?"

"Poor Liz," Beth said, and then she went to get ready.

Liz didn't know what to say, so she was glad for the distraction a bunch of kids trying to find helmets, goggles and gloves made. She put her helmet on and climbed up behind Drew, and she was thankful when he tucked his hand under her left knee.

"Some of your family's come around to the idea of us being a couple a lot faster than others have," he remarked.

"Yeah. Sorry about that."

"Why are you sorry?"

Because assumptions she was going to bear Drew a hockey team were a little premature, and made even more awkward by the fact she knew Drew really wanted that. Maybe not the hockey, but the kids. "It's a little soon for them to jump to conclusions like that."

His head made a little sideways motion that said *eh, not really,* and that worried her. Yes, really.

The four-wheelers started firing up, so Drew started theirs. The engine sounds were loud while they were all sitting there idling, so Liz relaxed against the seat and let the conversation go. Something to talk about on another day.

DREW WAS PRETTY sure the only thing that saved him from having *Water Ball Game of Doom* printed on his death certificate was the fact Ryan tried to spike the inflatable beach ball at him so hard he popped the damn thing.

Drew had known as soon as they got back from their ride and everybody started clamoring to go in the pool, that he'd be a target. Mitch was doing a really good job of respecting his sister's wishes, but that didn't mean Drew wouldn't pay. He had red splotches all over his torso, more than a few bruises and he was getting better at holding his breath by the minute.

"You broke it!" Bobby yelled at Ryan. "You broke the water ball."

"Do we have another one?" Danny asked.

Drew hoped like hell they didn't. He wasn't going to cry uncle, but he'd had enough water ball. He wanted to grab Liz, whose body in that swimsuit was one of the reasons he sucked at water ball, and go "take a nap" as some of the other adults did.

"Mom, do we have another water ball?"

"No," Lisa called. "That was the only one."

There were groans of disappointment, and then Bobby came up with a solution. "We can use the volleyball."

"No!" yelled every adult within earshot.

"What are we going to play now?" Bobby wanted to know.

"You could just swim around," Drew said, and he was pretty sure he heard Mitch and Ryan snicker.

He didn't care. Making his way to the edge of the pool, he sat on the middle rung of the ladder and let the small waves wash over him as the kids turned swimming around into some kind of water wrestling of doom match.

Liz caught his eye, twitching that swimsuit skirt at him, and he smiled when she winked at him. She was standing in the shallow end by the steps, watching Brianna splash around in her pink life jacket, and he tried not to feel anything at the sight of her and the little girl.

He hadn't been oblivious to the change in her mood when he was joking with her cousin about having a hockey team. He'd realized too late he pulled away from her a little bit when they were talking about babies, and he knew she'd noticed. But there was no sense in hiding how he felt because it wasn't a secret. He wanted kids and, judging by the way he'd pulled away from her without conscious thought, he didn't think she did.

She arched an eyebrow at him now and he realized he'd been staring at her. Pushing away from the ladder, he swam down the pool and ducked under the buoy line to float over to her. Her aunt reached out and pulled on Brianna's float so it moved like a boat. The little girl laughed and Drew also had a little bit of privacy to talk to Liz.

He was starting to like the Kowalski women a lot more than the men lately.

He sat on the step and pulled her down next to him. "How much longer do you think everybody will be in the pool?"

"If you think we can sneak out of here and be inconspicuous, you haven't been paying attention."

Drew laughed, knowing she was right. They'd been very careful about public displays of affection so her family could get acclimated to their situation, and trying to sneak off for a quickie while they were all in the pool wasn't going to happen. "I was thinking we could go for a ride."

"On the four-wheelers?" She wrinkled her nose. "I just started feeling clean again."

"In my truck." The big SUV with the seats that folded flat in the back and made for a nice amount of space.

"To where?"

"Wherever. Down some back roads."

He knew when she got his meaning because she laughed and slapped his leg. "You're so bad."

"Is that a no?"

Her eyes met his and he saw the same desire in them that he felt. "It might be nice to get away for a little while."

That was all he needed to hear. "I'm going to

go clean up since I have no interest in any more attempted drownings. Once you're done, we'll head out."

She gave him a look he was surprised didn't make his swim trunks go up in flames. "Half hour, tops."

He took some heckling for leaving the pool area but, since Liz didn't go with him, everybody lost interest before he'd gone twenty feet. After the fastest shower in the history of running water, he put on his flannel pants and a T-shirt. No buttons or zippers to slow him down.

Then he got to work on the SUV. He had a lot of work crap in the back, but he stowed what he could and set the rest in his tent so he could lay the backseats down. Then he threw in his sleeping bag and, after a moment's hesitation, his pillow, too. Then he waited.

It was another twenty minutes before Kowalskis started streaming up from the pool and, since he saw Liz helping Keri with Brianna's stuff, he knew it would be a few more minutes, at least.

More like fifteen. She gave him the *just another minute* sign before ducking into her tent. Then she was at the bathhouse for what seemed like hours, but was probably only five minutes. Finally, she was ready to go.

"What are we telling your family?"

"I told them we're going for a ride." He waited a few seconds, and then she blushed. "Okay, I told them you have to drive into town for cell reception to make a call and I'm going with you."

It was as good an excuse as any. Not that any of the other adults would buy it, but it was at least a solid pretense. "Let's go, then."

Of course they had to drive by where the family was hanging out to leave the campground and when Bobby ran toward his truck, he had to stop or risk running the kid over. He rolled down the window.

"Are you going to get pizza? Can we go?"

Of course all of the kids stopped to stare at him, waiting for his answer. "Um, I have to go make a business call. It's pretty important police business, so I can't have any kids around."

"In your pajamas?"

Drew looked down at his sleep pants. "They can't see my clothes over the phone."

"If we're really quiet, they won't see us, either."

The kid was tenacious. And smart. "But sometimes things go wrong, so we can't have any kids on a ride-along."

Bobby's shoulders sagged, but he recovered pretty quickly when his mom announced it was freeze pop time.

"Good luck with your very important police

business," Josh said, trying not to grin like an idiot.

Drew put up the window and hit the gas before the temptation to flip him off won. "Hell, that was awkward."

"You realize we're not fooling anybody, right?"

"I'm trying to pretend we are. I'm surprised Dad or Leo didn't pull me aside and ask me if I had a condom in my wallet."

Liz laughed. "At least they'd pull you aside. Rose was not shy about that when my brothers hit that age. And, um, you do have one, right?"

"I have two."

"Then let's get the hell out of here."

FOURTEEN

WITH THE RADIO on low, the air-conditioning on high and the road vibrating under the tires, Liz was afraid she might fall asleep. After already having his ass handed to him in water ball of doom, that could be a fatal blow to Drew's ego, so she shifted in her seat, trying to stay awake.

"Do you have any idea where you're going?" she asked when they'd gone a few miles north.

"Someplace where there aren't any Kowalskis." When she cleared her throat, he smiled at her. "You know, except for you."

"I'm guessing you didn't sneak down to the office and use the phone to make reservations at some five-star resort hotel."

"No, but when I threw the sleeping bag in the back, I threw a pillow in with it."

The way he said it made her laugh. "You're such a gentleman."

After a couple more miles, Drew signaled and then made a right turn onto a dirt road. He had to have known it was there, she thought, because he'd turned his blinker on before the road had even been visible. He passed by a couple of left-hand turns before making the third one onto a narrower, bumpier road and she realized it definitely wasn't random.

"Where are we going?"

"I asked the guy in the office where I could go and absolutely not be disturbed by anybody."

That didn't sound suspicious at all. "And did he ask why?"

"Nope. He asked me if I was trying to start a secret marijuana field and when I said no and explained that's frowned upon when you're the chief of police, he gave me some directions."

When he'd made another three or four turns and the roads had grown so narrow the brush was rubbing the SUV's doors, she started getting worried. "Did you write the directions down?"

"Nope."

"What are the chances we'll find our way back out again?"

"I don't care."

Neither did she, really. All that mattered was that, after days of torture, she was on her way to getting what her body was so desperately craving. It had been so hard being able to flirt and touch and kiss, but nothing more. She was ready for the something more part.

Finally, Drew pulled the SUV into a very small clearing and killed the engine. “Well, it’s not a five-star resort hotel, but it’s private.”

Since all she saw were bushes and mosquitoes out the window, Liz had to agree. “Definitely can’t crack the windows.”

“It’s cooler here, but if it gets hot, I’ll start the engine and let the AC run.”

With that covered, Liz unsnapped her seat belt and smiled at him. “You’re a man who knows how to get things done.”

“I guess that remains to be seen.” He arched an eyebrow and nodded in the direction of the back.

Liz was thankful he already wanted her badly enough to set up this little shenanigan because climbing between the two front bucket seats with their massive center console wasn’t one of her more graceful moments. She finally squeezed through and landed on the sleeping bag with a thud. A hard thud, since the flat deck of the dropped seats wasn’t exactly soft.

She watched him make his way through, biting her lip to keep from laughing. “We probably should have gotten out and come in through the back hatch.”

“With all the mosquitoes?” Drew grunted and

freed himself with a final push. "Consider this a test. See how much I want you?"

Once he was back there with her, it seemed a lot nicer. Maybe because he immediately yanked his T-shirt over his head and tossed it aside. With her hands on his skin, running over the muscles in his shoulders and arms, she didn't care where they were.

Drew plunged his hand into her hair at the base of her neck and hauled her in for a kiss. It was hard and hot and she slid her tongue over his bottom lip, making him shiver. Then he nipped at hers with his teeth and it was her turn.

"I've been waiting for this," he whispered against her mouth, "since I saw you again, sitting in that car in the rain with the fenders crumpled in."

"That wasn't my most sexy moment ever."

"Honey, there's nothing about you that's not sexy to me." He went back to kissing after that.

When his free hand slid up under her T-shirt and found naked skin, a thrill shot through her body. She pulled back from his kiss to toss her shirt in a pile with his, and he unhooked her bra. Sliding it slowly down her arms, he watched as the lace fell away to reveal her taut nipples. The lace went in the pile as he pushed her gently backward until she was lying on the sleeping bag with her head on the pillow. Then she kicked off her flip-flops so he could pull her shorts and panties down in one smooth motion. He threw them in the corner and the vehicle rocked as he removed his pants, as well.

"Here we are," he said, the corners of his mouth lifting as he settled himself over her. "Naked at last."

She laughed and ran her hands from his ass all the way to his shoulders. She loved the feel of his naked skin. "I've been imagining us naked for a while now. Reality's even better."

Bending his head, he sucked one nipple into his mouth while he caressed the other with his hands. His tongue and fingers teased and played, until she was squirming under him.

Then he blew softly over the damn nipple, which felt so exquisite she sighed and closed her eyes. "So tell me something."

His conversational tone made her eyes fly open again. "Now? You want to talk now?"

"No." He chuckled, the sound seeming to vibrate through his body. "I want to make you answer a question right now, while I have you at my mercy."

"Any statements made during sex cannot and will not be used against me. I'm sure they covered duress at your police academy."

"I want to know what word got you middle-named during dirty Scrabble."

Again? The poor guy. Whatever no-doubt-X-rated guess he'd built up to in his mind was a lot more exciting than the truth. "Never."

"Oh, that's too bad." He slid his hand down her stomach, stopping just short of going lower.

"What do you think you're doing?"

He made fake puppy dog eyes at her. "It makes me sad that you won't tell me. And when I'm sad I can't give beautiful women orgasms. It's a curse."

"I can't believe you're doing this." She laughed and punched him in the shoulder, which made him wince. "If there's no orgasm for me, there's no orgasm for you."

"Honey, I'm coming tonight or my balls will explode and there's nothing on this Earth that can stop that. The question is whether or not it'll happen while I'm inside you, watching your face while you beg me to take you faster and harder." The entire time he was talking, his hand was dipping to *almost* between her legs before retreating. "Which I'd be more than happy to do, of course… if I wasn't sad."

She hadn't come out here into the middle of nowhere to get a flippin' belly rub from him. "Fine! It wasn't the word that got me middle-named. I spelled Viagra."

He drew back, disbelief plain on his face. "I think you're lying because I'm pretty sure you can say that out loud."

"Yeah, you can. But what got me middle-named was asking Rose if I'd spelled it right."

It took him a second, and then he groaned. "That's cold."

"It was funny."

"It would be funnier if she wasn't sleeping with my dad." He frowned, and then shook his head. "No, I don't want to know."

"Next time, focus on what you're supposed to be doing instead of asking me questions about board games. Hello, naked here."

He grinned down at her. "I noticed. I like it."

In the fading light, she looked at his torso, then looked closer. "What did they do to you?"

He still had some red splotches on him, as well as a handful of bruises. The welts and the bruises all varied in size and severity, but it still looked like he'd run through a gauntlet of people taking shots at him.

"Water ball of doom," he said, looking down at his chest. "I played in a pickup game of football while I was at the academy on a day that was brutally hot and everybody's temper was short. Between injuries and dehydration, four ambulances were called to that field, and water ball of doom is still the most brutal sport I've ever played."

"They were hard on you," she said, running her hand over the marks. "Because of me."

"You, Liz Kowalski," he said, planting a hand on either side of her head so he could stare down at her, "are worth facing any amount of doom for."

She melted on the inside, and then the heat took over her entire body as he nipped at her jaw. And this time when he ran his hand down her stomach, he didn't stop. He stroked between her thighs until she whimpered.

"Do you like that?" he whispered against her mouth.

"Yes." The word was barely more than a breath, and she arched her hips into his touch.

He switched his kisses from her mouth to her breasts, alternating between licking and gently sucking on her nipples as his fingers slid inside of her, making her gasp. It was too much and she dug her nails into his shoulders as her climax shook her body. He didn't stop touching her until the tremors ceased, and then he kissed her again, harder this time.

"Damn," she said when she could breathe again, and he chuckled.

She tried rolling him to take the upper hand, but the space wasn't big enough for either of them to stretch out and he was stronger. Laughing, she pushed at his shoulder while hooking her leg over his hip, but it didn't work.

"This week has toughened me up," he said as he resisted. "You won't win."

Changing tactics, she slid her hand between their hips and curled her fingers around his erection. His body jerked, and she laughed when his muscles gave up resisting and they flopped over.

Now she looked down at him, as he had at her, while she stroked him. "Do you like that?"

Judging by the blush over his chest and the way his hand kept clenching and unclenching the corner of the pillow, he liked it a lot. "You are hell on my self-control, woman."

"I don't remember asking you to control yourself."

He reached out his hand and fumbled with the clothes until he came up with his pants and pulled a condom wrapper from the pocket. Liz felt her body grow hot in anticipation as she released him.

Once he'd covered himself, Drew hauled her up and over his body. He kissed her, his tongue dancing over hers as his hand tangled in her hair. She moaned against his mouth when he reached between them and guided himself into her.

Liz rocked, slowly taking more of him with each rise and fall of her hips. He kept on kissing her, his fingers tightening in her hair almost to the point of pain as he pushed up into her.

"So sweet," he murmured. "So sweet and hot."

She sat up, wanting to see his face, and he grabbed at her shoulder. "Don't hit your head on the roof."

Laughing, she rested her hands on his chest and moved her hips in a small circular motion. "Again, such a gentleman."

Groaning, he thrust upward hard, his hands cupping her breasts. "God, that feels good."

Yes, it did, and Liz sped it up a little as he squeezed her breasts. But Drew had other plans and she found herself under him again. The pillow was shoved out of the way, but she didn't care. He put his hands behind her knees, lifting her hips so he could drive into her.

She sucked in a breath as his strokes came hard and fast, his fingertips biting into her skin. Pressing her fingers into his thighs, she bit down on her lip to keep from screaming as the orgasm racked her body. Drew drove into her, his muscles quivering as he neared his own climax.

He growled her name as he came, dropping her knees and grasping her shoulders for leverage as he rode out the wave with stroke after stroke until he collapsed, panting, on top of her.

She ran her hands up his back and held him to

her, loving the solid, heavy sensation of his body crushing hers. Kissing the spot between his earlobe and his hairline, she stroked his hair as they caught their breath.

"That was so worth the paint on the side of my truck," he said as he rolled off of her.

"I think half the state's mosquito population is pressed against the windows watching us."

He chuckled and rested his hand on her hip. "With all your delicious skin on display, the rest of them will be along shortly."

"Whatever you do, don't open the doors or the windows or they'll find nothing but our skeletons."

"We're not going anywhere. In a few minutes, I'm going to start the engine to cool it off in here. Then I'm going to have a drink of water and give those mosquitoes another show."

She rolled onto her side and propped her head on her hand. "You only had two condoms. A double header means you have none."

"If we should find ourselves with privacy again before the trip's over or I get so desperate I drive to a drug store, there are plenty of games we can play without that piece of equipment."

"Then start your engine, Chief Miller, and let's play."

If Drew thought driving out of the campground with Liz was awkward, it was nothing compared to how conspicuous he felt driving back in. He could see by the smoke that the grills were fired up, and the family was all gathered together to get ready for supper.

"Great timing," he said, navigating the dirt roads up to their tents.

"I'm starving."

He realized she didn't feel as self-conscious about the whole snuck-off-to-have-sex thing as he did and tried to relax. After parking the SUV next to his tent, he decided to leave the sleeping bag and pillow in the back until later. Preferably until after dark. Whether the others had guessed or not, there was no sense in advertising what they'd been up to.

"Smells like chicken," Liz said as she climbed out. She took his hand as they walked down to join the others, giving it a squeeze.

"Hey, Liz, you're just in time," Terry said when everybody called out a greeting. "Can you help me with this coleslaw?"

And just like that, she was gone, leaving him to mill around with her family.

"So, Chief," Ryan said. "How'd that very important police business go? Get it all…conducted?"

Funny guy, that Ryan. "Conducted very well, thank you."

Bobby tugged at his shirt. "Did you get to put handcuffs on anybody?"

Mitch, who'd been mid-swallow from a can of soda, choked. The other guys started laughing at him, which earned them glares from the women until Josh finally pounded him on the back and Mitch got himself under control.

"No handcuffs," Drew told Bobby. Then he looked at his friend over the top of the boy's head. "This time."

Mitch flipped him the bird from behind the soda can, which made him laugh. It was going to take more than a cranky Kowalski to get under his skin tonight. Once he got his hands on that grilled chicken and coleslaw, Drew was going to be fully satisfied in every possible way. He knew it was temporary. He'd be itching to have his hands on Liz again in no time because, if he ever did get his fill of her, it wasn't going to be for a long, long time. But for right now, he was a happy man.

"Will you play ball with me?"

He looked down at Bobby, who was holding a tennis ball and smiling sweetly up at him. "Are you talking catch, or some kind of tennis ball of doom game that will leave me dying for a tube of muscle rub and a hot tub?"

"Just catch."

He wasn't sure he believed the boy, but the other kids were either helping with dinner or reading. Even if the game got rowdy, he could probably survive a one-on-one with a little kid. Maybe.

They moved out into the dirt road for space and Bobby lobbed the ball to him. Drew stepped in to catch it and then threw it back. They fell into an easy rhythm that reminded him of very long ago days when he'd done the same with his dad.

Last year, it had been the baseball glove he'd found in the garage that led to the end of his marriage. It had gotten him to thinking it was past time for him to have his own little boy to play catch with and he'd told Mallory that. She'd tried to put him off again and, for the first time, he'd really pushed. That's when she told him she'd never wanted to have kids and was afraid to tell him or she'd lose him.

Now he was starting over and, as Rose called for them to go and eat, he felt a little less satisfied than he had only twenty minutes before.

FIFTEEN

THE DAY BEFORE the Maine half of the family had to go home, Rose and Aunt Mary made it clear there would be family activities, not everybody going in different directions and doing different things. Once dinner had been eaten as a group, the guys could go ride if they wanted, but everybody was grounded until then.

Liz didn't mind. She spent a little time after breakfast cleanup doing her last load of laundry and then, after dumping it in her tent, she took a leisurely walk in search of others. She was almost to the screen house when Brian went by her, struggling to drag a cooler through the grass by one handle and, curious, she went and grabbed the other end to help him out. Or maybe to make sure he didn't have his little brother stuffed in it. "What's in the cooler, kiddo?"

"Drinks and ice." The poor kid was panting. "It's time for the Annual Kowalski Volleyball Death Match Tournament of *Doom*."

"The what?"

He repeated it, but it didn't sound any more appealing the second time around. She couldn't very well drop her end of the cooler and run off, though. The thing was even heavier than it had looked.

"I guess every sport needs cheerleaders," she said brightly.

"You have to play."

Great. "Can't you just call it volleyball? Does it have to be a death match tournament?"

"Of *doom.* It's more fun when it's a death match tournament of doom."

It took nearly half an hour to get everybody in place and it was too highly organized for Liz to slip away without anybody noticing. Chairs were lined up along the edge of the playground, close enough to the trees to catch some shade. Andy and Rose were playing, as was Uncle Leo, but Mary was sitting out so she could help Brianna cheer. Emma got to sit out because of Johnny, and Paige was, of course, excused from all activities involving doom thanks to her pregnancy, which was probably the worst-kept secret the family had ever not kept.

Everybody else, even little Lily, who was trash-talking her family members across the net like a pro in her squeaky little voice, was on the field.

It started out fun enough, but it didn't take long for their competitive natures to kick in and the game got fierce.

Kevin, who was hovering over his daughter like a linebacker, lifted Lily into the air and they both laughed when she hit the ball back over the net hard enough to get it by Rose.

"Score!" the little girl shouted.

They all laughed as they rotated positions. It was Liz's turn to serve and she got it over the net, though just barely. Since she hadn't played volleyball since high school, she considered it quite the accomplishment. Sean popped it up in the air and she sucked in a breath as Mitch launched himself in the air and slammed the ball back, right at Drew.

Drew turned so it slapped his shoulder instead of his face since the velocity was so high he'd never return it, and Liz heard the gasps around them. Fierce was one thing. Nobody was supposed to get hurt.

She watched Drew shake it off, picking up the ball and tossing it over the net to Beth, whose turn it was to serve.

But in the next volley, Drew had the opportunity to spike the ball back at Mitch. He didn't hit him, but Mitch's awkward attempt to save it made the rest of them laugh as he hit the grass. He came up red-faced.

"Time out!" Mary called from the sidelines. "Time for everybody to hydrate."

Liz was thankful for the cooling-off period her aunt had obviously seen the need for, but she didn't think it would be enough. There was a lot of laughter and teasing as they drank, but the two guys stood on opposite sides of the group, drinking their water in silence until it was time to go back to the game.

There were some whistles and catcalls in the audience as Drew and Mitch both peeled their damp T-shirts over their heads, but Liz saw it for what it was. She wouldn't be surprised if they started grunting and pounding their chests. Maybe pawing the ground. Idiots.

The two men engaged in a stare-down while they waited for their teams to get into position, and Liz wanted to cover her eyes when she realized it was Mitch's turn to serve. Drew's body was tense and ready for whatever her brother was going to dish out to him but, before anything could happen, Liz broke position and went to Drew. She put her hand at the small of his back so he looked at her.

"Stop," was all she said.

The ferocity cleared from his expression and

she felt the tension leave his back. "I'm not doing all the work here. I think it's time for Bobby to make a big play."

Everybody chuckled as Mike and Lisa's youngest flexed his muscles, posing for the cheering section on the sidelines. Before going back to her position, Liz made eye contact with Mitch and was pleased to see he looked a little chagrined.

The rest of the game—or death match tournament of doom, she reminded herself—passed in a blur of sweat, shouts, laughter and curse words that morphed halfway through being spoken into non-curse words that didn't fool anybody. The littlest ones and the older folks wandered to the sidelines as the volleys went on, but there was no quitting until the boys were done.

Finally Mitch's team scored the winning point, although Liz wasn't sure the scoring system was entirely accurate, and they all walked over to the shade and collapsed in the grass.

Liz flopped down next to Drew and rested her head against his shoulder while handing him one of the water bottles she'd grabbed as they passed the cooler. "Here. Drink."

Danny, Mike and Lisa's second son, pointed his drink at them. "Hey, you guys are both really tall. Your kids will be great at volleyball."

Liz felt the heat blooming on her cheeks as an

awkward silence greeted his words. Talk about zero to sixty.

"Depends on who they inherit their skills from," Drew said. "If you know what I mean."

Danny gave Liz the side-eye and then nodded. "Good point."

Liz slapped Drew's knee. "I'm not that bad."

"Honey, you're not that good, either."

Everybody laughed and, even though it was at her expense, it felt good to hear it and she hoped the better mood carried through the rest of the day. She really wanted, when everybody went their separate ways, for it to be on good terms. Or at least not bad ones.

As Mary had promised, once they'd eaten their last barbecued dinner as a family, the adults were free to go for a ride. After a very long day that included the pool, a water gun war and various other sports events of doom, most of them were content to sit by the campfire and supervise s'mores. But a few of the guys were going out.

Drew wasn't quite sure where he stood. Things had become more normal between him and Liz's family over the course of the day to the point he'd been pretty comfortable during dinner. But in a group made up of Joe, Kevin, Ryan, Josh and

Mitch—with no women playing peacemaker—he might not be as welcome.

"You in, Miller?" Mitch barked as he walked by. "Five minutes."

Good enough. He grabbed his gear and was ready to go by the time the other guys were. They all stopped on their way to the four-wheelers to kiss their women, so he did the same.

Liz was breaking chocolate bars into s'mores-size pieces in preparation for the evening when he stepped up beside her and kissed the side of her neck.

"I'm heading out." He snagged a piece of chocolate and popped it in his mouth.

She slapped his hand. "Those are only for people having s'mores. And don't forget, if you get too close to the other guys in mud, they *will* roost the hell out of you."

Since he had no desire to come back covered from helmet to boot in mud thrown off their tires, he made a mental note. "Maybe I'll roost them."

"They're not that easy to catch off guard." She lifted her finger to the corner of his mouth and swiped at it. "Chocolate."

"Let's go," somebody yelled.

"I'll be back." He tucked a strand of hair behind her ear and kissed her goodbye.

Once they were clear of the campground,

Kevin—who was in the lead—kicked it into high gear and they tore through the woods. Whenever they had to slow down for tricky terrain, Drew made sure he left enough space between him and Ryan so he wouldn't get wedged in behind him in a mud puddle.

Eight miles out, he saw Kevin's taillights get squirrelly through a break in the trees and then pull hard to the right. They all pulled in behind Kevin, who'd gotten his four-wheeler as far off the trail as he could.

"Think I punctured a tire," he said.

"I've got a kit," Joe called from the rear.

After inspecting the tire, the puncture was found and Joe opened up the plug kit. "This is going to take a while."

Drew tossed his helmet and gloves on the seat of his four-wheeler and grabbed a water from the storage box. He also found a candy bar and it made him smile to imagine Liz sticking it in there for him while he was getting ready.

Mitch walked over to stand next to him, mirroring his position of leaning against the ATV. "Heading home tomorrow."

"Yup." Drew took a swig of his water.

"I'll spend a couple of days at home playing catch-up on paperwork and email and shit, then

I've got jobs to check on in San Antonio and Philadelphia. Back to the grind, I guess."

"We'll be getting ready for Old Home Day." Drew hated the stilted conversation and the awkwardness between them.

"I'm probably going to miss it. Paige is a little disappointed, but it was more important to her I take this entire week off."

"It's a busy day for the diner, so she might work, anyway."

Mitch shrugged. "Probably. She might go in and help out Liz and Ava if it's busy."

"They asked the ATV club to ride in the parade to celebrate the trails opening, so they might be even busier than usual."

"Yeah. So…about Liz." Mitch stole Drew's water and took a long sip before handing it back. "Needless to say, walking in like that was a shock. You and her together didn't make any sense in my head. But now that I know and I've watched you guys be around each other, she seems happy. You guys look like a couple and it's less weird."

Drew nodded, not sure what he should say in response. Needless to say, Mitch coming around and even giving his blessing, so to speak, would be the best-case scenario. But the entire family seemed to have hopped on some kind of relationship express train while he and Liz were still at the station, trying to figure out their destination.

"What's going on?" Mitch's eyebrows furrowed, making him look even more serious. "Is there a problem with Liz?"

"No, there's no problem. I don't know how to explain it. Some of your family has looked at us and decided it's a done deal. There's even been talk of kids. But it's not like Liz and I have been together since your wedding. She went back to New Mexico and we had no contact at all until she moved back to town."

"So what are you trying to say?"

"Just that it's new. And, like any relationship, we're getting to know each other and figure out if we have a future and…we're not at the point you all seem to think we are. And that worries me because what if we don't get there?"

Mitch shrugged. "Right now you're in a goldfish bowl. Not only is her entire family here, but she's single while everybody else is doing the love and kids thing. That puts a big spotlight on your relationship. Once you guys are home, you'll only have half the family, so it'll only be half as bad."

Drew laughed. "It's not *bad,* really. I'm just afraid if we start getting to spend time together and realize we're not meant to be, I'm the asshole."

"And that would be different how?" When Drew looked sideways at him, Mitch laughed. A real laugh. "Sorry. My concern is that I know where you are in life. Mal did a number on you and now I get the impression you feel like you're running behind. You want a wife and kids, like, yesterday. I don't know quite where Liz is, but I don't think she's there."

"I don't think so, either," Drew agreed quietly. "And no, not yesterday, but kids aren't a *someday, maybe* thing for me anymore, either."

"None of us liked Darren. You know that. Maybe most of it was the fact he talked her into moving to New Mexico, but part of it was how his needs were what mattered in their relationship. Liz is putting herself first now and none of us want that to change." Mitch stole his water again. "If she decides she wants to explore her options and doesn't see having kids for another five years, what are you gonna do?"

"I don't know." He wished he could give Mitch some reassuring speech on how Liz was more important to him than anything, even his desire to have children, but he'd be full of shit.

His marriage to the woman he'd loved since high school hadn't survived his need to be a dad. Granted, that had the double whammy of her lying about having kids someday for their entire relationship, but if she'd changed her mind and told him she'd have a baby, he might have stayed. If Liz didn't want to have kids anytime soon, it would be a big deal.

"Talk about it before you get in too much deeper," Mitch said. "Your dad and our Rosie are together now, which means a whole lot of family time in your future. The less painful things end between you, if they do, the better it is for everybody."

"Hey, Doctor Phil, you gonna ride or what?" Ryan said. "Tire's good to go. Maybe."

Mitch handed Drew his water back. "For what it's worth, it's still weird, but I hope it doesn't go south."

"Thanks." After stowing what remained of his water and the uneaten candy bar back in the box, Drew grabbed his gear.

"I don't know what he hit, but he wiped out half my plugs," Joe said as he put his tools away. "I think it'll hold until we get back, but that tire's shot."

"It'll be fine," Kevin said.

"Maybe we should put you in the back."

Kevin buckled his helmet. "I could have four flat tires and you still couldn't keep up with me."

By the time Drew got his gear on, enough trash talk had been exchanged between Kevin and Joe that he knew it was going to be a wild ride back and plugged tire be damned.

He double-checked his helmet strap and adjusted his gloves before firing his engine. Then, one by one, they pulled back onto the trail in a spray of dust and gravel. Drew hit the throttle and prayed he didn't die.

LIZ HAD MIXED feelings about going home. On the one hand, it was time to get back to the new life she'd put on pause to be here. On the other, the time with her family had been amazing and part of her wished they could stay just a little longer.

"They're pathetic today," Keri said from her station, which was frying more bacon than Liz had ever seen in her life. And she'd worked in truck stops. "They're all sore and trying like hell not to show it."

"They're not hiding it well," Paige said. She was beating a huge bowl of scrambled eggs, which would be the first of several batches.

Liz rolled her eyes. "Drew told me he's never ridden that fast through the woods in his life. And Kevin knows these trails really well, so I guess he was moving right along."

"Don't tell anybody," Keri said, "but Joe asked me to tie his sneakers this morning."

The women all laughed and Liz glanced over at

Drew. He was sitting in one of the chairs, balancing a mug of coffee on the arm. When he saw her looking, he gave her a pretty feeble thumbs-up.

"I don't think Drew can actually lift that coffee up to his mouth," Liz said. "Maybe we should give them straws."

Aunt Mary slapped a stack of paper plates on the table. "Or maybe they shouldn't go out there and try to act like they're seventeen anymore."

"Hey, Gram," Joey said. "I don't ride like that."

"Only because you're behind slower riders," Lisa said. Her oldest son gave her his most charming Kowalski grin before taking off with a cup of orange juice. "They think I don't know what goes on when they go out with just dad and no mom. Last week, Danny had mud down his pants and leaves in his helmet."

They served breakfast and, after everybody had eaten their fill, the women sat and drank *their* coffee while the men tried to hobble their way through cleanup without moaning or groaning. They were horrible actors, but that just made the show all the more fun.

"I wish you didn't have to go home today, Liz," Aunt Mary said. "I mean, I wish nobody had to go home today, but especially you."

"I know, but I'm closer now. We'll see each

other a hundred times more than we have in the past. You'll probably get sick of me."

"Never. Mitch said something about leaving about four so you guys could have dinner on the road and still be home early enough to take showers and unpack the truck before bed, right?"

"Actually, I'm going to ride home with Drew and he has to work tomorrow, so we're leaving a little earlier." That got the attention of all the women sitting around them. There was some speculative noises dripping with innuendo and Liz felt her cheeks heat up. "Have you guys ever ridden in the backseat of Mitch's truck? If you were as tall as me, you'd ride with Drew, too."

"I wonder if he'll walk you to the door," Emma said, giving her an exaggerated wink.

"He's going to walk to my door several times since I'm going to make him carry stuff in." Then she intended to drag him into the shower and then into her bed, but she was sure they could fill in those blanks without specifics.

"We're done," one of the men declared, preempting what Liz knew was going to be a heap of teasing from the women.

"Where are the kids?" Drew asked.

"Quiet, isn't it?" Lisa sighed happily. "Leo took them down to the pond to do some fishing."

"Damn. I want to offer them money to break down my camp and pack it up."

Liz shook her head. "That's pretty lame, you know."

"You should know ahead of time my kids are brutal negotiators," Lisa said. "You might be surprised how much it'll cost you."

"I'll help you," Liz said. "I have to do mine, too."

It sounded like a decent plan, but an hour later she was hot, tired and ready to kill her tent with fire. "It came out of this bag, so it should go back in the same damn bag."

Drew laughing at her wasn't helping. "They never fit back in the way they came out."

"It's a scrap of nylon and some flimsy poles."

"You could always throw it in the Dumpster."

She put her hands on her hips and glared at the tent. "Then I'll have to buy another one for next time, because you know Rose and Aunt Mary are going to try to drag us back every year now that we gave in once."

"If we come back next year, we're coming in an RV. I don't care if I have to beg, borrow or steal one, but we'll have a bed, air-conditioning and a lock on the door."

Liz looked sideways at him, but he wasn't paying any attention to her. He was in the process of rerolling her sleeping bag because the way she'd done it, it wouldn't fit back in its zippered cover, and he didn't seem to be aware of the assumption he'd just made.

Rather than feeling uneasy, the idea Drew took for granted they'd be together next summer made Liz feel warm and fuzzy inside. Obviously he was easing up on his urgent mission to acquire a mom for his kids and relaxing a little.

He tossed the zipped-up sleeping bag in the back of his SUV and then groaned. "That hurt. Everything hurts. Remind me never to ride with your cousins again."

"We haven't even started on your tent yet."

"If we had an RV, we could just pile all the crap in it and shut the door. Then I could stretch out on the bed and take a nap while you drove home."

She snorted and tossed her duffel bag to him, laughing when it almost knocked him off his feet. "Maybe instead of an RV you should buy a four-wheeler with power steering and a good suspension so you don't hobble around like a ninety-year-old man after a ride."

His eyes lit up, of course, at the mention of new toys. "Hey, maybe we can do both. You should get one, too. Or I could get a two-up so you'd be more comfortable on the back. Longer wheelbase, though."

"You'd play hell trying to keep up in the rugged stuff with the other guys."

He started rambling about the pros and cons of different machines, so Liz turned her attention back to her tent. It was tempting to toss the entire thing in the back of his SUV and worry about repacking it later, but she didn't want it to get torn. Plus, it had become personal. The tent would fit in the bag, period.

SIXTEEN

DREW HADN'T THOUGHT they'd ever get on the road. The gauntlet of hugs, kisses and goodbyes alone had taken almost an hour, but he'd finally herded Liz into the SUV and driven away to waves and blown kisses.

Once they were on the road, she sighed and rested her head against the seat. "That was intense."

"I thought I was going to have to throw you over my shoulder and toss you in the truck."

"How very caveman of you. So it seemed like you and Mitch are doing okay."

Drew put his left hand on the wheel so he could hold her hand with his right. "I don't know about okay. There's still some strain, but we'll get there eventually."

"I still feel bad he hit you."

"That's between him and me. I don't want you feeling like you were in the middle of that."

She gave a humorless laugh. “How can I not feel like I was the cause?”

“Because shock was one thing, but that anger came from me lying to him.”

She sighed, turning her head to look out the window. “I don’t want to talk about it anymore. It’s behind us now.”

And he was happy to leave it there. “It’s going to feel unreal to go back to work tomorrow. I’ll be adding *of doom* to everything.”

“You can give speeding tickets of doom. Those are way more fun than regular speeding tickets.”

He squeezed her hand. “As long as none of them have your name on them.”

They opted for an early, drive-through dinner since they’d both need groceries after being gone a week. He laughed when she ordered one of the bottles of milk that came with a kids’ meal.

“For my coffee tomorrow morning,” she said, ignoring his mocking.

When he reached her house, he backed the SUV into her driveway to make it easier to unload her stuff and then killed the engine. “Wonder how long it’ll be before this picture’s on Facebook.”

“Well, now it doesn’t matter, does it? No more secrets.”

He grinned and leaned across the center console to kiss her. “I like that.”

After pulling a small stack of mail out of her mailbox, she grabbed a bag and went to unlock the door. He took her laundry bag and a bag of badly depleted snacks and followed her, going straight into the kitchen. She set the bag down, then dumped the mail on the counter.

"It's safer if you have your mail held at the post office when you're going to be away. When it piles up, it's obvious you're not home."

"Thank you, Officer Miller."

He pinched her ass. "Chief."

"Since I haven't been here very long, I'm not exactly rolling in mail."

"Don't call me if you go away somewhere and your house gets robbed while you're gone." She raised her eyebrow, and he chuckled. "Okay, I guess you do call me. But don't whine about it, or I *will* tell you I told you so."

He went to grab another load, but got side-tracked by his first view of her living room. It was filled with inflatable lounge chairs. The kind you blew up and used in the pool if it wasn't full of Kowalski kids.

"What the hell is this?"

A few seconds later, Liz appeared, her eyes wide. "What? What happened?"

He waved his hand at the inflatable chairs, surprised he had to specify those were what he was referring to. "Pool party?"

"Oh, those." Liz gave a breathless laugh, her hand to her chest. "I thought something horrible had happened. Busted pipes so the ceiling collapsed kind of horrible. Those are my chairs."

"You can't be serious."

"I got suckered into hosting movie night, but I only have the futon. Paige and Hailey brought those and we had umbrella drinks and watched *How Stella Got Her Groove Back*. It was very tropical."

"And now?"

"Now I have to give them more air every once in a while, but I like them. They're fun."

He wasn't sure about fun, but he was pretty sure if he sat in one, it would be a long time before he could get up again. "You don't have a pool float for a bed, do you?"

"Keep making fun of my furniture and you won't ever find out." She slapped him on the ass as she walked back to the door.

Furniture. Shaking his head, he followed her out for another trip. It only took a few more to get her stuff out of his truck and he closed the hatch. Then he shoved his hands in his pockets and wondered what he was supposed to do next.

Liz was inside and he couldn't leave without

saying goodbye, so either she was planning to come back out or she just assumed he would go back in. And, if he went back in, was she assuming he'd stay for a while?

When she didn't make an appearance after another minute, he locked the truck and went inside. She was in the kitchen, frowning at the pile of camping debris.

"I think I own more camping stuff than I do house stuff," she said.

"Depends on how you classify those chairs in the living room."

"Funny. You want a drink?"

So he was staying for a while. "What do you have?"

She thought about it for a few seconds. "Water?"

"Sounds good."

She grabbed a bottle from the fridge and handed it to him. "I'm glad I don't have to work tomorrow. I'm not ready to face four-thirty yet."

"I don't have to get up at four-thirty, but I do have to work tomorrow. And between now and then, I have to empty my truck, do a shitload of laundry, shower and sleep."

She leaned back against her counter, a naughty smile tilting the corners of her mouth. "You can save time and shower here if you want."

Oh, yeah. He most definitely wanted.

LIZ TOOK HER time soaping Drew down. It was a novelty, having all the time she wanted in the privacy of her own home, and she intended to enjoy every second she had him.

She started with his hair and he moaned, eyes closed, as she worked up a lather and massaged his scalp. The spot at the base of his neck made him suck in his breath, so she returned to it again and again, rubbing it with the tips of her fingers. When she tipped his head back under the stream, he let out a sigh of pleasure as the water washed the shampoo away.

Then she picked up the bar of soap and turned it over and over in her hands. Once they were lathered, she ran them over his shoulders and his chest before moving down to his abdomen. His muscles twitched under her slick touch, and his breathing grew rough as she made her way slowly and deliberately down his body.

Stepping very close to him, she put her hands behind him and soaped his back before running them over the firm mound of his ass. Her breasts rubbed his chest and his hands grasped her hips, holding her to him.

"You feel so good," he said in a raspy voice against her hair. "Is it my turn?"

"I'm not through with you yet." She wasn't

sure she ever would be through with wanting to touch him.

When he growled his impatience, she chuckled and re-soaped her hands. She did each leg next, enjoying the way he froze when her fingertips lingered near the tops of his thighs. Finally, she wrapped her hand around the hard length of him and stroked gently. Drew groaned and moved his hips toward her, urging her on.

She stroked a little faster, her hand sliding up and down his shaft, until he braced his hands against her shoulders and pushed her gently against the shower wall.

"It's my turn now," he said, and his hot gaze raked over her body.

Following her example, he started by washing her hair. Hers was long and thick, and it took him a while. She lost herself in the sensation of his fingertips massaging her scalp and then his hands working through the long strands, rinsing the shampoo out.

Then his lathered hands mimicked the path hers had taken. He ran them over her shoulders and her breasts. The soap made his skin glide over hers, and she whimpered when his thumb flicked over her nipple. She sucked in her stomach when his hand slid downward, her knees practically trembling in anticipation.

Liz had to grab on to his shoulders when he finally slid his hand between her legs. He caressed her there, working her into a state of desperate need, until the only thing keeping her from falling was being trapped between the shower wall and his body.

"The water's turning cold," he murmured against her ear.

"Don't care."

"Because it's hitting my back, not yours." He pulled away from her so he could reach back for the faucet handle.

"Wait, I'm still soapy."

Her rinsing wasn't as leisurely and sensual as his. She ducked under the water, which was turning cold even faster than she'd anticipated, even as he turned it to full hot to get the last few drops. The second she was clean, he killed the water, amusement all over his face.

"You're covered in goose bumps," he said.

"You should stop laughing at me and warm me up."

He grabbed the towel and wrapped it around her, trapping her to him again. "I can do both."

After patting them both down with the towel, he took her hand and led her into her bedroom. A fleeting thought went through her mind that the room looked so much like her bedroom at the lodge, it was almost as if they were making love in that spot again. Except this time they were alone, there was no rush and they weren't hiding anything from anybody.

But when he stretched her out on the mattress and covered her body with his, she stopped thinking about anything but the feel of his skin against hers. His mouth closed over her nipple and she arched her back at the sensation.

After the way he'd touched her in the shower, Liz was close and she wrapped her legs around Drew's hips. "I want you inside of me."

He kissed the hollow at the base of her throat, chuckling, and the sound tickled her skin. "Patience."

"No." She reached between their bodies to stroke him again. He was so hard and he groaned when her hand closed over him. With her other hand she reached for her nightstand and pulled out the condom she always kept on hand, just in case.

He took it from her and she sighed when she had to release him so he could put it on. She loved the feel of him in her hand.

Then he nudged her knees farther apart, and she remembered she loved the feel of him inside of her even more. He rocked his hips, pushing deeper with each stroke and she skimmed her nails up his hips to his back.

"You feel so good," he murmured, pushing her wet hair back from her face so he could see her eyes.

She lost herself in his gaze and in the feeling of him, raising her hips to meet Drew stroke for stroke. He quickened his pace, driving harder and faster, and when he hooked his arm under her knee, she gasped and clutched at his shoulders.

Her orgasm came hard and fast, taking her breath away. As it rocked her, she was barely aware of Drew saying her name in a low growl, his muscles tightening as he found his own climax.

He collapsed on top of her, his breath blowing hot across the sheen of sweat on her collarbone. She rubbed her hand up and down his spine, and he shuddered under her light touch.

"That was a great shower," he said after a few minutes. "It doesn't feel like that when Katie washes my hair."

She slapped his shoulder. "I should hope not."

"What?" He lifted his head, looking down at her with heavy-lidded eyes. "It's the same thing. She's washing my hair or you're washing my hair. Why doesn't it feel like that when she does it?"

"Because she's not naked?"

"Mmm. Maybe that's it." He slid off of her. "Be right back."

She was already sliding into sleep. There was nothing like a shower, an orgasm and your own mattress to knock you out after a week of sleeping on the ground. When the bed dipped under his weight, she woke up enough to snuggle against him and feel him kiss her hair, but then she was out.

The next morning, Liz stretched, not really wanting to get out of bed. She'd managed to ignore the alarm on Drew's phone pretty well, but she was aware the volume of the cursing and banging in her kitchen was increasing. After a quick detour to the bathroom, she went to see what the fuss was about.

It was about the coffee, which had been her first guess. Drew held up the jar of instant. "Is this really all you have?"

"It really is. Throw a mug of water in the microwave and voilà."

Because all of his stuff was still in his SUV, he'd put on the clothes he'd worn home yesterday, and he needed to shave. But he still looked delicious in her kitchen first thing in the morning.

"A man can't live on a cup of microwaved instant coffee," he grumbled. "I'm not sure a man can even *call* that coffee."

"Poor baby." She followed his gaze to the pile of mail spread out over her counter. Most of it consisted of brochures and info packets for various online classes. *Very* various. She couldn't figure out what appealed to her, so she was looking into everything and hoping something would stand out.

"Going back to school?" he asked, once he'd glanced over and knew she was aware he'd been scoping out her mail.

"Maybe. Not sure what I want a degree in, so I haven't signed up for anything yet."

"Not much of a job market in Whitford."

She shrugged, sticking two mugs of water into the microwave. It was a tight fit. "I pay Lauren rent month to month and my car will get fixed or replaced eventually."

He didn't say anything after that, which was fine with her. For starters, she hadn't had her meager allotment of caffeine for the day yet. And she didn't like talking about what she planned to do with her life because she didn't know and that was starting to worry her. She needed *goals,* dammit, and that was not something to worry about before coffee.

But after the microwave beeped and she'd handed him his mug, he nodded toward the brochures again. "If you don't even know what you want a degree in, why are you thinking about spending that kind of money?"

She shrugged. "Why not? A lot of people do it."

"Is this about your brothers? It's not a competition, and everybody just wants you to be happy."

"Maybe going back to school is what I want to do." It was way too early for this kind of conversation. "Since I don't have any groceries yet, I'll probably go to the diner for breakfast. Do you want to go?"

He looked at the clock on the stove and shook his head. "You know what? I still have to get home and shower and shave. And I hope to hell I don't have to iron a uniform before I go in. I'll just make something quick when I get home."

"Oh." She bet he wouldn't be running off if she'd said she was going to toss the school brochures and start having babies. "Okay."

He kissed her cheek and snagged his keys off the counter. "I'll call you later."

"Okay."

He paused in the kitchen doorway, maybe given pause by her lackluster response. "I really do have to go, Liz. But I'll call you later because I'll spend the whole day missing you."

That was what a girl liked to wake up to. "I'll be thinking about you."

He grinned and gave her a wink. "Good. That's the idea."

DREW FELT AS if he spent the entire morning playing catch-up. He'd been late to his first day back at work since he had to drive home first and empty his truck of camping debris, shower and put on his uniform.

When he'd arrived, the piles of paper awaiting his attention on his desk resembled a science fair mountain range project. He had dozens of calls to return and his email inbox had literally made him shudder. His paper inbox was spilling out of its plastic confines and he couldn't find the stress ball Barbara had bought him as a joke one year under the piles.

Between work and Liz, he could knead the hell out of that ball.

Spending the night and waking up in her bed had messed with his head in a big way. He'd liked it a lot and he'd already been thinking about stashing a real coffeemaker at her place so he could do it a lot more often. Maybe one of the units that brewed one cup at a time like they had at the station to cut down on tossed stale coffee.

Then he'd seen the brochures for online courses and that had segued into a pretty blatant reminder she wasn't tied to Whitford, or to him. If she got a better offer somewhere else, she'd be gone.

Now he didn't know what the hell to do. Was there any sense in pursuing a relationship with Liz and parking a coffeemaker in her house if she was just going to cut and run if her life's goal epiphany took her out of Whitford? When she'd implied she'd have no problem leaving town if a good job came along, she hadn't even hesitated. All he could infer from that was the fact she wasn't as invested in them as a couple as he was.

But if he put some distance between them now, what good would it do? He couldn't imagine trying to meet other women. He didn't want to date anybody but Liz, so any other relationship he tried would be doomed from the start.

Right now, he couldn't imagine not having Liz. But he was afraid he'd end up in the same place—with a woman who didn't want kids—only this time, it wouldn't be an unpleasant surprise. He'd have walked into it with his eyes wide open.

"You busy?"

He looked up to see Butch Benoit in the doorway and welcomed the distraction. Since the service station had finally upgraded to a pump that took a credit card, he hadn't seen Butch to talk to since the night he'd towed Liz's car. "Not too busy for you. What's up?"

"Wanted to follow up on an incident late last week, but Barbara said you might not have read the report yet."

Drew sifted through the piles until he found

the report. Bob Durgin had called Butch in to tow a vehicle that was illegally parked and the night after the owner coughed up the necessary fees to get his truck back, the service station had been broken into and some expensive tools taken.

"If you can give me a few hours, Butch, I'll look into this and get back to you this afternoon to see if Officer Durgin's made any progress. Barbara made sure you have what you need for your insurance, right?"

"Yeah. It's more a matter of principle than the money." Butch stood to go. "Oh, so you and Liz Kowalski, huh?"

Drew froze, then relaxed when he remembered he had nothing to hide anymore. At least it made sense now why a guy who knew that Drew would call him if he had any information on the case would show up at his office. "Facebook?"

"Yeah. Fran said it's all anybody's talking about at the market this morning. So how's Mitch taking that? And, before you answer, you should know Fran told me not to come home without some good, on-the-record gossip."

That was a warning that went without saying. "It was a surprise, but he's coming around to the idea."

"Huh. So you're officially a couple, then?"

Drew wondered if Fran had written out the list

of questions for her husband, or just drummed them into his head. “I guess we are.”

After Butch left, Drew rocked back in his chair and blew out a breath. Regardless of what the future held, being officially a couple with Liz felt good. And it felt right. Something that felt that good and that right would be too hard to walk away from, so all he could do was keep going forward and hope for the best.

He took out his cell phone and pulled up Liz’s number as he went to close his office door. Maybe he’d overreacted a little to the brochures on her counter, and it wasn’t as if she’d said she was leaving town. She’d just reminded him in a not-so-subtle way that she was still exploring her options. Instead of pushing or, even worse, pulling away, he needed to work on being one of those options.

She answered on the third ring, a little out of breath. “Hi, Drew. I was just thinking about you.”

He liked the sound of that. “Sexy thoughts, I hope.”

“Well, I was wishing you were here to carry my camping stuff and my laundry bag down to the basement and, since I find the way your muscles flex when you carry things sexy, let’s go with yes.”

“Not exactly what I had in mind.” He chuckled. “But whatever makes you wish I was there.”

"Are you coming here? Later, I mean?"

"I want to." He looked at the mountain of paper that had eaten his desk. "But I need to work late if I'm ever going to catch up. And your alarm going off at four-thirty's going to be a shock after a week off."

He heard her sigh over the phone and the disappointment made him feel wanted. "That's very grown-up of you. Will I see you at the diner tomorrow?"

"Absolutely. You should know, by the way, that Facebook struck again."

She laughed. "Of course it did. So I should brace myself for being the center of attention tomorrow?"

"Fran sent Butch in for an official comment under the guise of checking on a police report. It's out there now." He shifted some piles around as he talked, trying to sort things by priority. It all seemed high. "Sorry to put you back in the spotlight."

"Everybody knowing we're a thing doesn't bother me, Drew. It's kind of a relief to be able to talk about it."

"A thing, huh?"

"Yeah, we're a thing." He could practically hear the impish grin in her voice. "Don't you think the word *boyfriend* is a little high school?"

"I like it." He liked it a lot. But he heard a sharp rap on the door and Barbara stuck her head in, which meant it had to be important. "Crap, I've gotta go. I'll see you tomorrow, okay?"

"Can't wait. Good night, Drew."

He couldn't wait, either, and he thought about her more than he should have while dealing with the pile of paper punishment his department was determined to heap on him. High school or not, he liked the word *girlfriend.* Up until last year, he never would have thought it possible, but Liz Kowalski was his girlfriend.

Drew spent the rest of the evening whistling while he worked, much to the dismay of everybody else who worked late.

SEVENTEEN

"WHAT THE HECK is arugula?"

Liz smiled at her customer, ready with an answer since she'd already been asked that question at least a dozen times since writing *roasted chicken breast with arugula* on the specials board. "It's a leaf. Like baby lettuce, but with a little spicy flavor."

"Can I get the roasted chicken breast without the arugula?"

"Sure." The last dozen people who'd asked what it was had.

When she clipped the order slip into the rack and Gavin gave her a hopeful look, she shook her head. "Sorry, kid. Not an arugula crowd."

"It's a leaf! I can almost understand rejecting the cold melon soup. This is New England. Soup should be hot. But it's just a little arugula."

"I thought it was delicious." She'd had it on her lunch break. She didn't really get the whole arugula thing, either, but she liked to support Gavin.

"And the roasted chicken breast without the arugula is getting a lot of compliments. They like your seasoning."

Slightly mollified, the kid went back to his cooking and Liz glanced at the clock. It was almost time for Drew to show up, barring any police emergencies.

In the days since they'd gotten back to Whitford, they'd seen each other mostly during his lunch break. He had a lot of administrative stuff to catch up on after being gone for a week, even working through the weekend, and she got up at four-thirty in the morning. There wasn't a lot of time between when he was leaving his office and when she was going to bed, though they'd managed to sneak a little here and there. Like last night, when he'd stayed over.

And speak of the devil. The bell over the door rang and he walked in, looking sexy as hell in his uniform. From the neck down, anyway. From his collar up, he looked exhausted and maybe a little ragged around the edges. He'd grumbled more than a little when her alarm went off at four-thirty, even after microwaving his third mug of hot water for instant coffee.

Before taking a seat, he leaned across the counter and gave her a quick kiss. "Hello, beautiful."

"Hi, there. Let me guess. A salad with grilled chicken?"

"Actually, I'm going to have a cheeseburger today. Medium-well, but I'll have a side salad instead of fries."

"Wow." She arched an eyebrow at him. "Rough day?"

"Actually a good day. I'm getting a grant for most of the cost of an ATV for the police department, and the power sports shop is going to donate the rest of the cost. So I'm celebrating. As a matter of fact, I'll have bacon and extra mayo on that cheeseburger."

"You must be really happy to have a four-wheeler."

"To be honest, I'm the most happy about the paperwork being done," he said. "But it'll be nice to be able to patrol the woods a bit. Even if we don't have the manpower to have somebody out there all the time, knowing there could be a cop on the trails at any given time might deter some of the yahoos."

Liz ducked away to hang the slip for the cheeseburger before Gavin started grilling chicken for the salad. Then she grabbed Drew's diet soda and went back to the counter. "Did I tell you I talked to the insurance company?"

"No. How did that go?"

"I guess they sent somebody out while we were camping and they're totaling it. And they say it's not worth a lot. I knew it was coming, but a little part of me was still hoping to get it fixed. I guess Butch told them he couldn't even find the parts for it."

"Is it enough to put a down payment on something made in the modern era?"

She gave him a sour look. "It wasn't *that* old. And I'm not sure. I'm going to go online and research what's out there and go from there."

"I can help you out if you need it, you know."

"Thanks, but my car may have been ancient, but I'm fairly computer literate."

He shook his head. "I meant with the down payment."

"Oh." She wasn't sure what to say to that. You didn't make that kind of offer to a woman who hadn't been your girlfriend very long, if that was even the term he'd use. But, then again, he was a close friend of the family, so he might have made the same offer to any of them. "Thanks, but I'm okay. If I can't find something soon, I'll take the truck from the lodge so I don't rack up miles on the Mustang."

"You can drive the car as long as you need it." He took a sip of his soda. "Well, until mid-October or so. The heater in it sucks and she gets tucked away until spring in the garage before they start salting the roads."

A few other customers wandered in, so Liz was back and forth for a little while as he ate his lunch. A couple of people stopped to talk to him, and then his dad entered and sat down next to him.

"Hi, Andy," Liz said when she went over to set him up with a napkin and silverware. "Coffee?"

"Yes, please. I was in town and stopped in to say hi to Drew, but Barbara told me he was here. What's good on the menu today?"

She sighed. "We have a wonderful roasted chicken breast with arugula."

"I'll try it."

She wasn't sure she heard him correctly. "With the arugula?"

"Of course. Roasted chicken breast with arugula just isn't the same without arugula, now is it?"

As she went to give Gavin the good news, she heard Drew say, "Do you even know what arugula is?"

"Nope. But Gavin has yet to serve anything inedible, so I'll give it a shot."

Because it was almost time for Ava to take over, Liz left Drew and his dad to visit while she started doing her cleanup and making sure everything was stocked and ready for her. By the time she was done, so were the guys.

After cashing them out, she leaned across the counter so Drew could kiss her goodbye. “Are you going to stop by after work?”

“I have a meeting with a guy from the EPA later this afternoon. If it doesn’t run too late, I’ll be there. If it’s going to be long, I’ll text you.”

“Okay.”

When he was gone, she turned to go bus their dishes and almost ran into Ava. The older woman gave her a knowing smile. “It’s so nice to see Chief Miller smile like that. He’s a nice boy and Mallory was no good for him. You two are a much better couple.”

They were a pretty good couple, Liz thought. They enjoyed each other’s company, respected each other’s jobs, and certainly had sexual chemistry.

Ava put her hand on Liz’s arm. “And you’ll make the most beautiful babies. That Rose is a lucky woman. With the Kowalski looks and her Katie being so pretty and Drew being a looker, she won’t have a homely grandbaby in the whole damn bunch.”

Liz smiled, her cheeks feeling tight. Why did it always have to come around to babies?

DREW GRABBED THE huge box that had been delivered to the police department out of the back of the SUV and walked up to Liz's front door. He was saved from having to kick at her door for help when she opened it, and it gave him a jolt of pleasure to imagine her watching for him out the window. Or she'd heard his truck pull in, but he preferred the former.

"What is that?" She stepped back to let him and the box through.

"You'll see." He went straight to the kitchen and set the box on the floor. After using his pocket knife to slit the tape, he opened the flaps and pulled out a smaller box. "*This* is how you make coffee."

"You bought me a coffeemaker?"

He heard the confusion in her voice, which wasn't a surprise since he knew she was strict with herself. "It's one of those single-cup brewers and there's more."

Reaching back into the shipping box, he pulled out two boxes of the little cups, both decaf. She smiled when he held them up for her to see.

"Most guys start with leaving a toothbrush."

He shrugged. "I didn't have to because you had an extra in the drawer, so I went big."

"I hope it has directions."

While she started pulling the coffeemaker out

of its packaging, he took the last small box out of the bigger cardboard one and worked his way toward the stove. When he was certain all of her attention was on getting the brewer out of the plastic sleeve, he opened the cabinet over her range hood and stuffed the box in.

"What was that?"

Busted. He gave her an innocent look. "What was what?"

"Don't even try it. What did you put in that cabinet?"

"Coffee. The real kind. I was hoping to hide it from you so you wouldn't be tempted to drink it, but I *need* my coffee."

She laughed at him and went back to what she was doing. "You don't have to hide your coffee. Trust me, I felt crappy enough back when I was guzzling the stuff that I'm rarely tempted. Or I'm tempted a lot, actually, but I don't have too much trouble resisting."

"So you feel better now?"

"Yeah, I do."

"Was it all the coffee, or do you think it was making changes in your life?"

"All of it, probably," she said, shrugging one shoulder. "The coffee was the big thing, but I was also lonely and unhappy and had a lot of stress about it."

Drew stepped up behind her to wrap his arm around her waist. With his other hand, he pulled her hair to one side so he could kiss the back of her neck. "You don't seem lonely and unhappy anymore."

"Mmm." She relaxed against his body and he slid his hand over her stomach, feeling some of his exhaustion slip away. "Speaking of not being lonely, Rose and Andy invited us over for dinner. Just a small one in the kitchen, since the lodge has guests."

Disappointment surged through him, but he tried not to let her feel it in him. He did slide his hand away from the snap of her jeans, though, and back to her hip. "She did, huh?"

"I think she wants to gloat. I'm sure she's managed to convince herself—and half the town—that us being a couple was all her doing."

"So what time are we supposed to be over there?" Judging by the clock, it would be soon enough so they wouldn't have time to get naked before they left.

"I passed on the invitation. I told her you've been working overtime and that we just want a quiet night. Do you mind?"

He kissed the back of her neck again. "I don't mind at all. I've been looking forward to it, but I don't know how quiet it'll be."

"You realize that means frozen pizzas in the oven instead of Rosie's cooking, right?"

"Mmm-hmm." He was too busy nuzzling the side of her neck to make words, but hopefully she'd get the message. Frozen pizzas was a small price to pay.

"Okay, show me how to use this thing."

He lifted his head, scowling at the coffeemaker she'd just plugged in. "Right now?"

"Yes." She stepped away from him to set the temperature on her oven. "As tired as we both are, if we get horizontal right now, we won't have supper until tomorrow morning and I'm starving."

"Good point." He could wait a little while to get her naked, if the waiting involved food and coffee.

He showed her how to use the machine while the pizzas baked, brewing them each a mug of the decaf. As much as he preferred the high-test, her alarm was merciless and the sooner he fell asleep after sex, the better.

An hour later, they were snuggled on her futon, watching a DVD she'd popped in since she didn't have cable yet. He had his feet up on her coffee table and she was tucked under his arm with her head on his chest.

"The book was better," Drew muttered. They were watching *It,* which was based on his favorite

Stephen King novel. "I must have read that book ten times when I was a teenager."

"*Needful Things* was my favorite. It was more about people turning on each other, which was fascinating to me. Maybe because we live in a small town."

"I was always running with Mitch and your brothers, especially on our bikes, so I could imagine something like *It* happening to us. The clown was scary as hell, though."

He felt her chuckle vibrate against his chest. "You even had Katie, most of the time, since she was such a tomboy. The token girl."

"While you were with Rose, learning how to keep house and cook. Maybe you should have paid more attention." He kicked at the paper plates near his toe, bearing the remains of their frozen pizzas.

She slapped his leg. "Don't be a wiseass. Watch, this is a good part."

Drew slouched down a little more on the futon, trying to get comfortable. It was tempting to try out one of the blow-up pool floats still scattered around the room, but he didn't want to let go of Liz. When he'd told her he'd read *It* but hadn't seen the movie, she'd been so excited for him to watch it, he didn't have the heart to tell her what he really wanted to do was stretch out on the bed with her.

But this wasn't so bad, either. As a matter of fact, he could imagine doing it forever—coming home to Liz and having dinner and curling up in front of the television for a while. But, in his imagination, they'd need a few more frozen pizzas and the curling up would wait until the kids were tucked into bed.

His chest ached at the visual, so he tried to push it away. Kissing the top of Liz's head, he let himself feel content with holding her because ruining the here and now out of fear of the future was a stupid thing to do. And, right now, holding her was enough.

LIZ LINGERED AT the diner when her shift ended, chatting with Ava and a few of the customers. Drew wouldn't be out of work for several more hours, anyway, and when your house didn't have a lot of clutter, it didn't take a long time to clean.

She was starting to accumulate things, though. Like the coffeemaker Drew bought for her. And the extra razor and shaving cream in her bathroom. And, as of last night, a crisp WPD uniform hanging in her closet. Just in case he overslept on a night he stayed over, he'd said.

Part of her knew it made sense. He spent a

lot of time there and rushing in the morning because you didn't have anything you needed at hand could throw off an entire day. But another part of her was waving a yellow flag, urging her to slow down.

She loved spending time with Drew. Hell, if she was being honest with herself, she was in love with him and that scared the crap out of her. He seemed to be marching resolutely toward the finish line, which in his mind was marriage and babies, while she was content to go on as they were for a while. Spending time together, out of bed as much as in it, was enough for her since she was still adjusting to the changes in her life since leaving Darren and New Mexico behind her.

"You okay, Liz?"

She blinked at Gavin and realized she'd been standing in the kitchen with her keys in her hand for who knew how long. "Yeah. Just got lost in thought. I'll see you tomorrow."

Doing errands took up some time. She went to the library and visited with Hailey, who had a fresh stack of books to recommend to her. Then she went to the market to pick up a few things and visit with Fran. Since Fran loved to talk, Drew's cruiser was already in her driveway when she pulled the Mustang in.

He got out when she shut her engine off and opened her door for her. “How was your day?”

She climbed out of the car and kissed him. “It was another day. Better now.”

“I would have gone inside, but chiefs of police aren’t supposed to pick locks.” He winked at her, but she heard the seriousness in his tone. He was hinting at wanting a key.

“You know what they say. It’s only against the law if you get caught.”

He put his hands on his hips and gave her a stern look. “People who say that usually end up in trouble.”

“Again, only if they get caught.” She opened the trunk and he reached around her to grab the few grocery bags. She grabbed the library tote bag and followed him up the steps.

She felt slightly awkward when he had to step aside so she could unlock the door. Maybe she’d managed to put off the key conversation by being funny, but it was going to come up again and she wasn’t sure how she felt about that. Despite his toothbrush on her sink and his uniform in her closet, his having a key to her house seemed like a big deal.

“How was work today?” she asked once they were in the kitchen. “Any crime sprees?”

“Not today. Maybe tomorrow.” He helped her

unload the groceries, but he kept glancing at her. "You okay? You seem a little off."

Liz wasn't one to let things fester. If something needed to be said, she usually said it. But she wasn't sure she wanted to say something that might lead to a heavy discussion. They'd only been home from New Hampshire a week and it just didn't seem like it was time for the exchange of keys yet.

Not that it would be an exchange. She hadn't even been to his house yet. Logically, she knew it was probably because she got out of work first, but some part of her wondered if it was because it had been Mallory's house. Because it was the house he dreamed of filling with children and he didn't see her in it.

Which made no sense. He must think there was a chance she'd be that woman or he'd have moved on to a more likely candidate. It gave her a headache, trying to figure out where they stood.

He took her chin in his hand and tilted her head to face him. "Talk to me, Liz."

"Just had a long day, that's all."

"Don't lie to me. Please." The look in his eyes made her want to wrap him in a hug. "No matter how bad it is, just say it. Don't ever tell me what you think I want to hear."

"We're moving really fast," she finally said. "It just makes me nervous."

"Because I made a joke about breaking into your house?" He shook his head. "Or is it the uniform in your closet?"

"It's a little bit of everything, I guess. I just want to keep spending time with you without worrying that you're in the fast lane and I'm in the slow lane just trying to keep up."

He tossed his WPD cap on the counter so he could run his hand over his hair. "It's not a race. And I'm not trying to rush you. I know you're still exploring your options and I just want to stay near the top of the list, I guess."

"Why does it have to be a one or the other kind of list? I can't have you and explore other options in my life, too?"

"The time will come, though, when I'll ask you to commit to exploring those options in Whitford, though. This is my home and it's where I want to spend the rest of my life and raise my kids."

Liz turned and grabbed a jar of peanut butter to put in the cabinet. "See? Back to the kids."

"You know that's what I want in the future." He took the jar out of her hand and set it back on the counter before turning her to face him. "The future, Liz. I'm not stupid. You've been back, what? A little over a month? But I'm also not going to pretend having children isn't a big deal to me just because that's what you want to hear."

"That's not what I want, either. I just want some reassurance you're in this relationship for *me*."

"I'm here because I like spending time with you. Because there's nobody else I'd rather be with and nothing else I'd rather be doing. It's that simple, Liz." He looked at her, his jaw clenching for a few seconds. "If you want me to take my uniform home and give you some space, I'll do that."

"No." She didn't want that. "I like spending time with you, too. I want you to stay."

"Good choice." His expression cleared and he smiled at her. "Because I was going to fix that drip in your faucet while you made dinner."

"Plumbing skills are a very sexy quality in a police chief."

When he put his hands on her hips and hauled her in for a kiss, Liz sighed and wrapped her arms around his neck. Now that she wasn't feeling pushed, she was free to enjoy Drew without the nagging doubts rattling around in her head.

And she intended to enjoy the hell out of him tonight.

EIGHTEEN

DREW WANTED TO take the phone from his desk out to the parking lot, put it under the wheels of his truck and drive over it four or five times. Or quit. He could resign and go fishing until he ran out of money. Then he'd fish some more because he wouldn't have a lawn to mow and he'd need food.

His body was still adjusting to going to bed a little earlier and getting up a lot earlier, and today everything that came across his desk was pretending to be an emergency.

"Chief," Barbara's voice came from the doorway. "I really need an answer from you about scheduling the school emergency response drills because it takes time to pull it together and it needs to happen before school's in session again."

"I'm not here. I went home sick."

"That might work on the phone if you do the fake cough thing, but it doesn't work when I'm standing right in front of you."

He sighed and looked at the calendar hanging

on the wall to his left, which Barbara filled out for him. "You know my schedule. Tell the fire department to pick three dates and then you pick the one with the least amount of things scheduled around it."

"We're trying to coordinate with the state, too, so…"

He looked her in the eye and used his stern police officer voice. "Pass this to the fire chief. Tell him to contact the state and pick three possible dates and then you pick the one that works best for me."

"Yes, sir." She tilted her head, giving him a good looking over. "You know, you really need a haircut before the parade. Maybe you should go do that now. And by the time you're done with that, it'll be late enough so there won't be any sense in coming back."

He got *that* message loud and clear. And she didn't need to tell him twice. "I think you're right, Barbara."

"And while you're already being snippy with me, there's going to be a request for time off in your inbox tomorrow. Harry and I want to have a four-day weekend in Atlantic City for our anniversary next month."

"I will *absolutely* make sure that happens. And thank you, Barbara."

As soon as he walked out of the station, he felt a thousand times better. Most days he loved his job, but something about Old Home Day made everybody involved a neurotic mess. It was the same damn parade they'd been having every year for many decades, but every year the phone calls started rolling in with the stupid questions and the demands for information. Like he cared whether the horses were in front of or behind the tractors. Let the horse people decide.

Feeling the tension build up in his shoulders again, he pushed work and the parade out of his mind and took his time walking to the barbershop. It was hot and humid and they'd have a doozy of a thunderstorm later, but it was still better than being in the office.

Katie was sweeping when he walked in, but she set the broom aside when she saw him. "Hi, Drew. You have perfect timing. No line, no waiting."

"I don't have time for the works," he said, though he wished he did. Her hot foam shaves were amazing. "But Barbara says I need a trim before Old Home Day."

She snapped open a fresh cape. "Have a seat and I'll be quick."

Once he'd sat down and his uniform was protected by the cape, she set to work with the scissors. She was efficient and he liked that she took her cues from her customers. If they wanted to chat, she'd chat. If they were quiet, maybe lost in thought, she was quiet. Until he heard a buzzing in her pocket.

She pulled out her cell phone and looked at the screen. Then she growled, hit a button and slid it back in her pocket. "Freakin' stalker."

Drew looked in the mirror, trying to catch her eye. She put her hand on the top of his head, forced it straight and started snipping again. "Problem?"

"Yeah, you keep moving your head around and you're going to look like Vanilla Ice for the Old Home Day parade."

He snorted, imagining what that would look like on him. Not good. "You may have forgotten I'm the chief of police and one of the qualifications is caring less about looking like a rapper from the nineties than a woman snarling at a text from a 'freakin' stalker'."

She laughed and tilted his head to the left before picking up the electric trimmer. "While your powers of observation are indeed chief of police–worthy, that was Josh."

"Ah. I usually handle domestic issues," he said, keeping his tone light so she'd know he was kidding, "but since my dad lives in the house, I'll have to recuse myself and pass your case off to Officer Durgin."

She paused to give him a glare in the mirror. "You do that and he'd be in the state prison by morning. Sheesh."

The phone buzzed again, but she ignored it. "Is he having separation anxiety or what?"

"He's sexting me."

Thankfully for the hairline at the back of his neck, Katie had years of experience and lifted the trimmer before she said it because that surprised a barking laugh out of him. "Sexting? Seriously?"

"He must be bored today. Probably thinks I'll close the shop and go running home."

"Are there pictures?"

She laughed. "No. He's not that far gone."

"That's too bad. I'm sure I could have found some kind of legal reason to confiscate your phone and share the evidence with the other guys."

"Hey, you're supposed to keep things confidential."

"That's lawyers."

She yanked his head the other direction to trim over the other ear. "I haven't seen Liz in a couple of days. You guys go on a real date yet?"

That made him wonder if Liz had complained the last time Katie had seen her. "Not yet. It's hard with our work schedules because if I take her to a nice restaurant, that's a drive. And I don't think we'd get back before her bedtime. I'm hoping to be caught up by next week so I'm not working late. And if we go out on a night she doesn't work the next day, she might stay awake past nine."

"But you're still seeing each other, right?"

He smiled at her reflection in the mirror. "As often as possible."

"You should try sexting her."

"Yeah, because I want *those* messages being passed around the family. People post pictures of my car in somebody else's driveway on Facebook. No part of my sex life will ever be in transmittable data form."

"I hear you. You know, you don't have to drive to a fancy restaurant or anything. Pack a picnic lunch or something. Drive out to the lake with a quilt and some supper."

"Picnic, huh?"

"Or something like that. I'm just saying, going on a date doesn't have to mean dressing up and going into the city. All it has to do is make her feel special, like you're not taking her for granted."

She brushed off his neck and ears, and then removed the cape so he could get up. Then her phone buzzed again and she rolled her eyes at the ceiling. "I swear, I'm going to flush this phone down the toilet."

"I know the feeling. But, on the bright side, he's not leaving sex sticky notes on mirrors in public bathrooms."

Katie laughed as he handed her the money for the cut. "What is it with those Kowalskis?"

He'd known them long enough to know that was a question with no answer.

LIZ LOVED THE feel of the Mustang cruising the twisty, shaded roads that ran along the lake. It was more of a large pond, really, but it had always been called the lake. They wouldn't stop because Drew had snuck a few hours off and he wanted to enjoy them. According to him, every time he'd ever stopped at one of the beaches or boat launches on his time off, he'd ended up finding kids up to no good or somebody breaking a law.

It was enough feeling the cool breeze through the windows and watching him relax as he drove his baby. His hands were sure on the wheel and it was obvious he took a lot of joy in the vehicle.

"How come you don't drive this more?" she asked. "Even when you have time off, you drive your SUV."

He shrugged. "For a while it seemed like every

time I'd take her out, I'd end up being called in for some reason or another and have to go home to switch vehicles. I was planning to sell her at one point, too, so I think I'd tried to convince myself I didn't like driving her anymore."

"You were lying to yourself. I can tell you love her." When he grinned and gave a little shrug, she knew she was right. "Why were you going to sell her?"

"One of the many obstacles against having a baby Mallory threw out there was money. I thought if I sold it, we'd start a family."

"What changed your mind?"

"The economy. Not many people can afford this car and, before I got around to listing her nationally, I found out it wasn't about the money and, no matter what I did, it wasn't going to happen."

She wasn't sure what to say to that. While it didn't bother her too much on the rare occasion Drew mentioned his ex-wife, because everybody had a history, she didn't like when the conversation veered toward the fact they'd divorced because she didn't want kids.

They'd been on a pretty even keel since the conversation about the key a week ago, and she was perfectly happy to cut a wide berth around the subject of children. She'd been thinking about that a lot lately and, though she knew she wanted to have them *someday* and she knew she wanted to have them with him, she was afraid if she told him that, he'd start putting on the pressure for sooner rather than later.

"We don't really have enough time to drive into the city for dinner," he said, thankfully changing the subject. "I have some frozen burgers I can throw on the grill if you're not feeling too picky. Unless you want to go to the diner."

"No diner, thanks." She laughed. "I have tomorrow off, so I'll be eating frozen burgers tonight and oversleeping in the morning."

A classic rock song came on the radio and Drew cranked up the volume. Liz put her hand out the window, catching the wind as she sang along. It was almost a perfect night.

"I know my yard's looking a little ragged," he said as he pulled into his driveway. "I've been spending all my free time with this hot woman who wants to have sex with me a lot."

"You must be a lucky guy." She got out of the car and looked at his house. It was a simple Cape style, neat and well tended, except for the landscaping. The cream siding and cranberry shutters gave it a homey feeling. Then she followed him through the open garage and through the side door into the kitchen. “Too bad you don’t live closer. The kid who mows my lawn does a nice job.”

“It’s all the stupid flowers that are really a problem. I either have to start taking care of them or rip the beds out and make those spaces lawn again.”

“It would be a shame. Maybe the hot woman who wants to have sex with you should help you out on the weekends sometimes.”

He laughed. “In exchange for sex?”

“Or frozen burgers.”

Because she had to use the bathroom, she gave herself a quick tour of the downstairs. The house had the look of a divorced man’s house, with most of the touches that made it feel like a home gone. There was a couch, but no pillows or pictures hanging on the walls. There was a fireplace with no knick-knacks on the mantel. It was a family home with no family, and she could understand how he’d feel a desire to fill it with kids. A house like this should have little handprints on the wall and Legos on the floor.

Since Mallory had obviously taken the dining room set, Liz sat on one of the bar stools while Drew rummaged in his freezer.

He tossed the box of frozen burgers on the counter, then stood there scowling at it for a few seconds before looking up at her. "Do you think I take you for granted?"

She worried a lot about the pressure she felt to want children, but him taking her for granted had never crossed her mind. "No, I don't. Where did that come from?"

"I don't know. Katie asked if we'd gone on a real date yet and, when I said no, she said I should take you on a picnic or something to make you feel special, so you don't think I'm taking you for granted."

"I spent a lot of years with a guy who *did* take me for granted. Trust me, if I ever think you are, you won't have to ask. You'll know."

"I'm making you cheap frozen burgers on my grill instead of taking you someplace decent."

"I just want to spend time with you, Drew, and not in a car, even if it is the Mustang. I'd rather sit here and eat burgers. Besides, this is kind of a landmark date. It's the first time you've had me over to your place."

"I didn't know if it would bother you being here. You know, because it was Mallory's house." He pulled a knife out of a drawer and sliced the plastic wrapper on the beef. "I bought her out, though, so it's all my house now, but still…I didn't know if you'd be uncomfortable."

"It's just a house. And it's *your* house, so I'm

comfortable." When he rewarded her with a warm smile, she grinned. "It needs some fun, though. I could lend you some of my pool chairs."

He grimaced. "They're a little bright for my taste. And inflatable. When it gets cold enough to have a fire in the fireplace, they could melt. Come outside while I fire up the grill."

Liz followed him out the back door, to a small patio area. There were a couple of chairs and she curled up in one to watch him work.

IT DID SOMETHING to Drew, listening to Liz chatter about her day at the diner while he grilled the burgers. They had dinner together a lot, but it was different tonight because she was in his house.

They'd had their share of domestic bliss recently, making dinner and cleaning up together before settling in to talk or watch television. But this was the first time here, where he spent so much time imagining the future he wanted them to have. Even as he recognized it might be a small step in that direction, he had to tamp down on the desire to rush it—and her—toward making that dream come true.

When the burgers were done, they went inside to eat because the mosquitoes had realized there were humans outside and called in reinforcements. After pulling a bag of potato chips out of the cabinet to round out the romantic meal, they sat at the bar and ate.

"We should do this more often," Liz said after she'd pushed her empty plate away. "You made a good burger."

"Now my secret's out. I should have pretended helplessness to keep your expectations low."

Her laugh was low and sexy, echoing through his barren house and somehow seeming to fill it. "I'm not that easy to fool."

Since he was done, he shoved the paper plates in the trash and the chips back in the cabinet. Cleanup complete. "You want to see the rest of the house?"

A smile played at the corners of her mouth, and he knew he wasn't as subtle as he thought. "Sure."

After leading her up the stairs, he realized his come-on line wasn't the best idea. He didn't want to show her the smaller two bedrooms at the top of the stairs—the ones that were supposed to be for the family he didn't have. One had been made into a home office he almost never used. The other Mallory had used as a craft room and now it sat totally empty.

Instead he led her straight to the master bedroom, but she didn't seem to mind. He watched her look around the room, with the solid maple dresser and the king-size bed covered in plain blue linens. He wasn't much for decorating and had simply grabbed the first bed-in-a-bag set in a man's color. But at least he was good about picking up after himself and the room was neat.

"Bed looks comfy," she said, backing toward it with a come-hither look.

"Feel free to try it out. The sheets are really soft, too, so you might want to ditch the clothes to get the full experience."

Laughing, she yanked her shirt over her head and then grabbed his hand to pull him close. "Now we know why you went into law enforcement instead of real estate."

They got naked in a hurry, but he made love to her slowly, every touch and every kiss lingering as he explored her body. Having her in his bed triggered some primal desire in him and he wanted it to last as long as possible.

"You're killing me," she said, panting after the second orgasm he coaxed out of her.

He kissed her, his hand sliding between her thighs to see if he could get a third, but she had other ideas. She pushed at his shoulders, rolling him to his back and going with him. Once she was straddling him, she grinned.

"Enough playing around."

He reached under his pillow for the condom

he'd snuck there while they were undressing, and put it on. "You in a hurry?"

"Yes. I want you inside of me." She lifted her hips so he could guide himself into her.

Drew groaned as she slid over his erection, her slight rocking motions taking him deeper with every stroke. Reaching up, he cupped her breasts and watched her face as she closed her eyes and lost herself in the sensation.

He loved her.

The sweet physical sensations making his body tremble were intensified by that admission and he dug his fingers into her hips. The words fought to get out, but he bit them back. Maybe it was this house—having her in his bed—and he wouldn't risk losing this moment.

She cried his name when she came, her head thrown back and her eyes closed. He drove up into her, his own release racking his body until he couldn't think straight. The intensity threw him and, when she collapsed on top of him, he held her tight and pressed his face into her hair.

As they caught their breath, he reached between them and carefully pulled himself free. Then he kissed her hair and gave a low chuckle. "I bet I could have sold a few houses."

"I'd buy an entire housing development from you."

"I'll keep that in mind if the whole police chief thing goes south on me."

She lifted her head so she could see him. "It's too late, you know. Since you can't sell houses to anybody but me, you'd be broke in no time."

"I can't, huh?"

"No. I'd have to burn them down."

He laughed as she rolled onto her back. After disposing of the condom in the basket next to his bed, he reached to pull the blankets up, but she was already sitting up.

They could have this forever, he thought. Instead he watched her get dressed because she couldn't stay. He had to work in the morning and his SUV was in her driveway. If he took the Mustang in, she'd be stuck at his house with no vehicle, and she'd made it clear she wanted to sleep in on her day off.

So he threw some sweats on and drove her home, both of them content to listen to the purr of the Mustang's engine. She almost nodded off a couple of times, so instead of going inside with her, he kissed her good-night in the driveway.

"I feel like a teenager being dropped off after a date," she said, amusement coloring the weariness in her voice.

"I'll call you when I get out of work tomorrow and see what you're up to. Enjoy your day off."

After another long, slow kiss good-night, he watched her until she was inside and had closed the door behind her. Then he got in his SUV and drove home alone.

NINETEEN

On Saturday, Drew woke disoriented, not quite sure where he was until Liz stirred next to him and the pale blue walls of her bedroom came into focus. He didn't like waking up that way, but it had been happening more often in the week and a half since their frozen burger date. They usually stayed at her house because she was already finished at work when his shift ended, so she was home, but sometimes when she didn't work the next day, they'd stay at his house.

She made some mumbling noise he couldn't decipher, but which he assumed was her verbalizing a wish to go back to sleep.

If that was the case, he felt the same way. It wasn't four-thirty, but they hadn't gone to sleep for quite a while after they'd gone to bed and he wasn't ready to face the day. "I don't want to get up."

Liz's naked body snuggled tighter against his, playing hell on his resolve. "Then don't."

"And miss the Old Home Day parade?"

"It's a big parade. They'll be fine without you for one year."

He laughed and tried nudging her away. "I'm the chief of police, so I'm first in line. Not only would they notice I wasn't there, but I'm not sure they'd ever leave the staging area if I didn't tell them when to go. Besides, you have to work, too."

"I intend to sneak out and get fried dough. It was always my favorite part of Old Home Day, and I'm hoping the owner being my sister-in-law will keep me from getting fired." She rolled onto her back and stretched. The sheet started sliding downward.

Drew took the opportunity to get out of the bed so he wouldn't see the treasures the slipping sheet offered up to tempt him. He still had to get home and take a shower. And he couldn't remember if he'd ironed his dress uniform or not, dammit. It was too hot for it, but it was a parade and people expected him to look like a police chief.

By the time he had a coffee with Liz, drove home and then got ready, he'd be lucky if he got any breakfast. The parade kicked off at ten and he was usually at the lot they used as a staging area by nine at the latest to help keep the chaos level down. He was already rushed and running late, and he'd been awake maybe three minutes.

"This would be so much easier if you just moved into my house," he mumbled.

The silky sound of bedding shifting stopped. "What did you say?"

Nothing he'd really meant to say out loud. Or maybe he *had* meant to. It was the truth. "If you lived in my house, we could have stayed in bed another hour, at least."

He pulled on the spare pair of sleep pants he'd started leaving there so he'd have an excuse not to turn and see her face. Whatever came out of her mouth next would tell him everything. He knew her well enough to know she'd either agree it was a good plan, or she'd pretend she thought he was joking around.

She gave a small laugh, but it didn't sound very genuine. "Pretty sure you have to buy a woman dinner before you ask her to move in so you can sleep an extra hour."

He had his answer. "I paid when we were driving home from the campground."

"Because it was a drive-through and you were in the driver's seat."

Forcing himself to swallow his disappointment—which was dumb to feel anyway because it was too soon for that kind of move—he kept his tone light. "What time do you have to be in?"

"Ten. With the parade and all the events going

on, Paige says breakfast is always light, but there's an extended lunch rush, plus a lot of people wanting ice cream in the air-conditioning instead of from vendors. So Paige is opening and Tori and I will go in at ten and I'll probably work with Ava until closing unless it really drops off for dinner."

Drew rushed through his first cup of coffee, trying not to look at the clock a million times while Liz made small talk about the day. Finally, when he didn't have another minute to spare, he kissed her goodbye and did his best not to go *too* much over the speed limit on his way home.

By the time ten o'clock rolled around, he felt like his head was ready to explode. Whitford had been throwing Old Home Day parades since 1823. It didn't seem too much to ask that *somebody* in all those years write down the order the floats went in. And, in a first for the parade, they had almost forty four-wheelers show up in support of the ATV club, which was good. Many of the businesses in Whitford, but especially the Northern Star Lodge, the Trailside Diner and the Whitford General Store & Service Station, were seeing increased profits since they'd connected the trails to the town, so it was important to Drew there be a show of goodwill. It was even more important, however, he correct the dumbass who'd put the forty machines behind the 4-H kids and their calves.

Finally it was time to hit the sirens and mark the start of the parade. Moving at a crawl so slow it barely moved the speedometer, he pulled out onto the main street. His gaze was constantly bouncing from the road to the crowd to his mirrors and back to the road. People cheered and whistled while he smiled and waved. These were the moments, staging-area headaches aside, when he was damn proud to be their police chief.

When he got to the Trailside Diner, he couldn't help but look over. Liz and Tori were outside, along with the cook and a couple of what were probably customers, waving. He hit his horn and waved, waiting for her to blow him a kiss before turning his attention back to the road. If you were first in line for the town's big parade, with flashing lights and a siren, and you drove into something because you were checking out a woman, people noticed.

He spotted his dad, Rose and the Kowalskis, all sitting together on the hill by the library's monument. Hailey was with them, too, and they all waved and cheered when he rolled by.

It took nearly an hour to get everybody from one end of the town to the other and then, finally, it was time for the parade to disperse and for everybody to enjoy the festivities.

The first thing Drew enjoyed was a sausage from the first vendor he came to. He was starving because, just as he'd feared, he hadn't had time for breakfast. It wasn't exactly the breakfast of champions, but it filled the hole. Then he made his way through the town, talking to almost everybody and soaking in the good mood that everybody seemed to share.

When he figured any lunch rush Liz might have had was over, he found a vendor and bought two fried doughs. He sprinkled powdered sugar over both, then walked to the diner. There were still quite a few people inside, but most of them seemed to be having cold drinks and ice cream, just as Paige had predicted.

Liz's face lit up when she saw him and he held up the fried dough. "I didn't want you sneaking out and getting in trouble."

"You're the best boyfriend ever." She gave him a big kiss before taking the fried dough and biting into it.

Her facial expression seemed to imply she was enjoying the fried dough almost as much as she enjoyed sex with him, which made him shake his head. He wasn't a huge fan of fried dough himself, so he gestured at Tori, the other waitress.

"I was hoping that was for me," she told him, taking it and then making almost the same face as Liz after the first bite. "Thanks, Chief."

"No problem. I hope your customers don't mind you guys taking a few minutes to eat them."

"I don't think we really care," Liz said. "Do you care, Tori?"

She mumbled something with a mouthful of fried dough, then gave up and emphatically shook her head.

He helped himself to a cup of coffee since the servers were covered with melted butter and powdered sugar and needed to wash up. Once they'd done that and made a round of the tables, Liz joined him at the counter.

"Thank you for the fried dough. It was delicious."

"You're welcome. We had a bigger crowd than usual this year, so I was afraid they'd run out before you got some." He finished the last of his coffee. "Do you think you'll have to stay until closing? I'm wondering when I'll get to see you tonight."

He was surprised to see a guarded look come into her eyes. "I'm not sure. I'm probably going to work until closing and then I'm still opening in the morning, so…I'll probably go home, shower and go to bed."

"So I won't see you until tomorrow night?"

She was looking everywhere but at his face and he didn't need to be a police officer to know she was holding back. "Probably not. I'll call you at least, though I might be beat after this kind of two-day schedule."

Drew could take a hint. He dropped a dollar on the counter for the coffee and then kissed her cheek. "Just give me a call when you're ready to get together."

He walked back out into the sunshine, where his entire town sounded like a big, old party, and sighed. This morning, when he'd said something about her moving in with him, had been a big mistake. He'd pushed too hard, too soon, and she'd pulled back.

The question was how much.

LIZ KNEW THERE was a crossroads coming in her relationship with Drew. And she had the unfortunate feeling she was going to stand in the middle of the crossroad and spin around, not sure which way to go, until she got dizzy, crashed and burned.

And he knew it, too, she realized as soon as he walked through her front door the day after the parade. His smile didn't quite reach his eyes and his hello kiss landed on the corner of her mouth. "How was work today?"

"Quiet. Everybody expended all their desire to be out and about in town yesterday, I guess. How was your day off?"

He shrugged. "Mowed the lawn, stuff like that."

For the first time, she felt really awkward. "Do you want something to drink?"

"What are we doing, Liz?"

She gave one last attempt to avoid stepping into that big intersection. "Standing in my living room while you tell me if you want a drink or not?"

"We've fallen into a routine, but it's not a comfortable one for me. And I'm not sure how much of what we have comes from the way everybody else has assumed we're a couple."

"I…assumed we're a couple. Aren't we? We talked about spending time together. You're up to three uniforms in my closet now." She wasn't sure she'd breathe again until he answered.

"Of course we are. But we live in a place that doesn't offer a lot of options for dating, so we hang out here or at my house and it reinforces the routine."

"What routine?" He was losing her. "I know my getting up at four-thirty has been hard on you. It's an adjustment, I know."

He shook his head. "It's more than that. We're almost like a married couple who lives in two different houses. But when I mentioned you moving in with me, it threw you and you pulled away a bit."

"It took me off guard. I wasn't expecting that so soon."

"But is it too soon? Sometimes it's just right, Liz. The only thing living together would change between us is not having to rush through mornings."

"It would change me," she said quietly. "The only thing that would change for you is that you don't have to rush home in the morning. I would be giving up my house and my stuff and whatever I was going to do with my life because we both know you want children right away."

He ran a hand over his hair, sighing. "But what is it you're going to do with your life? Why is something you don't even know you want more important than our future?"

"Because it wouldn't be fair for me to have kids if that's not what I really want."

"You keep telling everybody you came home to be close to your family and figure out what you want to do with your life. I spent too many years married to a woman who didn't want the same things in life that I did, to risk being with a woman who doesn't even know what she wants."

She wasn't paying for what another woman had done. "What the hell am I supposed to do? Do you want a ten-year plan? Maybe I could do some spreadsheets and projection graphs."

"There's a big difference between projection graphs and basic signs of stability. You have inflatable pool toys in your living room, for God's sake."

"Hey, I *like* my furniture. It's funky and my friends gave it to me."

"It's not furniture. What it is, is temporary. You won't even commit to real chairs, but I'm supposed to think you're ready for a commitment to me?"

Temper flared through her. "I saw an old, plaid recliner sitting on the side of the road the other day with a Free sign on it. So if I go drag that into my living room, does that mean I'm good enough for you?"

"This is the most ridiculous conversation I've ever had in my life."

"Feel free to end it at any time."

"Is that what you want?" He locked gazes with her, his eyes sad. "For me to end it?"

An ache started in her chest and she had to resist rubbing at the spot. "I meant ending this conversation and you know that. I feel like you're looking to pick a fight and you're going to keep picking until I throw you out."

"And I feel like you're coming up with excuses not to address what I'm actually trying to say."

"Because what you're trying to say isn't something I want to hear," she admitted. "You're talking about a level of commitment that scares me. I'm not stupid, Drew. I know inflatable pool floats are not furniture. I accumulated a bunch of stuff that meant nothing to me over my life and I tossed it out. You saw for yourself that everything I owned fit in my car. I let everything else go, but those blow-up chairs are bright and fun and, most importantly, they were from new friends—Paige and Hailey—to celebrate a fun night in my new house to start my new life."

"I know you're not stupid."

"They make me smile. I've never owned anything before that made me happy just to look at them. I want the freedom to explore what else is waiting in my new life."

"I don't understand why a child with me can't be a part of your new life."

His single-mindedness was the match that lit her temper. "Does it even matter that it's *me* or am I just convenient? Hey, Liz had sex with me once, so she'll do it again and I'll have a baby."

Some of the color drained from his face and his jaw clenched. “Is that what you think? You think I’m just looking for…what, an incubator? That any woman will do?”

“That’s how it feels right now.”

He shook his head, staring off at a space over her shoulder. “I knew getting involved with you was a mistake right from the beginning.”

That hurt more than she could ever have imagined, even though she understood what he meant. She’d known it, too. She wasn’t ready to be involved with a man who wanted to be on the fast track to a wife and family, but she couldn’t resist him and she’d done it anyway.

And now they’d both pay.

“You should go,” she said quietly.

“Liz, I—”

“You should go now before anything else gets said that can’t be taken back. We’re going to have to be around each other for a long time, so the less ugly this gets, the sooner we can maybe be friends again.”

“I don’t want to be your friend. I want to be your husband.”

She hadn’t thought she could feel any worse than when he’d said she was a mistake. “No, Drew. You want to be the father of my children first and everything else after. I may not know what I want in life, but I know I don't want that."

He stared at her for what seemed like forever, sadness so heavy on his face. She knew he cared about her. He might even love her. But she also knew he was going to turn and walk out her door because she wasn't what he needed.

Knowing it was coming didn't make it hurt any less when he did.

DREW SPENT THE night sitting on his couch, staring at the empty fireplace and wondering how his life had gone totally to shit in such a short time.

It was his own damn fault. Once he'd brought up their living together and she'd pulled away, he felt compelled to clarify their relationship. Where they were and where they were going. But he'd screwed it up so badly, it would never be fixed.

When his alarm went off, he got up off the couch, showered and got dressed for work. He thought about calling in sick, but the idea of sitting alone in his house all day made his skin crawl. Then he went to work.

"You okay, Chief?" Bob Durgin asked when he walked by the officer's desk.

Drew didn't stop walking. "Yeah. Just Monday blues, I guess."

He forced himself to offer Barbara a smile and

a wave so she wouldn't follow him into his office to cluck over him. Being fussed over would just make him feel worse because he didn't deserve sympathy. He'd been a jerk and then, instead of trying to figure out the right thing to say to de-escalate the conversation, he'd walked out on her.

He put his bad mood to work, plowing through paperwork, making calls and getting results. Anything to keep his mind busy so he would stop replaying the nightmare of last night over and over in his mind. Everything he shouldn't have said. And everything he should have.

Working for three solid hours, he almost managed to push losing Liz into the dark recesses of his mind a few times. But the look in her eyes when she'd realized it was over haunted him.

"Hey, Chief?" Barbara stepped into his office just before her lunch break started. "Josh Kowalski was just here. Asked me to give you these and said they appreciated it a lot, but it's in your driveway and his sister's all set now."

He knew what was in her hand before she tossed the keys to the Mustang on his desk. "Thanks, Barbara."

"You okay? You look a little off."

A little off was an understatement. More like upside down, inside out and sideways. "Just tired. And I hate paperwork."

"You always hate paperwork, but you don't always look this bad. The last time was when your wife…oh. Do you want a cupcake?"

"No, thanks." Sugar wasn't going to help him now. "But I don't feel so hot. After your lunch break, I might go home and I might not come in tomorrow."

"No problem. I'll be quick."

She ended up grabbing takeout, which she brought back to the office. Free to leave, Drew closed up his office and headed for the SUV. He wasn't sure if word of their breakup would have gotten around yet, but he still walked at a fast pace with his head down to avoid conversation. And once he was in his vehicle, he pointed it toward home.

His heart broke all over again when he saw the Mustang sitting in the driveway, just as Josh told Barbara it would be. He unlocked the door and lowered himself into the driver's seat. Though the car had been his for twenty years, it would forever be tied to Liz in his mind now.

It smelled like her, and when he ran his hand over the dash, all he could think about was how amazing she looked driving it. The car had suited her and seeing her drive it had suited him.

But it was over. She'd booted him and now

she'd booted his car. Drew bent his head, resting his forehead on the steering wheel, and stayed there for a while.

TWENTY

Liz did what she'd always done to cope with heartbreak. She went to Rosie. There had been countless bouts of tears and high drama in her teenage years that the woman had soothed away, but she didn't know if even Rose's magic could work on this pain. None of that drama had begun to compare to really and truly having her heart broken.

She parked the truck she'd borrowed to replace Drew's Mustang in its usual spot next to the barn and walked to the back door, which opened into the kitchen. That's where she expected to find Rose and she wasn't wrong.

The older woman set down the pan she was washing back into the soapy water and dried her hands before opening her arms for a hug. Liz walked into her embrace and instantly felt a little better. Not a lot, but it was better than sitting in her house alone, feeling sorry for herself.

"I thought maybe I'd see you today," Rose said,

"and I made two dozen mini pumpkin muffins for you, honey."

"I hope you don't have plans for them because I might eat them all."

Rose let go of Liz and nudged her toward the table to sit down. "If you eat them all, I'll hold your hair while you throw up and then I'll make you some more."

"You're the best, Rosie."

"I think we'll try talking things out before we try the gorge-on-pumpkin-muffins-until-you-vomit route, though."

A couple of minutes later, a plate appeared in front of her bearing warm pumpkin muffins cut in half and slathered in butter. Then a glass of milk.

"There's no talking it out," Liz said after she'd demolished three of the mini muffins. "We want different things and we suck at figuring out how to talk about that, I guess."

"There's a start. You want different things. What does Drew want?"

Liz rolled her eyes. "Everybody knows what Drew wants. He wants children. That's what he wants more than anything."

"And what do you want?"

"I don't know." That was the worst part. She just wasn't sure, no matter how much sleep she lost thinking about it. "I was thinking about getting a degree if something interests me. Or at least taking some classes."

"You can't do those things with Drew while having a family?"

"So many women want to do things but, once they have kids, they never do."

Rose pushed another muffin at her. "That's true. And very many women have kids and still do the things they want to do. But here's maybe the most important question. Do you even *want* to be a mother?"

"Yes." She didn't even have to think about it. "I really do. But I have to figure out what I want to do with my life first."

Rose frowned and slapped her hand on the table. "Child, exactly what is it you think you're supposed to be doing?"

"I don't know!" Liz heard herself getting louder and tried to moderate her tone. "*Something.* I changed my whole life, Rosie. I'm starting all over and what's the point of leaving everything behind if I don't *do* something going forward?" She could feel herself unraveling on the inside.

"You finally left Darren after all those years because you were unhappy. You gave up almost everything you owned and drove all the way across the country alone to come home because you were unhappy. It seems to me the point of all that was to be *happy*."

"Well, I screwed that up in royal fashion, didn't I?" Liz popped the entire half of a muffin in her mouth, and then had to drink some milk to swallow it.

"Are you happy living in Whitford?"

"I love it here. I love being near you guys and friends from when I was younger. I don't have any regrets about moving back."

"How do you feel about working at the diner?"

"I love it. Really. The customers are great and I adore Gavin and Tori. Even Ava and Carl a little, though I don't know them as well."

"So you love your home and you love your job. How do you feel about Drew?"

Liz breathed in through her nose, then slowly blew the breath out through her mouth. "I love him."

It felt good to admit it, even if it was too late. She couldn't pinpoint exactly when it had happened, but she'd fallen in love with him along the way and she'd been too stubborn to admit it.

"So what are you chasing that's more important than all that love?"

"It's so hard, Rosie. Look at the rest of the family. They own businesses and they're successful and I feel like…less somehow."

She felt stupid saying it, but Rose covered her hand and squeezed her fingers. "Call Mitch and ask him what the most important thing in the world to him is. Ask him what makes him happy. Call Ryan. Call any of your brothers and ask them what makes them happy."

"I don't need to ask them," Liz said. "I know what they'll say."

"You know I'm not into sports as anything other than a reason to sit and knit in front of the television, but even I know what a hat trick is."

"Three scoring shots in one game," Liz murmured. "Love my town, love my job and love my man."

"Not bad for starting over."

"He walked out, Rose. It was pretty horrible, and what am I supposed to say? Yeah, I was stupid and stubborn and didn't know what I wanted."

"That's pretty much what you say, honey. Love's messy and people are messy and sometimes stupid and stubborn happen."

"Is it just me," Liz asked, "or do they seem to happen to Kowalskis a lot?"

Rose sighed and took a pumpkin muffin for herself. "Oh, honey, you have no idea."

DREW DIDN'T HAVE any more to give. Unable to sleep again, he hadn't bothered going to work.

And he'd burned through the energy he had left by going through every flower bed and pulling weeds and clipping off dead blossoms. He raked mulch and fixed paving stones that had shifted. He mowed, then he got the weed trimmer and did the edges of the lawn. His yard looked amazing and he'd almost exhausted himself to the point of numbness.

Almost. He'd yet to find a way to achieve a total lack of feeling. Alcohol was tempting, but he was afraid if he started, he wouldn't stop. He'd tied one on the night Mallory packed up her belongings, but he'd had Mitch to go to. Mitch had not only kept him from doing something stupid while he was in his alcohol fog, but he'd made sure Drew limited it to one night.

Instead he took a shower, washing away the sweat and grime of a day outside. Then he poured himself a glass of water and went into the living room to stare at the television for a while. He didn't know what he was watching, and he didn't care.

When there was a knock on the door, he ignored it just like he'd been ignoring his cell phone. There was a good chance it was Barbara, his dad or Rose, trying to do a wellness check or offer him company. He didn't want company.

But after a second knock, the door opened and

Mitch walked in. "You're not answering your phone and you look like hell."

"Hey, come on in. So nice to see you."

"Shut up." Mitch walked right past him, into the kitchen. A few seconds later he came back with two beers. He set one on the coffee table in front of Drew, then sat in the recliner with his. "Okay. Now talk."

"About what?"

Mitch pointed at him. "Don't be an asshole. I was in Philly, but Paige called and said you're having woman problems. I'm your best friend, so I'm here. Talk."

For a few moments, Drew wasn't sure he'd be able to. The fact Mitch thought Drew needed him and had come without question choked him up and he had to blink a couple of times and clear his throat.

"This is weird," he finally said. There was that word again, but it always seemed to fit.

"You're telling me." Mitch popped the cap off his beer and took a long swallow. "But friends listen to friends whine about their women problems, even if the woman happens to be my sister."

"I appreciate it." And he really did. It probably wasn't easy for Mitch to make the effort. Or the travel and work arrangements.

"Unless it's a sex thing. I don't want to hear about sex things."

"We definitely don't have any problems with sex."

Mitch grimaced and took another swallow of beer. "Not sure I wanted to know that, either. Why don't you stick to telling me why you want to be with her and she wants to be with you, but you're not with each other."

Drew wasn't sure he could explain how he felt. "I never planned to be with her, but it went sideways on me. Like when you're racing down an unfamiliar trail and all of a sudden there's a corner and you're sideways, getting passed by your ass end."

"You know what helps with that? Slowing the hell down."

"Funny how you always figure that out when your wheels are coming up and you're about to roll up in a ball."

"Just means you were going too fast in the first place."

Mitch wasn't very good at the whole shoulder-to-cry-on thing. "It hasn't been fast, though. I mean, yeah, us hooking up at your wedding was a total broadside. Never saw that coming. But since then, it's been a slow burn."

"Drew. I'm here for you, really. But there were

meetings and then phone calls and then flying and then driving. This whole careening sideways, broadside, burning thing is starting to go over my head. What the hell is the problem?"

"She thinks I'm just looking for a baby mama and I accused her of not being mature enough to make a commitment because she has inflatable chairs."

Mitch blinked. Took another sip of his beer, then blinked again. "Are there really inflatable chairs or is that another metaphor thing?"

"She has a collection of those inflatable chairs that float in pools because she didn't have enough furniture to host movie night. I'm surprised you don't know about them, since your wife and Hailey bought them for her."

"Sometimes my wife talks, but I don't listen. I just nod. But tell no one."

Drew snorted and opened his beer. "Maybe I should have tried that. Just kept my mouth shut and nodded."

"Is any of it true? Are you just looking for a mother for your children?"

"You know I want kids. But that's not why I fell for Liz. I mean, if I just wanted a woman to have babies for me, I probably would have picked somebody a little more…settled."

"Somebody who doesn't have inflatable chairs."

"Exactly." Drew pointed at Mitch. "This is why I like you."

"Then again, there are people who might think it would be cool to have a mom who's fun and doesn't give a crap what other people think if something makes her happy."

"Now I like you less. Stop drinking my beer."

"Get over the chairs. Those don't mean anything and you're using them as some kind of inflatable wall between you."

He was right, Drew thought. "Why am I doing that?"

"Hell if I know. My degree's in engineering."

"I love her."

"That," Mitch said, tipping his beer bottle at him, "I do know. Did you tell her that?"

"No. I was too busy pushing her away before she could push me away."

"Are you going to tell her?"

As badly as he'd been hurting, he couldn't imagine the pain if he went and told her he loved her and she threw him out again. "Maybe I should have another beer or two first."

Mitch laughed. "Oh, hell no. You're not talking to her tonight. You're not in great shape, buddy, and tomorrow's a brand-new day. Hopefully one you'll face sober and without the bloodshot eyes and the mangy look that comes from either doing a shitty job shaving or, you know, actually mange."

Drew laughed, a real laugh that cheered him up and actually made him feel some hope everything would be okay. "I'm glad you came, Mitch."

"I'm sorry I punched you in the face."

"I'm sorry I broke your sister's heart."

Mitch looked at him, then gave a regretful shake of his head. "I think that breakage was mutual, my friend. But you can ask me or Ryan or Sean or Josh or even our cousins, and we'll all tell you the same thing. Swallow your pride and be willing to lay your feelings out there with no shame, because it's worth it. And she's worth it."

LIZ WAS PRETTY sure she'd never eat another mini pumpkin muffin. Well, for at least a week anyway. But she did feel better after the time she'd spent with Rose yesterday. She'd slept decently last night and, once she was sure she was on solid emotional ground, she was going to reach out to Drew and see if they could talk.

For now, she sat on her futon, drinking her decaf coffee and reading the newspaper's classified ads. If she didn't find a good used car soon, she was going to need a second job just to put gas in the truck.

When her doorbell rang, she frowned and set the paper aside. Maybe Rose or Paige had come to check on her. Her sister-in-law had told her to take a few days off to get her feet under her before facing the gossip mines and she hadn't taken no for an answer.

But, as she walked to the door, she could see the outline of a light bar across a big SUV through the curtains and her heart turned over in her chest. It was Drew, and it was too early to be a casual visit even if they hadn't just broken up.

She smoothed her hair, which was a wasted effort, then pulled open the door. He looked as tired and wrung out as she felt, and she stepped back. "Come in."

"I love you."

She'd expected words. Maybe an apology. More explaining. She hadn't expected him to stand there with such serious eyes and hand her his heart.

"I love you," he said again. "I want to have babies. I want to have *your* babies. I want a daughter with your blue eyes and your laugh and I want sons who live to kick my ass in water ball. I want little children of doom running through my house."

She smiled, feeling how shaky it was because she was trying to hold back the tears.

"But more than that, Liz, I want you to be my wife. Holding you and loving you for the rest of my life is what will fulfill me. You once told me you wanted to turn a man inside out. You do that to me. You turn me inside out and upside down and a little bit sideways."

"I love you, too," she told him because it was the truth and it seemed to important to get it out there in case she fell apart before she could say anything else.

"When I said getting involved with you was a mistake, that was a lie. It was a lie I was telling myself and then I told it to you. What was a mistake was not being willing to take a chance on us without some kind of guarantee we would be okay. I was scared to believe in what we have. I was so afraid of putting my faith in love again only to find out it wasn't real. I still am."

And she wasn't? But she knew Mallory hiding her true feelings from him was something he'd probably never get over. "I've never lied to you, Drew. I never will."

"Not deliberately. But what if you finally figure out what you want to do with your life and it's not here? Or it's not with me?" The ragged emotional fear in his voice tore at her heart.

"I know now that figuring out what I want to do with my life was just a way of saying I'm looking for the thing that will make me happy. Or I *was* looking." She reached out for his hand. "I was happy with you. I'm not happy without you. It's that simple."

"I want you to marry me, Liz. I want *us* to be a family and, when the time comes that we're ready to have kids, then our family will get bigger. Until then, I don't want to spend another minute without you."

"Yes," she whispered, looping her arms around his neck. "I want to marry you and have children of doom to kick your ass in water ball. I want a loud and messy and crazy life with you."

He pulled her close and kissed her until the hurt drained away and all that was left was love and hope for their future. Then he kissed her some more.

"You should tell Rose as soon as possible," he said once he decided to let her breathe. "My dad's checked on me about twenty times and I think it's Rosie's doing."

She smiled up at him. "I saw the curtains across the street move and what I think was a camera. I think we just had our engagement portrait taken and it'll be up on Facebook before you can come inside and shut the door."

"Good. I want everybody to know," he said. But he stepped inside and nudged the door closed with his foot. "I love you and I don't intend to ever hide that."

"I love you, too."

When he lowered his mouth to hers again, she sighed happily against his lips. Sure enough, within a few seconds, her cell phone started to ring, and then his right after that.

"Ignore them." He laughed, and then took her hand to lead her inside. "Let's go get loud and messy and crazy."

* * * * *

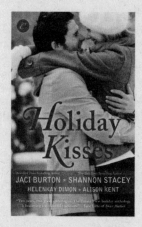

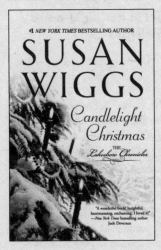

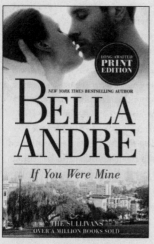

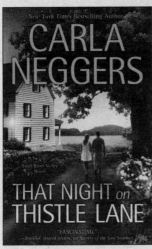